"I was a damned fool."

"I should never have suggested such a charade. I'm being torn in pieces, and you sit there looking angelic and serene—don't you care?"

"Mel, you know I care," she whispered, the tears brimming over now, for she ached with longing for the kind of love she knew she must refuse.

"Yes, I know you do. Forgive me. The whole thing is iniquitous. If only I could marry you!"

"That's impossible," she said steadily. "And you ought not to think of it."

A WELL-MATCHED PAIR

Sheila Bishop

FAWCETT CREST · NEW YORK

A Fawcett Crest Book
Published by Ballantine Books
Copyright © 1987 by Sheila Bishop

ISBN 0-449-21733-7

Manufactured in the United States of America

First American Edition: July 1989

CHAPTER ONE

The carriage had been moving very slowly for some time, and what seemed so extraordinary, the horses made hardly any sound on a road already blanketed with snow which was getting deeper every minute. Only the wheels continued to creak. Snowflakes the size of moths flew against the windows and clung there, so that Edith, peering through the glass, could make out nothing but a landscape of whirling whiteness. She had no idea how far they had come. Then the carriage stopped rather suddenly and a bandbox fell on her feet.

She could hear people shouting in the road. When she banged on the front of the chair wanting to ask John the coachman what was happening, he paid no attention, and when she tried to open the door on the offside, it was stuck. She was not frightened, simply annoyed at being shut in, apparently forgotten, when something unusual was going on. The shouts were not unfriendly. She was straining to catch the words and still peering through the window, when the nearside door was opened, and a voice said,

"I'm afraid you'll have to leave the carriage, ma'am. May I help you down?"

Edith turned quickly. "Has there been an accident?"

"Not a very serious one. There's a wagon over-turned and your coachman can't get past. In any case, there are deep drifts ahead and you would not be able to continue."

He was a broad-shouldered man, almost burly in his greatcoat and muffler, with strong irregular features and an engaging smile. He spoke with the manner and accent of authority. He held out his gloved hands to Edith, and lifting her out, began to carry her away from the coach.

"Please put me down, sir!" she said. "I am well able to walk."

She felt she was being treated like a helpless baby, but the burly gentleman took no notice. She now saw that they had stopped beside a pair of wrought-iron gates, and a little Gothic lodge that seemed faintly familiar. She also caught sight of a wagon tipped on its side, and a group of men gath-ered round.

"Here we are," said her rescuer, putting her down. "Mrs. Mapley will take care of you for the time being—won't you, Mrs. Mapley?"

"To be sure I will, Mr. Sam," said the lodge-keeper, welcoming Edith into her cottage. "Come and sit by the fire, miss. You'll be glad to get warm on such a perishing day."

The door was shut behind Edith before she had time to speak, and the gentleman in the greatcoat was striding off to join the party in the road. Ev-erything had happened so quickly that she felt be-wildered. She gazed round the small dark kitchen, identifying various soft sounds and movements: a hissing kettle, a purring cat, a baby in a cradle.

"Please tell me, where am I? What is the name of this place?"

"You're at Seddon Park, Mr. Dampier's house, miss."

Of course. Now she recognised the gates and the

lodge, which she had glimpsed often enough, travelling between her grandmother's house in a Hampshire village and her father's rectory in the small market town of Cotebury, not far from Bath. It was a distance of fifty miles, and Seddon was roughly half-way between the two places, so that the Dampiers lived too far off to be on visiting terms with either Canon and Mrs. Bruton or old Mrs. French, but Edith had heard her mother say that they were people of consequence.

"Was that Mr. Dampier?" she asked.

"Oh no, miss. That was Mr. Sam Palgrave, Mrs. Dampier's cousin, miss."

Edith sat on the high-backed settle, nursing the cat, which was like a particularly soft, warm muff. She was a small slim girl of eighteen, made strikingly pretty by the contrast between her auburn hair, fair skin and brilliant blue eyes. She was only half aware of this, having led a very quiet life under the eye of parents who frowned on vanity and affectation.

Presently Mr. Palgrave came back into the cottage with an older man who introduced himself as James Dampier.

"I have been talking to your father's coachman, Miss Bruton, and he tells me you are bound for Cotebury. I'm afraid there is not the smallest chance of your getting through today. You will have to remain here for the present. My wife and I will be delighted to put you up."

"But I can't do that! It is very kind of you, sir, but I must get on. I have been staying with my grandmother over Christmas, and my father sent the carriage to fetch me home. I shall be expected at Cotebury this evening."

"I don't think you will," said Mr. Palgrave, who had been standing in front of the fire, his coat gently steaming. "This hard weather is coming in from the west. It must have been snowing at Cotebury for many hours, and when you don't arrive, your parents will assume that the whole country is snowbound and that you never set out from your grandmother's."

Edith saw the sense in this, though she asked if she might have a word with the coachman. He was fetched, and agreed emphatically with the gentlemen. They'd never get through today, nor he wasn't wishful to risk the reverend's horses on such roads.

"Nor the reverend's daughter either, I hope," said Mr. Palgrave very softly, so that only Edith could hear.

Mr. Dampier repeated that they were all welcome to stay at Seddon Park. "And we will soon get you up to the house, Miss Bruton. I will send two of the men to bring my mother's sedan-chair for you."

"That will be quite unnecessary, sir. I am very well shod for walking."

Edith kicked back her skirt and displayed her well-polished half-boots. The gentlemen surveyed them politely.

"You know, James, I think it will save time and trouble if I take Miss Bruton straight up to the house on foot. It is hardly snowing at present."

Edith was grateful for this support from Mr. Palgrave, and was ready to step out beside him, rather enjoying the adventure. The carriage drive lay at a right-angle to the turnpike road, besides being protected by a high wall, so there were no impassable drifts to block their way.

Sam Palgrave glanced down at her, smiling. "You were not at all pleased by the summary way I abducted you from your carriage! I hope I have redeemed myself by saving you from a ride in Lady Anne Dampier's sedan-chair."

Edith laughed. "I could not imagine myself arriving in such a state, like a lady of quality going to a ball! Tell me, if you please, sir, are there a great many other people in the house besides Mr. and Mrs. Dampier?"

"Well, there is a fair-sized party, but they are all very agreeable. You will like them."

She hoped he was right. At any rate she liked him, and walked happily beside him under the network of bare branches, her cheeks tingling in the cold air. Only when she saw the house was she a little daunted. It was a high, geometrical building of red brick, more imposing than she had expected.

Mr. Palgrave took her into the empty hall and helped her out of the scarlet woollen cape she had been wearing for the journey. He took off his own coat and hat. He was not so burly after all, but looked strong and athletic, and his tightly curling hair had that very bright fairness which might have been red when he was a boy.

"I expect they are all in the library," he said. "Come along."

He took her into a room which seemed to be absolutely crammed with people of every age from seven to seventy, talking, reading or playing games. As the door opened, they stopped in order to stare at the newcomers. Sam Palgrave put a reassuring hand under Edith's elbow and guided her towards their hostess.

"I've brought you a visitor, Pen. Miss Bruton is on her way to Cotebury, but the roads are becoming dangerous. There are ten-foot drifts at Peter's Cross already. James and I have persuaded her she should not go any further. I'm sure you will agree?"

"Certainly she must not do anything so foolhardy! My dear Miss Bruton, I'm so glad we can offer you shelter. You must have had a very disagreeable drive. Do come and sit by the fire and get warm."

Mrs. Dampier could not have been kinder. She was a tall, handsome woman, the mother of about half the children who gathered round to gaze curiously at the young lady rescued from the snowstorm.

Various ladies in the party asked Edith about her journey and told her how frightened she must have been, which made her feel a fraud, for she had not been at all frightened, at least not until now, when faced by such a large audience of kind but inquisitive strangers. She had to explain about her grandmother, who did not like to be uprooted at Christmas but did not care to travel during the winter. That was why Edith herself had been staying at Cobdene and was now on her way home.

"And your father is the rector of Cotebury," said Mrs. Dampier. "A friend of mine, Mrs. Wells, has just taken a house in that neighbourhood. My dear governess, who has recently been left a widow. I don't suppose you have come across her?"

Edith had to admit that she had not met Mrs. Wells. She asked rather anxiously whether her valise would be brought in from the carriage, for it would be dreadful to find herself in this grand company with nothing to wear but the clothes she stood up in.

"Oh yes, that will be seen to. And where is your maid, by the way? Did she walk up here with you, or is she still at the lodge?"

"I haven't a maid," said Edith, flushing slightly.

"Did you come all this way alone?" asked one of the other ladies, more in wonder than disapproval.

"Miss Bruton was very safe in the care of her father's coachman and groom," said Mr. Palgrave, who had stationed himself behind her chair, apparently ready to act as her champion.

There was a straight-backed old lady watching Edith from the other side of the fire. Her hair, piled up under her cap, was as white as the powdered wig she would have worn when she was young, and everyone treated her with great deference.

"Are you related to Sir Harley Bruton, child?" she enquired.

"Yes, ma'am. He is my uncle."

"He suffers from poor health, I understand."

"Yes. It is very sad."

In fact he was almost a recluse, and she hardly knew him or the fine old house in Dorset, standing in its own park like this one.

"And what is your Christian name?" asked Mrs. Dampier. "I cannot keep on saying 'Miss Bruton'. It sounds absurdly stiff."

"I am called Edith."

Several people exclaimed with interest and pleasure. Such an unusual name, so romantic. Had it not belonged to a Saxon princess?

"Edith Swan Neck," suggested Mr. Palgrave.

Edith Bruton knew that Edith Swan Neck, as well as being romantic, was also decidedly improper, having been the mistress of King Harold. She was sure that Mr. Palgrave knew this too, even if no one else did.

Presently it was time to change for dinner, and she was shown into a warm, firelit bedroom. As soon as the candles were lit, she saw that her valise had been unpacked and the best of her dresses laid out on the bed for her to wear. She dressed anxiously, rather dreading the ordeal of the evening.

She knew she was a little out of her depth. Although he was the brother of a baronet and fairly well off, her father's unworldly character had kept their family within a circle of close neighbours and old friends, and as there were no large estates near Cotebury, they did not have the entrée to any great houses. She realised that the Dampiers and their guests belonged to the world of fashion. They really

were surprised at the idea of a girl travelling without a female companion, even in her father's carriage. Not because of any risk of impropriety (they
would not be unduly strait-laced), but because they
could not envisage a household where a young lady
did not have her own maid. Edith put on her blue
silk dress and went downstairs, feeling she would
much rather have joined the children in the schoolroom.

She was relieved, when they took their places at
the long dinner-table, to find that she had Sam Palgrave beside her. They talked about the rival merits of town and country.

"Do you live in London, sir?"

"I am obliged to, when the House is sitting. I am
one of those despised legislators everyone loves to
abuse!"

She was impressed, and wondered how old he
was. She found it difficult to guess. Actually he was
thirty-one.

"Are you a Whig or a Tory?"

He was amused by her directness. "I support the
present Government, but don't mention the fact
above a whisper, for they are all Whigs here!"

For a moment she took this seriously, and then
saw that he was teasing her. If he was a Member
of Parliament, of course his relations knew which
side he was on. And it seemed they were all good
friends. Edith's father was a lifelong Tory, and he
detested all Whigs as dangerous revolutionaries.
Could it be that people in the great world were less
extreme?

"I was born a Whig," added Mr. Palgrave, further confusing her.

"I thought men always stayed in the same
party?"

"They do as a rule. Let me help you to some hare
pie." He spooned a liberal helping on to her plate,

before going on. "If I'd been old enough in '89, I'd have cheered with the best for Liberty, Equality and Fraternity. By the time I became aware of politics, the case was altered. We'd witnessed the Terror, fought the Republicans and seen the greatest of them set himself up as a tyrant. That's why I supported Mr. Pitt, and why I feel obliged to support his successors until we have finished with Bonaparte."

Then a footman came between them to fill her wine-glass, and Mr. Palgrave was claimed by his other neighbour.

Edith looked down the table and across to the faces opposite, between the spires of candlelight. She had realised by now that she was the youngest person present, the only unmarried girl in the company. This was to her advantage, though she did not know it. The Dampiers' guests included four married couples, two bachelors, and two much older ladies, both widows: Lady Anne Dampier and her friend, the Dowager Lady Woodruff. Three of the couples had young children with them.

This was not the sort of house-party where the husbands and wives played hide-and-seek through the upstairs passages in the early hours of the morning. Everything was on a much more domestic footing. Even the bachelors were not likely to create havoc: Sam Palgrave was known to have his own preoccupations, while Mr. Fitzroy cared for nothing but whist and shooting. So the unexpected arrival of a young girl, far from creating jealousy, provided a distraction for the group whose plans had been spoilt by the weather. They had all decided to be kind to her. The man on her other side began to talk to her about skating. By the time the covers were drawn and the children came in with the dessert, Edith was quite happy to be a young lady at the dinner-table.

* * *

The next two days were delightful. Edith had never enjoyed herself more. She spent a good deal of time in the schoolroom, helping the older children to fit together a dissected map of Europe, and playing racing games. But this was no penance, for a good many of the ladies and gentlemen came and joined in, notably Mr. Palgrave, who was a great favourite with his young cousins and generally managed to overexcite them, so that in the end, Mrs. Dampier told him to go away.

He did go, taking Edith with him. He showed her a portfolio of Italian prints in the library. Later, he taught her to play billiards.

"Odd to see Sam so taken," James Dampier said to his wife. "Do you think there's anything in it?"

"I hope there may be. She is a charming little creature!"

"He doesn't care for young girls, as a rule."

"Much better if he did."

Dampier did not need to enquire what she meant, and two other keen observers had noted what was going on. "That is a very pretty behaved young woman," said Lady Woodruff approvingly to Lady Anne Dampier. "She might be made into a good wife for a public man, if Palgrave had the sense to see it. Her father will inherit the baronetcy when that poor sickly brother dies."

"Do you suppose she has any fortune?"

"Not at present, perhaps, but she must have something eventually. And Palgrave doesn't need money; he has plenty of his own. What he needs is a wife who will make him a comfortable home and induce him to stay in it. You know that as well as I do," said Lady Woodruff with a sigh.

"Plenty of young women have set their caps at him."

"Yes, and how exactly like a man to ignore them

all and pay marked attentions to this child, who is here only by chance and does not even know that he is flirting with her!"

Edith did know that Mr. Palgrave was flirting with her in the gentlest and most circumspect way. She did not know what this meant, if it meant anything at all, and was not sure if she wished to respond. She was not quite such a newborn kitten as the older people thought—at least her eyes were open. There were men, even in Cotebury, but the ones in her circle were inclined to be very young and entirely dependent on their fathers, so when they began to talk a lot of extravagant nonsense, she never paid much attention. Mr. Palgrave was different. She wished she could get to know him better. And so she might, if only the hard weather continued long enough.

It had stopped snowing, but the cold was more biting than ever. Mrs. Dampier said they must dance to keep warm. In fact, they would have a ball. There were eight children in the house between the ages of ten and fourteen, and with most of the older people prepared to dance, they could muster nine couples, a respectable number. One of the mothers volunteered to play the pianoforte, Lady Anne and Lady Woodruff provided an audience, with the little children clustered round their feet, allowed to watch for the first half-hour. Only Mr. Fitzroy retired to the library in disgust to read the *Gentleman's Magazine*.

Everyone else went flying up and down the drawing-room, looping through arched arms, swinging with clasped hands so that the lustres quivered in the chandelier overhead, and the lines of dancers were repeated infinitely in the sheets of gold-framed looking-glass that faced each other from wall to wall.

Edith danced only twice with Sam Palgrave. He

was kept busy partnering the married ladies and their little girls, while she was chosen in turn by all the little boys and their fathers, but somehow she always knew where he was in the set, while every time they met, she felt a keener pleasure.

"Did you enjoy yourself, Miss Edith Swan Neck?" he asked, when the dancing was over and the children had been sent to bed.

"Oh yes, indeed I did." She added after a moment's thought, "I don't think you ought to call me that."

"A pity. It suits you to perfection. You carry your head so well."

"I have to do what I can, being so small."

She half-hoped for a second compliment, but he was pulling back one of the heavy shutters to take a look at the weather outside. The air was clear and still, and the full moon shone with an almost blinding light. Across the pure white lawn a small classical temple gleamed icily pale against the darkness of an evergreen shrubbery. Edith gazed at this enchanting vision.

"How pretty the temple is. I wish I could go and explore it properly!"

"You would be disappointed, my dear," said Mrs. Dampier, coming up behind them. "You would find a shabby old folly that is hardly worth noticing in daylight. James's grandfather built it, and I am afraid we have not kept it up as we ought. What you are seeing now is just a trick of the moonlight."

"Not entirely," said Sam Palgrave. "The moon does lend a singular beauty to the temple, but it is the presence of the snow, the extreme coldness of the night adding a necessary touch of remoteness, which completes the illusion. We none of us really want to leave this comfortable house and go out into that freezing landscape. That is the contradiction that makes it so desirable. A truly romantic prospect has to be inaccessible."

"What a cynic you are!" said his cousin.

Edith hardly took in what they were saying, except to hope that the excessive cold would keep her here, a willing prisoner.

Next day she had a disappointment.

In spite of the low temperature it was no longer snowing or blowing, and gangs of men had been at work, digging out the drifts on all the turnpike roads. The mail coach had come through in the early hours, leaving word that the Bath Road was now open. This meant that Edith's carriage would be able to reach Cotebury.

"I shall have to be on my way," she said reluctantly at breakfast.

The Dampiers said at once how sorry they would be to see her go, but they did not attempt to detain her. Her parents were expecting her, and once the roads were known to be open, they would become really anxious if she failed to arrive.

Edith stole a glance at Mr. Palgrave, who had become unusually silent. Dreary arrangements were made for her departure. The carriage was to be round in half an hour. Mrs. Dampier went to give orders about hot bricks, an extra rug and a luncheon basket.

Going upstairs, Edith found a housemaid packing her clothes, and started wondering what vails she ought to give the servants and whether she had enough money. Behind this minor worry, she felt sad and flat. Once she left Seddon Park, she did not suppose she would meet any of these people again. She had not known them quite long enough to establish the sort of permanent connection which would make them eager to keep in touch with her. Not wanting to waste the last precious minutes, she started downstairs again, and had reached the first landing when a voice called to her from an open doorway.

"Come in here for a moment, child. I want to talk to you."

It was Lady Woodruff, sitting in her dressing-room and writing letters at a folding escritoire. Edith did not want to talk to the old lady when she might be spending a few more minutes with Mr. Palgrave, but good manners compelled her to go in.

"I am sorry you are leaving us," said Lady Woodruff, "though I am sure your parents will be thankful to see you safe and sound. Tell me, how many sisters have you?"

"Two, ma'am," said Edith, a good deal surprised. "Lizzie, the eldest, is in the West Indies. She is married to a naval officer. Then there is Emma, and I am the youngest. We have a brother, William, who lives in Oxford. He is a fellow of his college."

"And your sister Emma is still at home?"

"Yes, ma'am."

What odd things old people wanted to know! There was no need to explain that Emma never went away if she could help it. She was only happy among familiar scenes, and papa said she was more use to him than his curate. That was why Edith had been chosen to pay the Christmas visit to their grandmother.

"Since your mother has one daughter to keep her company, perhaps she might be prepared to spare you for a little longer? I wonder if you would care to spend a few weeks with me at my house in London."

Edith could hardly believe her ears. "It is very kind of your ladyship to ask me. I hardly know what to say. Though I should like to come, extremely." She was almost inarticulate from surprise.

"My own two daughters have been married for many years," said Lady Woodruff, "and their girls are not yet old enough to enjoy the pleasures of rational society. If you would care to pay me a visit, I will write to your mother at once and you can take the letter with you. I shall be returning to town in a fortnight, and provided your parents approve, I will send my travelling chaise over to Cotebury to collect you the day before I mean to start."

Edith repeated her thanks, still feeling bewildered and a little overwhelmed. She had gathered from the other ladies in the house that the Dowager Viscountess Woodruff was a person of consequence. Her elder daughter was called the Honourable Mrs. Gordon, and the younger was a beauty who had made a great marriage: she was now the Duchess of Melford. They all lived at the centre of the fashionable world. She could not think why she herself had been singled out for such an invitation, but she was determined to accept if her parents agreed, and she was pretty sure they would. It had struck her immediately that if she went to London in February, Mr. Palgrave would be there too, attending the House of Commons.

CHAPTER TWO

Woken by the pounding of heavy thuds somewhere below her window, Edith opened her eyes on
an unfamiliar patch of wallpaper and a blur of winter light coming from the wrong direction, and
knew she was not in her own bedroom at home. So
where was she? At grandmama's? Or Seddon Park?
Then she remembered. She was in the second-floor
spare bedroom of Lady Woodruff's house in Hertford Street, just off Park Lane.

Her parents had made no difficulty about her
paying Lady Woodruff a visit. They saw the flattering invitation as a proof that she must have ac-
quitted herself very well when pitchforked into a
world of fashionable strangers. She had been four
days in Hertford Street, long enough to know that
the commotion on the front doorstep was most unusual and that the servants would not like it. The
pounding had stopped. Someone had opened the
door. She could hear the sound of voices.

Edith told herself it was vulgar to be inquisitive;
what was happening downstairs could have nothing to do with her. She stretched in her comfortable
bed and pulled the quilt up to her chin, contem-
plating her London adventure. So far they had not
done anything very notable, but the town itself was
an entertainment, and since she was used to deal-

ing with old ladies, she got on well with Lady Woodruff, who was easy to talk to and not always thinking about her health. She had announced to Edith that they would go to the play on Thursday, to see Mrs. Siddons as Lady Macbeth, and she had asked Mr. Palgrave to accompany them. The immediate future looked rosy.

Presently the housemaid came to call her, bringing a message. "Her ladyship says, would you be pleased to look in on her, miss, as soon as may be. Before you go down to the breakfast-room."

Accordingly, Edith got up at once, presented herself at Lady Woodruff's door as soon as she was dressed, and was admitted. She expected her hostess to be still in bed, and was surprised to find her already up and seated at her dressing-table, giving directions to her maid, who was carefully bringing out stockings, gloves, stoles and other items from the chest of drawers and laying them carefully on a sofa at the foot of the bed. A footman came in, carrying an empty trunk.

"Your ladyship wanted to see me," said Edith, gazing round her in astonishment.

"There you are, child. A most unfortunate circumstance—not the black lace, Gibbs; I shan't want that at Wakeland. I have just received an express letter from my sister, Lady Moresby. I dare say you heard the postboy. I must set out for Northamptonshire immediately after breakfast."

Edith was completely taken aback. She asked, "Is it a case of serious illness? I am very sorry."

"There has been an accident. Not to any member of the family, however. As to my nephew's state of health, that has never been called in question, which makes the situation all the more delicate."

Edith was more mystified than ever. After a moment she said, "Is there anything I can do to help, Lady Woodruff?"

The old woman seemed too distracted to answer. She suddenly looked much more frail, more like grandmama, no longer the wealthy hostess who could give her young guest such a privileged taste of London life.

Edith thought, I'm an encumbrance now; she wants to be rid of me. She was gripped by a sense of bitter disappointment, much worse than she had felt on the morning at Seddon when they had heard the roads were open again, because this time the blow was so unexpected, and she had stupidly built up too many high hopes round this visit. She also felt puzzled and slightly aggrieved, because the cause of her disappointment was not even going to be explained to her. However, she must make the best of it and behave as well as she could.

"You will be wanting me to leave," she said, trying not to sound dismal. "I'm afraid I don't know how to make the arrangements for my journey."

Lady Woodruff seemed to focus on her for the first time. "Good gracious, child—you've only just arrived! I'm not sending you home again. I shall not be gone above a fortnight, and while I am away, you can stay with my elder daughter in Grosvenor Street. I would leave you here, if I could think of some suitable person who could come and act as your chaperon at short notice, but I can't, so I've sent round a note to Valeria to tell her of your arrival. It is all settled."

Edith's spirits revived, though she felt obliged to say that perhaps Mrs. Gordon would not wish to have an uninvited guest foisted on her.

"Nonsense!" said Lady Woodruff firmly. "She will be delighted." Then she set out on her journey in her own travelling chaise, drawn by four post-horses and accompanied by her maid and footman. Half an hour later her town carriage came round

to convey Edith the short distance to Grosvenor
Street.

Edith felt nervous and disorganised, deprived of
her benefactress and about to find herself uncere-
moniously dumped at yet another strange house. If
only she understood what was happening! It did all
seem very odd.

Put down at a tall house in Grosvenor Street, she
was shown into a slightly gloomy north-facing hall,
where she was asked to wait while a footman went
to announce her presence. He moved towards the
staircase, and then paused.

Voices could be heard approaching from the floor
above, though the speakers were not yet visible,
being still beyond the corner of a gracefully inclin-
ing curve.

"I don't know what mama can have been thinking of," said a woman's complaining tone that was
plainly audible. "Saddling herself with this little
nobody who hasn't the faintest claim on her! It was
all on a par with her going off to the Dampiers at
Christmas, when I'm sure we would have been glad
to have her and I expect you would, too. Which
wouldn't signify, only I am to be landed with the
nobody, if you please, while she goes to succour
Aunt Moresby!"

A much softer voice said something placating,
which Edith could not hear properly. She was too
stung by the wounding contempt of the first
speaker, undoubtedly Mrs. Gordon, and the un-
pleasing view of herself as a tiresome interloper,
encroaching and unwanted. She would have liked
to turn and run, but was held back by the prosaic
difficulty of opening the heavy front door and carrying away her various pieces of baggage on foot.
So she stood rooted in misery as Mrs. Gordon came
round the corner of the staircase, saw her, and
stopped dead. She was a thin woman, with sharp

features and a high colour which increased with
the awkwardness of the moment.

"Miss—Miss Bruton," she said in a strained, artificial voice. "They did not tell me you were here."

She cast an angry look at the unfortunate footman, as though he were to blame.

Edith curtsied, but said nothing. If she had
opened her mouth, she could only have said, You
don't want me here; I'll go away. But she knew very
well that under the rules of polite society, she must
pretend not to have heard Mrs. Gordon's outburst
of frankness, while Mrs. Gordon must pretend to be
pleased that she had come. It was all a charade of
horrible hypocrisy.

"We will go into the morning-room," said Valeria
Gordon, recovering a little. She crossed the hall and
ushered Edith in ahead of her. "Do be seated, Miss
Bruton. We are all at sixes and sevens, and your
bedchamber is not ready yet. We have only just returned to town ourselves."

While observing the conventions of hospitality,
she was quite prepared to make her unwelcome
guest feel uncomfortable.

A third person had accompanied them into the
room, the woman to whom Mrs. Gordon had been
talking as they came downstairs. Edith had not
looked at her properly. Now she spoke for the first
time, in an unusually low, sweet voice.

"I have been wondering, Valeria. Would it not
suit just as well if I were to take charge of Miss
Bruton instead of you while mama is in Northamptonshire? You know we always have plenty of room,
and I should be glad of her company."

Looking for the first time at something beyond
her own confusion and discomfort, Edith found herself gazing at the most beautiful woman she had
ever seen. She was tall and fair, somewhere in her
mid-twenties. Her face was a classical oval with a

straight nose and a mouth which, because it was a little too curved and laughing, broke the paralysing rule of absolute perfection. Her eyes were almond-shaped and a very clear, luminous grey.

She met Edith's glance, and asked, "Would you like to come and stay with me, my dear?"

"It is very kind of you, ma'am. Your grace," mumbled Edith. "I will do whatever is least troublesome to everyone."

She had grasped who this vision must be: Lady Woodruff's younger daughter, the Duchess of Melford, and she would make a very much more agreeable protector than her cross elder sister! But it was impossible to hint at this without appearing rude.

"Well, you are not likely to cause me the smallest trouble. So I shall steal Miss Bruton from you, if you can spare her, Valeria," said the Duchess, with a faint undertone of amusement which could hardly be called malicious.

Mrs. Gordon looked rather ashamed of herself and made a slight demur. "If you are quite certain, my love. I should have been delighted to have Miss Bruton here, but you know James does not care for strangers about the place when he has the gout, and what with a dinner-party tomorrow and the new governess wanting everything changed in the schoolroom, I am driven out of my wits."

"I am sure Miss Bruton understands perfectly," said the Duchess. "We must not keep you talking when you have so much to do."

A few minutes later, Edith found herself in the ducal carriage, on her way to Melford House.

"You must not mind my sister," said her new acquaintance as soon as they began to move. "Of course you heard what she was saying on the stairs; you could not help it. I felt so sorry for you. She talks in that extravagant way when things are going wrong for her, and Mr. Gordon can be very difficult."

"I am sure it is a great imposition for anyone to have a total stranger wished on them."

"Not for me! It is a great diversion, and I am sure my mother would have sent you to us in the first place, only we are expecting an addition to the family. She has an absurd idea that I ought to lie on a sofa all day with my feet up, just because I had several miscarriages when I was first married. But that is all in the past. I have a daughter who is six years old, and a son of four."

Edith would not have guessed that the Duchess was expecting a child; she gave no sign of it, and her figure was more elegant than most women's. It would be impertinent to ask when the new baby was due, but surely it could not be for some months.

The carriage had brought them down Park Lane and half-way along Piccadilly. They now turned right, down the broad thoroughfare of St. James's Street, with the gentlemen's clubs and the old palace at the foot of the hill.

"I know you are called Edith," remarked the Duchess. "How do you like having such an unusual name?"

"I used to find it a trial, but I am becoming reconciled," said the owner of the name as she remembered Mr. Palgrave calling her Edith Swan Neck. "At least it is better than being Jane or Lizzie, like everybody else."

The Duchess laughed, and Edith was struck by the idea that she might have made a gaffe.

"I hope your Grace is not . . ."

"Oh no, my dear! We share a similar distinction. My parents saw fit to christen me Arethusa!"

Melford House lay between St. James's Street and the Green Park, occupying all four sides of a hollow square. They drove through an arched gateway, across a cobbled court and under a porte-cochère, so that although it was raining a little, they left the carriage without getting wet. They went up the steps and into the hall, and here the Duchess addressed a formidable individual who looked too grand to be a mere butler.

"Miss Bruton has come to stay with us, Blake. Would you please tell them to prepare—let me see ... the blue bedchamber, I think. It will suit your pretty colouring," she added to Edith.

The idea of having a room chosen for her as though it was a dress seemed to Edith just one more marvel in a morning which, after starting so badly, had turned into a fairy-tale.

The Duchess took her upstairs and into a beautiful small drawing-room overlooking the park, where the satinwood furniture was inlaid with medallions showing ivory figures in the classical attitudes of ancient Greece. Similar medallions, hand-painted, appeared on the pale green wallpaper. A lady was sewing by the window.

"Maria, I have brought Miss Bruton home with me," announced the Duchess. "My mother sent her to Valeria, but I could see it would not answer. This is Mrs. Jarvis, Edith."

Mrs. Jarvis was fashionably dressed, with an eager manner and large prominent eyes. She got up and made rather a parade of moving chairs and cushions about so that everyone could be comfortable.

Edith could not make out whether she was another visitor or some kind of very superior companion. The Duchess spoke so pleasantly to everyone that it was impossible to tell their exact status.

Presently a light luncheon of poached eggs and minced chicken was brought in, and afterwards Mrs. Jarvis escorted Edith to the blue bedchamber, which was even more charming than she expected, with painted canework chairs, and a sofa bed set sideways to the wall under its own little coronet and veil of pale blue silk.

"You will find everything you need here," said Mrs. Jarvis.

"I'm sure I shall. The Duchess is so kind!"

"Oh yes, indeed. She has the sweetest nature in the world," said the older woman in a rather sentimental manner. "She is an angel!"

She was certainly beautiful enough for this description, though it was slightly shocking to a clergyman's daughter, and not entirely accurate. In spite of her sweetness, there was a touch of frivolity about the Duchess that was likely to make her, Edith could not help thinking, better company than most angels.

Left alone in her new domain, she began to explore, opening all the drawers and presses, admiring the pattern on the china jug and basin, and gazing at herself in the long cheval-glass. After this, she did not know what to do next, so she decided to return to the Grecian room, where she had been taken when she first arrived.

She found her way back after only two wrong turnings. There was no sign of the Duchess or Mrs. Jarvis, and the only person in the room was a gentleman reading a newspaper. He was holding it up in front of him, so that she could see nothing but his long legs in elegant pantaloons. This must be the Duke, she thought, and prepared to retreat hastily, rather than stay and have to explain herself. Just as she felt for the door-handle, the gentleman lowered the newspaper, and she found herself gazing at Mr. Palgrave.

"Good God!" he said. "Edith—Miss Bruton! What are you doing here?"

"The Duchess of Melford has asked me to stay. Lady Woodruff has had to go to her sister Lady—

Lady Moresby at . . . I forget exactly; somewhere in the Midlands."

"Yes, I know. She sent me a note. But she was arranging for you to stay with Mrs. Gordon."

"Mrs. Gordon didn't want me," said Edith, aware of sounding like some pauper child being hawked round the parish.

She had realised with a sense of chilling dismay that Sam Palgrave was not at all pleased to see her. He had risen to his feet as a matter of politeness, but he was frowning, and it seemed as though he had nothing more to say to her. In the hiatus of silence, an uncomfortable sequence of ideas flew into Edith's mind. He had been pleased enough with her at Seddon Park, where everyone had made much of her: the little girl brought to them out of the snowstorm whom they never expected to see again. Mr. Palgrave had paid her the kind of attentions which might have turned her head (well, perhaps they *had* turned her head just a little), thinking he could safely forget the whole episode as soon as she went away, and here she was in London, less than a month later. Very likely he found her presence a tiresome embarrassment. Such a possibility had not occurred to her before, but it struck her forcibly now. Pride demanded that she should appear cool and independent. She strolled over to the window and looked out.

"I find this such an enchanting prospect," she remarked, in what she knew to be a silly voice.

In fact it was decidedly dreary, because it was still raining and there was no one about in the park except the sheep, huddling together in sodden misery.

"I am very privileged to be here," she added.

"Anyone is privileged who is received at Melford House," he said gravely.

"Have you known the family long?"

"I was at Eton with the Duke."

They were now joined by the Duchess, who hurried in, saying, "I am so sorry I was not here. Have you introduced yourselves? Edith, this is Mr. Palgrave."

"Miss Bruton and I are old friends," he said, before she had time to reply. "We met at Seddon Park during the famous snowstorm."

"Of course! How stupid of me to forget."

"And we were to have met again at your mother's house tomorrow night," he continued. "Lady Woodruff intended taking Miss Bruton to see Mrs. Siddons."

"Now that I did not know. Have you never seen her, Edith? What part is she playing?"

"I think it is Lady Macbeth, your Grace."

"Then we must certainly go. And you'll come with us, won't you, Mr. Palgrave?"

"With the greatest pleasure, Duchess."

The following evening, Edith was seated in the Melfords' box at Covent Garden, pushed into the place of honour by the Duchess so that she could get the best view of the stage, and gazing across the candlelit well of the theatre towards the heavy velvet curtains and the proscenium arch, full of a delicious expectancy. The Duchess was next to her, Mrs. Jarvis beyond, behind them a young man called Preston, and Colonel Waters, a half-pay officer who had been wounded early in the war and more or less lived at Melford House.

Sam Palgrave, behind Edith, began to talk to her very much in the easy way he had at Seddon Park. His mood of uneasy coldness had apparently passed.

"Have you had a pleasant day? What have you been doing?"

"I went shopping with the Duchess in Bond Street, and then we played with the children."

They were a charming pair: Lady Harriet Mount-Stephen aged six, and the four-year-old Marquess of Barlington, known in the family as Bar. Harriet was a sturdy, fair little girl, not pretty but very affectionate. Bar was a slim, dark child, strong-willed and lively.

Edith had not yet met the Duke, who seemed to be living in the house in a state of invisibility as far as she was concerned, but she had seen a portrait of him painted by Lawrence and hung at the head of the grand staircase: tall, graceful yet commanding, almost unbelievably handsome, the stormy darkness of his colouring subdued by an air of civilised calm. Could he really be as splendid as that? She was wondering whether she could ask Mr. Palgrave, or whether the question would seem ill bred, when the curtains parted and the play began.

The meeting with the witches on the blasted heath sent a shiver through Edith's imagination, but it was nothing to the shock of wonder and awe she felt when Lady Macbeth came on, reading her husband's letter. Sarah Siddons's voice had a deep and thrilling music, and her presence was so compelling that while she was on the stage it was impossible to look at anyone else. Edith leant forward and let herself absorb the play through every nerve. During the interval a good many people came to visit the Duchess in her box, but Edith was hardly aware of them. She remained in her chair, talking to Mr. Palgrave about Shakespeare.

"I used to think it might be better just to read the plays, so that the poetry would not be diminished by the actors, but I never saw acting like this!"

"Neither did Shakespeare, I imagine! Strange to think that the first Lady Macbeth was a boy."

"And the witches, too. I expect boys liked playing those parts. They are horrid, aren't they? But I was

far more frightened by that terrible knocking on
the door. I forgot it was coming, and it made me
jump."

"I know it did. I was watching you."

"You ought to have been watching the stage!"

"No, I think not."

He did not expand this remark, but it was so ev-
idently a compliment that she could not ask what
he meant without appearing either greedy for admiration or very simple-minded. However, he had
clearly returned to the mood of their original acquaintance.

"When we met yesterday, you did not seem so
enchanted to see me."

She could not resist saying this, but was sorry
almost immediately, for the frown came back and
he glanced away from her.

"You are very young still," he said quietly. "I
know you will not care to be told so, but it is true.
I should not like you to be exposed to situations you
cannot deal with yet. I don't want you to be hurt."

What could he mean? What could threaten her
while she remained under the protection of the
beautiful Duchess of Melford? Of course, she had
been brought up to believe that the world, especially the world of wealth and fashion, was a dangerous and corrupting place. Men and women could
be cruel in the most subtle ways. Mrs. Gordon could
have made her miserable if she had remained in
Grosvenor Street, and there were other ladies of
quality cast in a different mould, irreligious and
brazen, with their lovers and their gaming debts.
It would be very uncomfortable to be thrown into
such a set. But the Duchess was not at all like that.
Edith was sure she was not only kind and gentle
but also very good. So what had Mr. Palgrave been
hinting at? It was impossible to ask; the curtains

had parted once more and they were carried off again into a world of barbaric terrors.

When the play was over, they all went back to Melford House. In the library they found two gentlemen seated in front of the fire, playing chess. One of them jumped up at once and bowed to the Duchess. The other rose a good deal more reluctantly, as though he was annoyed by the interruption. He still held a black knight in his hand.

This dark, elegant, composed gentleman was undoubtedly the original of the Lawrence portrait: Julius MountStephen, seventh Duke of Melford.

"Well," he said in a cool, rather clipped voice, "are your nerves all torn to shreds? How was the divine Siddons?"

"In very good form," said Palgrave. "You should have come with us, Mel."

"Not I. She rants too much, and it's an abominable play."

Edith was shocked. The Duke had just noticed her. After a somewhat alarming scrutiny, he said to his wife, "Arethusa, are you going to present me to your friend?"

"This is my husband, Edith. Miss Bruton is the young lady who has been staying with mama. You remember, I told you."

"How do you do, Miss Bruton. I hope you are enjoying your stay in London?"

"Very much indeed, your Grace."

Edith was annoyed to find that her manner sounded childish and insipid. Colonel Waters set a chair for her, and Mr. Palgrave came across to sit beside her, which took her by surprise, for a moment earlier he had seemed about to settle on a sofa next to the Duchess. Edith was seized by an entirely new idea. If Mr. Palgrave thought she was in some sort of danger at Melford House, was it the danger of falling in love with the Duke? He was

certainly handsome enough to break any number
of hearts. It was flattering. It was flattering to suppose that Sam Palgrave should be so concerned
about her, and rather amusing to think that he
would prefer to have her in Grosvenor Street, where
the gout-ridden Mr. Gordon did not sound a very
fascinating rival.

The Duke, meanwhile, reminded of Lady Woodruff's trip to Northamptonshire, was asking his wife
how soon she expected to hear from her mother.

"Not for two or three days, I should think. I cannot help hoping that poor Moresby's trouble may
not be so serious as my aunt made out."

"Poor Moresby? I don't know why you should call
him that; for, as far as I can see, he is not entitled
to the adjective, apart from the fact that he is always in debt."

"Well, my dear, he is very much to be pitied, for
he is not entirely in his right mind."

"That's a mere excuse," said the Duke impatiently. "He is not mad. He is ill-natured and self-
indulgent. He behaves like a brute whenever he
gets drunk, and this time he has gone too far and
half killed one of his servants."

"Yes, Mel. I know. It is very shocking."

The Duchess's eyes had filled with tears. Edith
was gazing at them in astonishment. In the excitement of the last two days, she had stopped wondering why Lady Woodruff had been obliged to leave
London in such a hurry. This dreadful story fully
explained her agitation.

"Let us change the subject," said the Duchess.
"Edith does not want to hear about such distress-
ing matters."

"I am sorry if you are distressed," said the Duke,
speaking directly to Edith. "Though I can't imagine why you should be. Unlike my wife, you don't

suffer from the misfortune of being related to Lord Moresby."

Edith did not answer. She sensed that the sneer was directed, not at her, but at the Duchess.

Two footmen were bringing in the supper-table. Soon Mr. Palgrave fetched her a plate of cold chicken and a glass of wine. She was pleased that he should be so attentive, though she could have told him that she did not need to be guarded against a non-existent temptation.

She did not like the Duke of Melford.

CHAPTER THREE

It was over a week before a letter arrived from Lady Woodruff, and when it came, the mixture of good and bad news was unexpected. Lord Moresby's troubles were over for the time being. He was not going to be arrested for murder. He had attacked one of his servants in a drunken fury and felled him with the butt of his gun. The man had been at death's door; now he had recovered and had been lavishly paid to keep his mouth shut. The dissolute peer had been thoroughly frightened and was very subdued. All this was satisfactory, but meanwhile, Lady Woodruff, walking in the formal garden at Wakeland, had fallen down some steps and broken her leg. She was laid up in her nephew's house, being cosseted by her sister and quite unfit to travel.

"Oh, poor mama!" exclaimed the Duchess, who had been reading part of this letter aloud to the small party assembled in the breakfast-room: Mrs. Jarvis, Edith, the Duke and Colonel Waters.

Everyone had something sympathetic to say, though in the Duke's case the sympathy was rather astringent.

"I always thought it was unnecessary for her to go jaunting off like that in the dead of winter. She would have done better to stay at home."

"She wanted to comfort my aunt, which I can understand very well, for I am sure I should need the support of my family if I were so unlucky as to have a son like Moresby."

"Good God, what a horrible prospect!" commented the Duke, stirring his coffee.

Edith thought him quite heartless.

Colonel Waters said soothingly, "It is some reassurance that Lady Woodruff is well enough to write."

"Yes, though I think she must be suffering a good deal. Some of the words are so scrawled that I can hardly make them out, and she seems to be worrying herself over trifles, as people often do when they are in pain. She has had my letter, and she seems unreasonably put out to find that Edith is here with us, instead of in Grosvenor Street as she thought. Which is quite absurd, for what difference can it possibly make?"

"What difference, indeed?" echoed Mrs. Jarvis. "I am sure Edith is sensible of your kindness in taking her in. Are you not, my dear? It is sad that your visit to London must be curtailed, now that dear Lady Woodruff is bound to be fixed in Northamptonshire until she is quite recovered. Perhaps she will invite you again on some future occasion."

Edith was considerably taken aback. She felt great concern for poor Lady Woodruff, and had not yet started to think how the news might affect herself. It was true that the old lady was her real hostess in London, and that she was merely to be befriended by one or other of the daughters during a brief emergency. The situation had now changed, but surely there was no need for Mrs. Jarvis to point this out, as though she herself had neither the good sense nor the good manners to act on her own initiative! She flushed with mortification.

"Of course I know that there is no longer any question of my staying in Hertford Street, and I will write to my father today and ask him to arrange for my journey home. If your Grace will give me a frank," she added, not quite looking at the Duke.

"I will frank any number of letters for you, my dear Miss Edith. Though not if you intend to tell your family that we have tired of you after a mere ten days and mean to turn you out of doors. I never heard such nonsense! I am sure the Duchess does not want to part with you."

"No, I don't! My dear Edith, you have seen nothing of London yet, and we have made so many plans. As for you, Maria . . ." The Duchess turned a surprisingly fiery glance on Mrs. Jarvis, "I don't know what you can be thinking of!"

"I'm sure I beg your pardon. I see I have presumed too far." Mrs. Jarvis jumped to her feet and rushed out of the room.

Edith felt thoroughly uncomfortable, and so, she thought, did two of her companions.

The Duke merely said, "If I were in Maria's shoes, I should not go around telling other people's guests when they ought to leave. She is hardly in a position to speak! She has been here five months, and I for one should be glad to see the back of her. It's high time you dropped her a hint."

"Oh, Mel—how can I? Poor Maria, she has no proper home of her own, and she is not made very welcome at her brother's house in Norfolk. And you have not had to endure her so very long. You were away in Ireland for three of those five months."

The MountStephen family had estates in Limerick, and the Duke went over there every year to hunt.

"Well, keep her if you must. Your unresisting good nature never ceases to astonish me!" The Duke glanced at Colonel Waters. "If you have finished, John . . ."

The Colonel rose at once, and the two men went out together, leaving the Duchess alone with Edith. The Melfords never had servants in the room at breakfast-time. The flowered service was set out on the large round table, everything necessary for a London breakfast within reach, and on a convenient side-table all the paraphernalia for making tea or coffee: the two silver pots and, gleaming above them, the graceful silver urn, still bubbling gently.

The Duchess sat lost in her own thoughts—not very happy ones, to judge from her expression. Then she pushed aside her plate and smiled at Edith.

"So that's all settled, my love. You are remaining here, and we are delighted to have you."

Edith was still not certain if this was true. The Duchess had just demonstrated that she was incapable of asking a guest to leave.

"I wish my mother were here to tell me what I ought to do," she said frankly. "I don't wish to be encroaching, and I cannot help wondering why Mrs. Jarvis spoke of my going home, unless it is what everyone would expect."

"I'm afraid Mrs. Jarvis is jealous."

"Jealous?" repeated Edith. "Of me? Good heavens, why?"

"Well, you are very pretty."

This, though flattering, seemed a complete irrelevance. Edith could not see how any comparison could be drawn between herself and a widow of thirty-seven with two sons at Winchester. In what way could such a woman be affected by the prettiness of a girl of eighteen? It was all very puzzling.

The Duchess watched her with interest. She did not find it necessary to say that it was her own liking for Edith which had aroused poor Maria's jealousy. Arethusa Melford had always been one of those rare creatures who inspired devotion whether she wanted to or not, and she often found it very tedious. Of course she knew that Edith, too, had fallen under her spell, but hers was the natural admiration a girl would often direct towards a woman half a generation older than herself and which would help to form her mature taste and judgement. Edith would never sink into a sentimental adoration for a member of her own sex.

So she said in a rallying voice, "You are not to worry yourself about Maria. Youth is the one quality that no one values until they have lost it. If she gives way to an occasional irritation of nerves, you must take no notice. It will not last long."

Edith hoped the Duchess was right. She could not help feeling a little awkward the next time she met Mrs. Jarvis, but the older woman was as smiling and insinuating as ever. She seemed to have forgotten the whole episode.

Letters passed between London and Cotebury, and with her stay at Melford House assured, Edith was plunged into a sequence of pleasures: drives, visits, plays, shopping expeditions. The Duchess insisted on buying her ravishing clothes and ornaments which she did not know how to refuse, and it was true that she needed more dresses to fulfil all their social engagements.

In particular there was a ball at another great London house, where the splendour of the guests and their surroundings fairly took her breath away. Just to be in the same room as so many famous people was exciting in itself, but it was the brilliance of the lights as much as the brilliance of the company that dazzled her, glittering on the jewels of the women and the orders of the men, so that the continual sparkle and movement made her almost dizzy. The fashionable dresses were well worth studying. All were designed with the same outline: low neck, tiny puffed sleeves, high waist, straight narrow skirt with perhaps a short train, though the variations were many and fantastic. Edith thought the Duchess the most beautiful woman there. She wore a tunic of silver gauze, classically draped over a slip of pale green satin, with a net of diamonds on her shining hair. She looked like a mermaid. Edith herself wore white, almost compulsory for young girls, and was content to remain one of a large throng.

She was introduced to a niece of the hostess, whose name was Fanny Oxenham. Her mother, Lady Jane Oxenham, was a particular friend of the Duchess. Fanny was a healthy English rose, pink and well rounded and pleased with herself. While she talked platitudes to Edith, her eyes were continually searching for young men—summing up, rejecting, inviting.

A partner was presented to Edith, a young dandy called Richard Weare.

"He is a detestable fellow," whispered Miss Oxenham. "I pity you!"

So it was rather strange, when they found themselves neighbours in the set, that she spent most of the dance squabbling and bantering with Mr. Weare, who ought to have been attending to Edith. Not that it mattered. Edith found him tiresome and conceited. She had caught sight of Mr. Palgrave in the distance, and hoped he would dance with her soon.

She had reckoned without the well-meaning officiousness of the Oxenhams. Countless young men were produced for her to dance with, and though it was pleasant never to be without a partner, she did not find them at all congenial. They either despised her for not knowing the other people in their circle, or they told her boring hunting stories. Of course

Mr. Palgrave could have come and claimed her, but he did not do so. He danced once with the Duchess and then retired into the card-room.

The Duke did not dance with anyone. He talked to his friends or walked about, looking supercilious.

"So romantic," sighed one of the girls. "If only he wasn't married!"

Edith did not think this would have made much difference. Unmarried, he had probably been even more disagreeable.

At the end, when everyone was leaving, they all said what a pity it was that there could be no more balls until after Easter. Tomorrow was Ash Wednesday, and there would be no dancing during Lent.

Edith did not really mind. She had not enjoyed herself very much. While in a ballroom, she realised, her youth was a disadvantage, for she was expected to dance with young sprigs in their early twenties and she did not find them at all amusing. She had made the interesting discovery that she preferred older men.

The restrictions of Lent suited her very well, because once formal entertainments ceased, there was more time for quiet meetings of close friends. Sam Palgrave was constantly at Melford House. He was one of a select group who was always shown up to the private apartments without ceremony, so she saw a great deal of him.

She thought about him a good deal, too. She felt an instant concentration of pleasure as soon as he came into a room, and he had the power to make everything more interesting and delightful than it was already. And when he went away, she felt suddenly flat. No one else had ever awoken these sensations in her before. Did this mean she was in love? She thought she must be.

She had hardly asked herself this question, when

she found herself thinking less of her own feelings and more of his. For Sam's courtship, if it was a courtship, was proceeding very slowly. He would sit and talk to her for hours on end, sometimes seriously about politics, sometimes it was just gossip or nonsense, a return to the teasing flirtation he had begun at Seddon. But, inexperienced as she was, she thought as time went by that a man in love would have committed himself a little further by now. Probably he thought a girl of eighteen from a country parsonage would not make the sort of wife he needed. Humble about her own merits, she was not inclined to blame him. Yet when he smiled his charming smile and called her Miss Swan Neck, she did think she might learn to live in his world and make him happy.

She would have liked to confide in the Duchess, but was held back by her own diffidence. Sam was an old friend of the Melfords, a contemporary of the Duke; probably they had never even thought of his making such a match and would be astonished at her presumption.

Though once, hurrying into a room, she had come on the Duchess and Mr. Palgrave talking earnestly in low voices. They broke off immediately, which made her think they had been talking about her.

Several days later the Duchess asked her, "Would you like to hear a debate in the House of Commons?"

"Very much indeed. But I thought it was impossible, that ladies were not allowed."

"It is not impossible, merely very uncomfortable. We have to go up to the top of the building and look down through the ventilator. Sam Palgrave is hoping to speak tomorrow night," added the Duchess, elaborately casual. "I thought you would like to hear him."

The following evening, they were escorted to the

Palace of Westminster by Colonel Waters. After toiling up an immense number of stairs, they finally reached a large, dark garret directly above the chamber of the House. It was badly lit by a single lantern and a candle in a tin candlestick, and it took Edith several seconds before she could make out the raftered roof of a one-time chapel and a curious sight in the centre of the room: a group of ladies standing on chairs pressed up against a kind of wooden sentry-box made of planks standing on end.

The Duchess took Edith's hand and led her quietly forward. They climbed on two vacant chairs and peered over the open top of the wooden shaft. Edith found they were looking down through a hole in the floor, past the hanging lights of a chandelier, at the Mace lying on a table, and two clerks writing. They could also see the tops of the heads of three gentlemen on the Government front bench and three more facing them on the Opposition side. One of the Ministers was on his feet, and in spite of the unusual angle, she was able to recognise Lord Castlereagh, who had been pointed out to her at the ball.

Castlereagh was speaking about the war. Presently he said something which annoyed the Opposition and they interrupted him, baying like a pack of hounds. Through the din came the resonant command: "Order! Order!" This was Mr. Speaker, invisible to the ladies round the ventilator.

Edith leant against her plank and listened for what seemed a very long time. She was not able to understand all the speeches, and she was disappointed at not being able to see Sam, but patience was rewarded, for eventually she did hear his voice.

He was attacking a member who had spoken contemptuously about the achievements of the Army in Spain, and he did this by making the Honourable Gentleman sound ridiculous. The members on both sides were amused. They laughed, and allowed Sam to continue with an impassioned plea that Englishmen should learn to give their soldiers the heartfelt support they had always accorded to the Navy.

Edith was much impressed by what he said and the way he said it. He spoke much better than most of the back-benchers, who stumbled and faltered a good deal.

"Do you think he will ever be in the Government?" she asked the Duchess as they were driving home.

"Why not? I think it very likely. And then we shall all grow proud of knowing such a distinguished person."

The Duchess already knew all the men in the present Ministry; she was laughing gently at Edith's awed expression.

She leant back in the carriage, and Colonel Waters said, "I hope the evening has not been too tiring for you?"

"Not in the least, my dear friend."

Edith felt guilty. The Duchess ought not to have been standing all that time in her condition. The new baby was not expected until the beginning of September, but her pregnancy had become increasingly prominent almost overnight, so much so that her sister wondered whether she was carrying twins.

Next morning, Edith felt guilty once again when the Duke discovered where they had been and expressed his annoyance.

"Why do you always have to be careering about the town?" he demanded. "Wearing yourself out when you ought to be nursing your health. If you were in pursuit of pleasure, I might understand even if I did not approve, but attending sacred con-

certs and hanging over that infernal ventilator—
it's downright folly!"

"I shall come to no harm, I promise you," said
the Duchess, who always met her husband's criti-
cisms with the soft answer that was supposed to
turn away wrath.

This made Edith think, or at least hope, that the
Melfords were on happier terms in private than an
outsider was able to detect. The Duke had an irri-
table, impatient temper, and perhaps she knew she
need not take him too seriously.

"That's a stupid promise to make!" He sounded
crosser than ever. "We shan't know what harm
you've done until it's too late. Anyone might suppose you were hoping to lose the child."

This time his harsh words did penetrate her serenity. She became very pale and seemed to shrink
into herself. "Mel, don't say that," she whispered.

The Duke seemed slightly ashamed. "My dear
girl, you know I did not mean . . ."

Edith heard no more, but whisked herself out of
the room and closed the door. She dawdled in the
corridor, and when the Duke presently came out,
she accosted him.

"Your Grace?"

"Yes?" He stopped. "What can I do for you, Miss
Edith?"

"I only wanted to say, sir, that I am afraid it is
my fault if the Duchess has been overtaxing her
strength. She has arranged so many pleasant ex-
cursions for me, and I am afraid I have been too
selfish to consider the consequences. I'm sorry."

He studied her attentively, as though he was
bringing into focus something he had never looked
at properly before.

"So all this gadding has been for your benefit? I
wonder what inspired my wife to take you to the

House of Commons," he said with an astringency
Edith did not care for.

She said stiffly, "Her Grace knew I should be very
much interested in the speeches."

"Oh? And who was speaking?"

"Lord Castlereagh," said Edith glibly. She struggled to remember some other names, but could come
up with only one. "And Mr. Palgrave."

"Ah—Mr. Palgrave!" said the Duke. He laughed,
and walked on.

She gazed after him, flushing furiously. Horrid,
sarcastic creature! Perhaps he had been given a
hint that she had lost her heart to Sam Palgrave,
and it was plain that he rated her chances pretty
low.

While they attended the Lenten sacred concerts together, the Duchess discovered that Edith was in-
tensely musical. In spite of this, she had never had
much chance to play the pianoforte; at home they
still had an old-fashioned harpsichord. The Duchess
had instantly decided that she should have lessons
from a first-class music master. He came three
times a week and in between she practised hard,
enchanted by the effect of producing such sounds,
so resonant, so sustained, so various in their im-
pressions of light and dark after the rather thin,
wiry notes of the harpsichord. There were several
good instruments in the house, one in a long narrow saloon only used for receptions. Here she could
play away for hours, confident that she was not disturbing anyone.

She was trying to learn a Haydn sonata one afternoon, when the door opened and Sam Palgrave
looked in.

"I guessed it was you," he said, smiling.

"You mean you heard a terrible succession of

wrong notes, and you knew at once who was the perpetrator!"

"Not at all! I caught the sound of a joyful allegro, and I thought to myself: there is the little swan."

"I wish you would not call me . . ."

"I beg your pardon, Miss Bruton," he said with mock humility. "I did not address you as a swan, for I know you do not like it. I was simply describing my thoughts, and you must know that is how I always think of you."

"You talk a great deal of nonsense," she said, trying not to laugh, and twisting round on the stool so that she could look at him.

He was standing between her and the window. She saw him almost in silhouette, except that his eyes were very bright, full of amusement and, she thought, affection. He did not speak, just stood there watching her, and the moment prolonged itself until she felt slightly awkward. She gazed round the room, hunting for something to say.

"What a lot of paintings there are in this house," she remarked fatuously.

"There are a great many more at Rythorpe, the ancestral mansion of the Dukes of Melford in the north of England."

"I suppose you have been there often. Is it very beautiful?"

"That's hard to say. The setting is very fine indeed—in the grand manner, you know. And where nature itself is so grand, there is a sort of wildness that triumphs over all that formality. The house is decidedly odd. I believe the first Duke designed it himself, after getting drunk in the company of Sir John Vanbrugh."

Edith had no idea what this meant and was just about to ask, when he said abruptly, "How much longer will be be staying here? Your parents must be anxious for your return."

And you seem anxious for my departure, she thought. She would not say this aloud. Nothing would induce her to make the kind of provocative statement that demanded compliments and reassurance. She bit her lip and stared at the keyboard.

Sam moved round so that he could see her face more clearly. "Are there any good inns in Cotebury?"

The question was so extraordinary that she was completely taken aback. "Why do you want to know?"

"Because, when you are at home once more, I should like to make a pilgrimage to your birthplace. So that I can call on you and make the acquaintance of the rest of your family."

"I see," said Edith untruthfully, gazing up at him in a state of delight and mystification. Wasn't he going to say any more?

He took a step forward, bent, and kissed her twice; once on the cheek and once, a lingering kiss on the mouth. This was a new sensation for Edith, delicious and bewildering.

"Dear Swan," he murmured. "I can say no more at present. Be patient and trust me."

There was a rattle of the door-handle. They both heard it, and when Mrs. Jarvis came in a moment later, Edith was once again practising her sonata and Sam was standing decorously beside her, turning over the pages.

CHAPTER FOUR

Once she had time to think out what Sam had said, Edith was seized with a tremendous elation. He was intending to visit her at Cotebury and that could mean only one thing. For although a man might flirt with a girl in any number of London drawing-rooms without committing himself, it was a very different matter to seek her out in her own surroundings unless he had the excuse of being a family friend or a near neighbour. If Mr. Samuel Palgrave arrived in Cotebury with the sole intention of calling at the rectory, where his only acquaintance was the Rector's youngest daughter, then her parents would assume he had come to make her an offer of marriage.

But why did he ask me to be patient? she wondered. Why can't he say what he means straight away? She supposed it had something to do with her being so young, a state of existence she did not value so highly as everyone else seemed to. Sam thought he ought to make sure of her parents' approval before he said anything definite, and of course it was true that if she wrote home from London, saying she wanted to be engaged to a man they had never met, papa and mama would be thrown into consternation. Even though they must welcome the idea of Sam as a son-in-law, they would not be easy until they had met him.

This delay almost made Edith want to go home at once, but it would be rude and ungrateful to bring her visit to an abrupt end after the Duchess's extraordinary kindness, especially at this moment when the Duchess herself seemed out of sorts. Her energy flagging at last, her size increasing daily, she looked washed out and anxious.

"Do you think she is ill?" Edith asked Mrs. Jarvis.

They were sitting in the Grecian saloon; Maria Jarvis was embroidering a chair-seat and Edith was dressing a doll for little Harriet MountStephen, who had become very much attached to her.

"Women in her condition suffer a great many minor ills, as you'll find out all in good time, my dear. And when you consider the agitation she must be feeling, there is not very much to make her cheerful at present."

"But what is the matter? Why should she be agitated? Do you think she is afraid of losing the baby?"

"No," said Mrs. Jarvis with an odd sort of laugh. "*That* is not what she is afraid of."

Edith would have liked to know more, but did not ask. She did not greatly care for Mrs. Jarvis, and felt there was something false and uncomfortable about her manner which was always too ingratiating. It was easier to lapse into silence and think about Sam.

"You at least have pleasant thoughts," said her companion pleasantly.

Edith realised that she had been sitting idle, the doll's dress forgotten and a silly smile on her face.

"I dare say you here been thinking about some young man?" Mrs. Jarvis was tiresomely coy. "I wonder who it can be? Mr. Richard Weare, perhaps, or one of the Liftons."

Edith did not answer.

"Well, I see you don't mean to tell me, and it's no concern of mine. So long as you don't fall a victim to that wicked fellow Palgrave! But you would not be so foolish."

Aware that she was blushing, Edith asked stiffly, "Why would it be foolish for—for anyone to become interested in Mr. Palgrave?"

"Oh, my dear child, surely you must have realised after spending nearly two months in this house! You must be aware why he comes here so often. Or perhaps not . . . Never mind Mr. Palgrave; forget that I spoke."

"How can I forget, after such hints? Please tell me what you mean."

"I never talk scandal," said Mrs. Jarvis primly. "Surely you can draw your own conclusions. You don't suppose Palgrave comes here every day to see you?"

This was exactly what Edith did suppose. What else could draw him so frequently to the ladies' part of the house? An uncomfortable new possibility slid into her mind.

"Are you suggesting that he might be in love with the Duchess?"

"There—you knew all the time, you sly girl! Why pretend to be so innocent? There is no need to keep up appearances in front of me. Of course it's very shocking and not what your mama would like, I dare say, but you cannot be implicated. The affair has been going on ever since the Duke went to Ireland, and there has been no scandal."

"The affair," repeated Edith, gazing at her in horror.

"Though perhaps I should give you one word of warning," added Mrs. Jarvis, who was enjoying herself very much. "I don't think you should make opportunities to be alone with Palgrave. Her Grace would not like it, and if she caught you trying to flirt with him, she would probably pack you off home straight away. She would have a perfectly good excuse. Girls who pursue men soon get a bad character."

The unfairness of this would normally have sent Edith into a rage. Just now she was too stunned to protest. Could it possibly be true that Sam and the Duchess had been conducting an intrigue before she ever met either of them? No, she would not believe it. And yet ... And yet ... She remembered her first day at Melford House, and how she had come upon Sam very much at home in this room, and how put out he had been at finding her established here. He had not wanted her to come to the Melfords, he was anxious to know when she was leaving, and anything he had to say to her must wait until after she had left. Taking all these facts together, it did seem as though he was playing a double game.

She was deeply distressed, and not only by the idea of Sam as a heartless philanderer. The Duchess, too, whom she had come to like so much and then to love; could she possibly be such a hypocrite, such a wanton?

Edith sat screwing up her sewing in her hands, aware of that hateful woman watching her. She's been telling me all this for the pleasure of tormenting me, she thought. So perhaps it isn't true after all. Somehow she knew there was no comfort there. She had been blind before, but once the situation had been pointed out to her, she was obliged to recognise what she might have seen all along. She must get out of the Grecian room before she disgraced herself and delighted Mrs. Jarvis by bursting into tears.

She was just about to move, when the door opened and the Duke and Duchess came in together. They had been visiting one of his great-aunts, an elderly eccentric, and the Duchess was laughing, so that her look of strain and pallor and the awkward prominence of her figure could be forgotten for an instant, while her face was young and eager, framed in the curled feathers of her bonnet.

"Lady Augusta is fiercer than ever. She has armed her footman with a bow and arrow in order that he may shoot her neighbour's pug. I don't know what will happen if . . . Why, Edith—what's the matter?"

"Nothing, your Grace," mumbled Edith unconvincingly, too late to conceal her woebegone expression.

If she made for the door she was going to be intercepted, so she did the next best thing. Her scissors had slid off her lap, so she stooped and began to grope for them on the carpet. The Duchess glanced at Mrs. Jarvis.

"What have you been saying to her? I've told you, I won't have her teased and made uncomfortable."

"I don't know what you mean," protested Mrs. Jarvis, high and shrill. She was a little frightened, but still able to bluff. "All young girls have moods and fancies, and I must say it is very strange, whatever happens in this house, the blame is always put on me. It is very wounding to be treated so, and I feel it, I assure you. It is not pleasant to live in a place where one's good intentions are valued so little."

These reproaches might have been enough to deflect the Duchess, who hated scenes. Unluckily, the Duke decided to intervene in his most caustic manner.

"If you don't like it here, Maria, you have an excellent solution. You can leave whenever you choose. No one is compelling you to remain."

"Mel, that is a cruel way to speak to Maria," said his wife, who had become a little breathless. She sat down heavily on the nearest sofa, as though suddenly weary. "Do consider what you are saying."

"I have considered. Maria has been here over seven months, which is quite long enough, and if you won't send her away, I must, for I can see she is having a bad effect on your nerves. You think I don't notice such things, but I do."

Maria was now brick red and she had changed from whining self-pity to belligerent spite.

"Since your Grace is so observant, I wonder you haven't discovered that it is your wife's conscience that is plaguing her, not her nerves! Deceived husbands are such fools."

Edith had straightened up. She looked apprehensively at the Duke, who did not seem unduly shaken by this revealing utterance.

"Set your mind at rest. No one is deceiving me," he told Maria with a contempt that touched her on the raw.

"You flatter yourself," she retorted, "if you think you know all that has been going on. I am not speaking merely of your wife's passion for Mr. Palgrave. What of this child of hers whose birth you expect in September—won't you be surprised when it arrives two months early?"

Melford took a step forward. "What are you implying?"

"I prophesy that you will have an addition to your nursery in July, and that the infant will prove uncommonly well grown for a seven-month child. For it was conceived last October, five weeks after your Grace went to Ireland and seven weeks before you returned."

"You poisonous bitch!" he said, and then swung round on his wife. "Arethusa, is this true?"

She had covered her face with her hands. Across the room, Edith could just catch her answer.

"I'm sorry," she whispered.

The Duke turned back to Mrs. Jarvis, his face grim. "You can go and pack your trunks. You are not spending another hour in this house. And don't go spreading this story all over town! I warn you, if a word of it gets out, I shall stop paying your sons' fees at Winchester and they will have to leave. Your husband was a friend of mine, and for his sake I undertook to educate his children, but if you decide to set up as my enemy, I shall consider the obligation cancelled."

Her moment of triumph over, the tale-bearer had already begun to have regrets and to make excuses, trying to put her conduct in a more favourable light.

"I've done nothing to deserve your displeasure. I felt obliged to tell you the truth. I thought it was my duty."

"Get out," said the Duke. Mrs. Jarvis fled. He caught sight of Edith, and added, "You, too."

As she crossed the room she saw him, out of the corner of her eye, go up to his wife and drag her hands away, so that he could look into her face.

"Why didn't you tell me?"

"I was afraid."

"You had good reason to be afraid," said the deadly quiet voice, "and you haven't saved yourself by adding cowardice to all the rest."

Outside in the passage, Maria Jarvis was inclined to be hysterical. Quite forgetting how she had taunted Edith, she now wanted her sympathy. Edith shook her off without compunction, and almost ran to the only sanctuary where she could be safe and private, her own bedchamber. She flung herself on the bed and buried her head in the pillow, like a child trying to shut out in darkness and solitude events that were too horrible to accept. But, of course, they wouldn't go away.

She was not sure how long she lay there, stupidly struggling against reality. Presently a maid came in to lay out her dress and help her to change for dinner.

Edith said, "I have a headache, Betty." Which, by now was true. "Would you please say I don't feel well enough to dine."

"Very good, miss. Shall I bring you something light on a tray? Is there is anything else you require, miss?"

Edith settled for the tray, to save argument, and Betty went away. She had shown so little surprise or curiosity that it seemed likely the whole household knew already what was going on. If Mrs. Jarvis had already been turned out of doors, they must know that. Probably the Duchess too had taken refuge in a headache and gone to bed.

What would happen to her now the Duke had discovered her guilty secret? Would he compel her to endure the public shame of a divorce, or merely send her away to live in seclusion on one of his estates? Either way, it will serve her right, thought Edith, hardening her heart. She had been brutally disillusioned by two people she had trusted, and though the greatest pain naturally had been caused by the perfidy of Sam Palgrave, it was the Duchess's transgressions which shocked her to the core. She would not have minded Sam having a mistress or two in his past (provided they were in the past), but women who took lovers were outside the pale. At least they were outside the pale in the country society to which the Brutons belonged.

She had understood from her parents' sober warnings that some worldly people treated these matters with an irreligious levity, and since com-

ing to London she had caught glimpses of several
ladies, still clinging with desperate bravado to the
fringes of society, who were pointed at and talked
about but not invited to the best houses. She remembered a supper party where a certain Mrs.
Penrose had arrived, rather tipsy, in search of her
former lover, whom she had assailed with a mixture of insults and grovelling entreaties. Edith had
not seen much of what happened, because she and
Fanny Oxenham and several other girls had been
hustled into another room by their hostess, but she
had gathered that Mrs. Penrose was a well-known
adulteress, and in knowing this she had felt an increased sense of worldly wisdom. What she did not
realise was that Mrs. Penrose and her kind were
sneered at and ostracised, not for taking lovers, but
for taking them in such a hubbub of notoriety and
behaving so badly in public. It had not yet dawned
on her that there were a good many quiet, well-
regulated liaisons going on all around her. So she
saw the Duchess of Melford as a unique example of
wickedness, sunk in sordid depravity like any of
the Penrose sisterhood, yet worse, because she had
somehow managed to hide her vices behind a screen
of false propriety.

I hate her! thought Edith. I hate him, too. And I
despise him. How could he be so taken in?

Betty brought her supper and set it out on a small
table. Edith managed to eat a bowl of soup and half
a roll. After this her headache felt better, and with
the return of energy her sense of loss and resentment grew stronger.

Presently there was a rap on the door. She called
out, thinking this was Betty once again, come to
fetch the tray, but when she turned her head, the
Duchess was standing just inside the room. She had
a chintz wrapper dragged round her as though she
had just got out of bed. Her beautiful fair hair was

tumbled, and her face had the naked, unprotected look brought on by much weeping.

She said, "They told me you were ill, and I am sure it is the effect of hearing the terrible thing I have done. You must be so shocked and disgusted, Edith. Try not to condemn me too harshly."

"Oh, I am quite recovered," said Edith, scrambling to her feet. "And it is not for me to condemn you; I suffered no injury. Your Grace need not concern yourself on my account."

She knew her voice sounded hard and unyielding, but she could not help it. She was determined to pretend that Palgrave's defection meant nothing to her.

"I should never have brought you here. My mother did not wish it. That was why she tried to send you to Valeria."

"Does Lady Woodruff know?" Edith was startled.

"She suspected me of falling into temptation, but didn't know how far. Or about the baby. Maria was the only person who guessed that."

Edith's mind was racing. So that was why Lady Woodruff brought me to London, she thought, suddenly enlightened. She saw that Palgrave liked me when we were at Seddon, and she hoped I could lure him away from her daughter. What a stupid venture! As though I could compete against the famous beauty. There was an alternative. If Sam Palgrave and Arethusa Melford refused to part, their relations would do everything in their power to head off scandal, and one way to achieve this would be for Sam to marry a young wife, a girl too green to understand what was going on under her nose. Edith stood dumbly sorting out these ideas, and feeling that everyone had conspired to make a fool of her.

The Duchess watched her for a short time and then slipped away like a ghost.

* * *

By ten o'clock next morning, having breakfasted in
her room, Edith felt she could not endure her self-
imposed prison a moment longer. It was craven to
lurk here as though she were the person who had
done something to be ashamed of. She must go out
to face the world and make some sort of arrangement for her departure from Melford House.

At this hour of the day they generally visited the
children in the nursery, so she went there first. If
she had to encounter the Duchess, the presence of
Harriet and Bar would put a veto on awkward con-
versations.

The Duchess was not there, rather to her relief,
and the first person she saw was six-year-old Harriet, standing in the middle of the floor and sending
up a forlorn wail, something to do with mama.
Edith checked. Had the Duke already taken some
drastic step to punish his wife's infidelity? Was this
already being visited on their poor little uncompre-
hending children? But the trouble was not so serious after all.

"Lady Harriet is in a terrible taking about Mrs.
Dampier's party, miss," explained Nurse. "Now
hush up, Lady Harriet, do, or Miss Edith will think
you are a great baby! Her Grace does not find herself well enough to go with the children, and what
must my young lady do but decide she dare not go
without her mama."

"Dear me, it would be a great pity if you were to
miss Georgie Dampier's birthday party," exclaimed
Edith, rallying to Nurse's aid in a bright, cajoling
manner. "It is sad your mama does not feel very
well, but you will have Nurse with you, and Bar."

"It's not the same," lamented Harriet between
sobs.

Edith knew it was not the same. The nurses
would be there in the background, but in the

drawing-room where the other children's mothers
were assembled, Harriet would feel lost. She was
going through a phase of shyness, quite irrational
but none the less real.

"Couldn't Mrs. Gordon take them?" she asked.

Nurse reminded her that Mrs. Gordon had gone
to Northamptonshire to see Lady Woodruff, still
languishing with her broken leg.

Lord Barlington appeared from the other nursery, careering towards them on his hobby-horse and
shouting, "Seedif! Seedif!"

It was the nearest he could get to "Miss Edith"
and had become her nickname with both children.

Abruptly Harriet stopped crying and said, "Seedif, why can't you take us to Georgie's birthday?"

Edith was in no mood for a party, and the Dampiers' London house was the last place she wanted
to go. It would be too reminiscent of Seddon Park
and the happy days she was only too anxious to
forget. All the same, she felt a deep compassion for
this little girl and boy whose family life was under
threat, although they did not know it. It would not
be much of a sacrifice to go with them to Berkeley
Street. Firmly crushing down her own self-pity, she
decided to ask if the Duchess would agree to this
plan.

She approached the Duchess's bedchamber by
way of her dressing-room, which was used less for
dressing in than sitting in, a misnomer everyone
understood. The Duchess of Melford's dressing-room
was painted the palest primrose yellow. Her chaise-
longue, tea-table torchère and escritoire were all
made to match, exquisitely delicate and fine. The
only person in the room was the Duke, whose height
made him look intrusive and out of proportion as
he searched through the pigeon-holes of the escritoire and looked in the drawers.

He saw Edith was making for the bedroom, and said, "You can't go in there!"

She stopped and faced him. What was he doing? Looking for love letters? She supposed he had every right to do so, but it was horrible all the same.

Meeting her gaze, he said in a more conciliating manner, "I don't wish to prevent your seeing my wife, but she wishes to be left alone."

"Very well, your Grace. I only wished to ask the Duchess whether I should take the children to the Dampiers this afternoon. It's Georgie Dampier's birthday. Harriet and Bar have been looking forward to it, but they are too shy to go without their mother. At least Harriet is. Bar is not afraid of anything."

I'm chattering, she thought. Irritating this cold, arrogant man who is bored by feminine trivialities. But he did not seem irritated.

"Would you take them? I'd be uncommonly grateful. I'm trying to find out my wife's engagements so that I can cancel them, but I don't know where to look. It's damned awkward."

Edith joined him at the writing-table, and after shifting a few papers found the leather-bound book in which the Duchess made a note of her many social engagements. As she handed it to him, her well-trained impulse to be helpful took charge of her again.

"Would your Grace like me to write the necessary excuses to these people? I could do so, if you would tell me exactly what to say. I think if I wrote it might seem less . . . less particular."

"That is certainly true. You are a sensible girl." added the Duke, surprising her a good deal.

She felt she was entitled to the praise, but was surprised at his troubling to express it. He was a good deal less lofty than she'd ever known him before. Well, he had been knocked off his pedestal of impregnable superiority with a vengeance, deceived by his wife, and his friend, on the point of accepting their bastard child as his own. It struck her for the first time that she and Melford were both in the same boat, the two victims of that unscrupulous pair of charmers. Though, of course, his situation was far worse than hers. She wondered what he meant to do. Remembering his voice as he confronted his wife yesterday afternoon, remembering uncomfortably how she had looked a few hours later, crushed and defenceless, Edith could not help feeling a tremor of sympathy for the wretched Arethusa in spite of everything.

The Duke gave no hint of his intentions, simply telling her how to word the various letters she was to write. Edith wanted to raise the matter of her own departure; the sooner she got away from Melford House the better, but they were interrupted by a footman announcing Dr. Chalfont. This was the family physician, and she could see that the Duke was anxious to talk to him at once.

She made herself scarce and composed civil notes to Mrs. Dampier and various other ladies, saying that the Duchess had been ordered a complete rest, wondering as she wrote how long this convenient platitude would be sufficient to paste over the cracks in the Melford's marriage.

Later that day she travelled the short distance to Berkeley Street with Harriet, Bar and Nurse. Harriet wore a white muslin dress with pink ribbons, and a silk shawl round her in the carriage. She was nervous and silent. Bar wore a jacket and pantaloons of cherry red silk. He was noisy and exuberant.

As soon as they were upstairs in the Dampiers' drawing-room and Harriet caught sight of her friend Georgiana Dampier, she miraculously forgot all her fears. She rushed to join a game of musical chairs and was soon whooping and shrieking with the best. Edith need not have come.

However, the Dampier children were pleased to see her. They encircled her, telling their young guests, "This is our snow lady that came to us out of the storm."

"No, she isn't! She's Seedif," said Lord Barlington.

"You mustn't contradict, Bar. It's rude," Edith told him, thinking it was a pity no one ever said this to his father.

The ladies asked well-meaning questions about the Duchess. How many of them realised that her troubles were far more serious than the ailments of pregnancy? Mrs. Dampier knew, Edith was sure of that. After all, she was Sam Palgrave's cousin. So she was not entirely unprepared, at the height of the party, when her hostess murmured in her ear, "There is something I must say to you. Let us slip away for a few minutes. We shall not be missed."

Edith followed her down a short flight of stairs and into a room on the half-landing. She could hardly refuse, though she did not want to answer questions or take part in any discussion of the sordid intrigue and its likely results. She was working out ways of saying this without seeming discourteous, when she found that Mrs. Dampier had bundled her into the little writing-room and closed the door on her. She was not alone. There was a man sitting on a chair by the window, who stood up as she came in. It was Sam Palgrave.

"No!" said Edith, backing away.

"Edith, I'm so sorry. If you will let me speak to you."

"No!" she repeated. "You can have nothing of interest to say to me, Mr. Palgrave."

"I want to explain . . ."

"There's no need. I know the whole miserable

story already." She was standing right up against the door, so could have left easily enough, but remained because she had an urgent desire to speak her mind. "You made love to your friend's wife while he was out of the country, you conspired with her to pass off your natural child as a legitimate MountStephen, and when I arrived at Melford House after Christmas, you made up to me simply to distract attention from your frequent visits to the Duchess. I think you are contemptible!"

"Yes, I am contemptible," he agreed in a quiet, flat voice. "But that is not exactly how things fell out."

Staring at him, she seemed to be seeing a stranger. All his lively humour had vanished; it was no longer there, even as an undercurrent, and without that sparkle and the laughter lines, she thought his features quite ugly. She supposed she had never seen him entirely serious before, yet she had never even realised that when she had considered marrying him. Which did not say much for her ability to choose a husband!

He was desperate to give his explanation, such as it was. "Arethusa and I carried on a long-standing flirtation, a harmless game based on real, though innocent, affection. For a brief space last autumn matters got out of hand. It was my fault; I was selfish and reckless. We soon came to our senses, decided that we must call a halt and meet simply as friends. She did not tell me there was going to be a child—at that time, I doubt if she knew. None of this is any excuse for the way I have treated Melford, but I never meant to hurt you, Edith. When we met at Seddon in January, I believed myself free to marry. I had parted from Arethusa, and the only loyalty I owed her was to keep my mouth shut and safeguard her reputation. I began to fall in love with you straight away, when we

walked up the drive in the snow, do you remember?
When we met at Melford House, I was confused and
alarmed."

"I dare say you might be," said Edith, aware of
the waspish note in her voice.

"I soon became certain that you were the one girl
I wanted for my wife. Yet I couldn't bring myself
to make my feelings plain at Melford House with
Arethusa looking on. That is why I kept wishing
you would go home, so that I could visit you in your
own family and become your declared suitor. I dare
say this two-faced manoeuvring makes you despise
me more than you do already. I don't expect you to
understand everything that relates to me and Arethusa, but I wish you could believe that, with you,
I was always honest, not playing a shabby game. I
wasn't using you as a decoy, to protect her."

Edith did not trouble to consider his protestations seriously. She resisted belief because she had
lost faith in her own judgement and was afraid of
being talked round. What did it matter, anyway?
Not heart-broken so much as disillusioned and disgusted, she collected herself to end the interview
on a note of icy self-command.

"I never asked to hear the details of your association with the Duchess, Mr. Palgrave. The less
said on that score the better. As for your profes-
sions of being in love with me, I suppose I ought to
say I am honoured, but it would not be true. In fact
I wish to end our acquaintance, and I hope never to
see you at Cotebury, or anywhere else." The last
part of this declaration had the effect of a slight
come-down.

Palgrave said in a curiously desolate voice,
"Make your mind easy. It is very unlikely you will
ever see me again."

Edith went out on to the staircase. She could hear
the shrill, excited voices of the children on the floor

above, among them the little MountStephens. She was able to crush an impulse of charity towards Sam Palgrave. His disgraceful seduction of Arethusa Melford had started a train of events through which a great many people were going to be hurt, some of them far worse than herself.

Edith slept badly. She kept waking, her nerves clenched, her mind churning over and over the events of the last two days. At six o'clock she was disturbed by the sound of a pair of horses clip-clopping over the cobbles right up to the front door, an unusual happening so early in the morning. At the stable end of the courtyard there was always something going on: grooms taking horses out to exercise, a wagon of farm produce coming in from the country, but no one normally came or went by the main entrance before breakfast.

Because she was edgy and restless, she got up and looked out of the window. From her room on the first floor, she was gazing down at right-angles into the arch of the porte-cochère. She could just see the horses' heads and the light glinting on their harness. The vehicle itself was out of sight, but she had a distinct view of two men coming down the steps of the house: the Duke and Colonel Waters. They disappeared, there was the sound of a door being shut, and a moment later one of the town carriages drawn by a pair of bays, with a liveried coachman and footman on the box, crossed the courtyard and went out by the main gate.

Edith was surprised. She could not think where the Duke and Colonel Waters could be going at such an hour. Unless it was to some sporting event out of town—though this seemed a curious thing for the Duke to do at a moment of crisis. Besides which, he wouldn't have gone in a closed carriage. He would have ridden, or driven his curricle.

She got back into bed, vaguely disturbed though not knowing why. She spent the next hour sadly reliving all her encounters with Sam, right up to the last one—the day before at the Dampiers'. How changed he had been! Guilty and hangdog now that he had been found out. The news must have shaken him. For the first time, she began to wonder how it had reached him. A warning message from his mistress? Or an angry accusation from her husband, that was more likely. Edith sat upright in bed, rigid with horror as she thought of the one assignation gentlemen kept very early in the day. The Duke had gone to fight a duel with his wife's lover! He had taken Colonel Waters with him to act as his second, and they had driven off in a closed carriage in case he had to be brought back wounded or even dead. And she recalled Sam saying with terrible desolation that it was very unlikely she would ever see him again.

She now felt she had been needlessly cruel to a man who might at this moment be facing death, if he was not dead already. She could hear his voice saying, I'm sorry, Edith. He had called her "Edith" yesterday; he had never once said "Swan".

She got up and dressed, though there was nothing she could do except lean on the window-sill and wait for the carriage to return. She could foresee nothing but disaster. If one of the duellists was killed, would the survivor be put on trial? She knew this could happen, even to a peer. Men used to escape across the Channel, but that wasn't so easy with Bonaparte in control of the Continent. And how would the Duchess feel, with two men's ruin on her conscience, as well as her own?

Edith went on leaning out of the window until her elbows were sore. Then at last she saw the carriage enter the gateway and move sedately towards the front of the house. She waited no longer, but

ran out of her room along two corridors and down
the stairs, arriving in time to see the Duke come
through the front door, looking perfectly calm and
unruffled.

He handed his hat to an attendant footman, said
something to Colonel Waters, who was just behind
him, and vanished through a door which led by a
private staircase to his own apartments.

Edith didn't think he had seen her. The hall was
immense, and very ornately decorated. She hurried
towards Colonel Waters.

"What happened?"

He took her arm and led her out of earshot of the
servants, but made no pretence of misunderstanding the question.

"Palgrave deloped. Fired in the air."

"And the Duke?"

"Hit him in the arm. A flesh wound. Nothing
dangerous, thank God."

"He might have been killed!"

"No," said Waters decidedly. "The Duke is one
of the best shots in England. He could kill a man
intentionally—he could not do so by mistake. As it
is, Palgrave has lost a little blood and will have to
carry his arm in a sling for the next week, but the
injury is so slight that he will be able to fob off
awkward questions—put it down to a fall from his
horse, or some such thing."

Edith's relief was so intense that she felt quite
dizzy. Gradually this strangeness subsided into a
new anger against Sam, because she had been
tricked into feeling sorry for him. She breakfasted
alone. Presumably the two men had eaten some sort
of a meal before they went out.

She was on the point of leaving the breakfast-
room, when the Duke came in and said, "I should
like to talk to you, Miss Edith, if you can spare the
time."

As though she had any other occupation which could possibly take precedence over his wishes! He pulled out a chair from the table, sat down and looked around.

"Is that coffee still hot? Will you pour me a cup?"

She did as she was asked, spilling a little in the saucer. For some reason she always felt clumsy in the presence of the Duke of Melford. She did not know why, for she was neat-fingered and tolerably self-possessed. Other men did not reduce her to a state of silly incompetence. Perhaps it was his air of conscious superiority which intimidated her, allied to his superb good looks. That classical marble profile seemed impervious to the admiration of lesser mortals, the level dark brows rejected emotion. However, she filled the cup, substituted a clean saucer, and resumed her seat.

As she watched him stir the coffee, the light winked on the great signet ring he wore on his fourth finger. There was a curious fascination about that well-kept hand, which had so lately gripped a smoking pistol. The hand that had held Sam Palgrave's life in its power and then spared him. She shivered inwardly.

At last he said, "I'm sorry you have passed two such disagreeable days. You have been distressed by all the details of a family scandal—which you cannot have wanted to hear—and then left to your own devices. I'm afraid I have been very remiss."

"It's of no consequence, sir," she said, embarrassed.

"Well, it ought to have been of consequence to me. My only excuse is that I have been too taken up in trying to find a way out of our difficulties. I suppose you realise the chief of them? I cannot accept this child as a legitimate MountStephen. It is out of the question."

Edith understood. The baby, if a boy, would become in law the second heir to the dukedom, and though no one would care to put such a painful thought into words, there was always a chance that Barlington would not live to inherit the title. He was a sturdy, vigorous little boy, but he was only four, and such dreadful things did happen to children. The Duke himself had no brothers, but he had plenty of MountStephen cousins, and he could hardly be expected to risk their being cut out by another man's bastard. She supposed there would have to be a very public and humiliating divorce, with all the opportunities and dates made plain. But what was he saying now? She listened increasingly bewildered.

"I have consulted Dr. Chalfont, our family physician. He has a trusted colleague, a Dr. James, who has opened up a small spa on the site of some mineral springs at a place called Strenton near the Welsh border. I don't suppose the waters do much good at any of these new places, but they are probably harmless, and by great good fortune the Strenton water is reputed to benefit women who have trouble in bearing children. We are going to give out that my wife's condition is causing anxiety and that Dr. Chalfont has recommended her to try the waters at Strenton. A secluded house will be rented for her, and she will live there quietly with Dr. James in attendance. There will also be a very discreet midwife, whom Dr. Chalfont assures me we can trust. These two, and perhaps her maid, will be the only persons present when the child is born, which must happen some time in July. Since it is generally believed that the Duchess expects to be confined in September, everyone will take it for granted that the birth is almost two months premature, and the news of the infant's death will hardly seem surprising."

"Its death!" repeated Edith with a slight gulp. "Surely, sir, you don't intend . . ."

"To murder the wretched brat? Calm yourself, Miss Edith, I only intend to make away with its presence in my family pedigree. Nothing worse, I assure you."

"I beg your pardon," she said, scarlet in the face. "I did not really suppose you meant anything more sinister. But what is to happen to the poor little thing?"

"The poor little thing will be put out to nurse, and then placed in some poor but respectable family where it will be properly cared for and educated. I shall make every necessary provision. You need not think it will be neglected or ill used."

"And the Duchess," she asked after a moment's hesitation. "May I know what is to happen to her?"

"She'll travel up to Rythorpe as soon as she is recovered from her lying-in. We always go north in the summer." He caught her quick, uncertain glance, and laughed. "Oh, I see how it is! I am cast for all the villains' parts—not Herod merely, but Othello! My dear child, do use your wits. Why do you suppose I am going to all this trouble: conspiring with doctors, renting houses, trying to keep my wife hidden for the rest of her pregnancy? What would be the point if I meant to abandon her at the end of it? The baby can be spirited away and reported stillborn, but unless she remains out of sight, no one will believe the story of the seven-month child, and once the gossips started calculating, it would be known that I could not be the father. I am trying to arrange that, once this episode is over, she can return to her natural place in the world without a shadow on her character."

Edith sat as though paralysed by astonishment and a certain degree of shame. It struck her that

Melford, with more to forgive than she had, was showing a far greater degree of Christian charity.

He got up and walked round the table. She could feel him standing behind her, his hands pressed on the back of her chair.

He said more gently. "You are not used to situations of this kind, and of course you ought not to be. No doubt you have been taught that women who make this particular mistake have to pay for it with a lifetime of misery and disgrace. When it actually happens, you know, we are not always so severe. Her worst action was to try and deceive me about the child, but if that is put right, I can learn to forget the rest. Do you understand?"

"Yes, your Grace," she whispered, a good deal mortified.

"Good. Because there is something I want to ask you."

"If you wish for a promise of silence . . ."

"No, that is not what I meant. I was taking your discretion for granted—you are not a Maria Jarvis. What I want from you is a great favour, a request Arethusa would like to make, only she will not do so because she is afraid that you find her situation so repulsive that you will not wish to accept."

What could he mean? He had moved away from her chair and a little further back, to stand in the window embrasure. She turned to look at him.

He said, "Would you go down to Strenton and stay with her, see her through this ordeal?"

"Go to Strenton?" She was absolutely horrified. "Oh no, I could not! I should not be of the smallest use. It is out of the question."

"Is it? I'm sorry."

Edith was left floundering. She had been very much shocked by the Duchess's adultery, which she felt unable to condone. At the same time she was honest enough to admit that her reluctance to go to

Strenton had less to do with morality than a horrible kind of jealousy. She had imagined herself happily and successfully in love with Sam Palgrave, and did not want to spend the next few months cooped up with the woman who had shattered all those dreams, waiting for her to bear Sam's child.

"I don't wish to be disobliging, but I don't see why the Duchess should want me. She must have many closer friends of her own age?"

"That's the main problem. Her sister and her closest women friends all have husbands and children of their own. If she was dangerously ill, there are half a dozen who would come to her at a moment's notice. But she is in no immediate danger, and our story is that she is simply going to Strenton to take the waters. People are always going to take the waters somewhere or other; it is hardly a cause for alarm. But if my sister-in-law or Mrs. Dampier or Lady Jane Oxenham were to throw up everything and go with her, it would cause a great deal of speculation, just what we hope to avoid. And whoever volunteered to go would find it hard to appease her own family without giving the game away. So you seemed such an excellent choice, because you are staying with us already and Arethusa has become so much attached to you."

And since I already know her wretched secret, that would mean one less person to confide in, thought Edith with a new-found cynicism. All the same, she saw the point of what he had said. She felt trapped.

"If your Grace will give me a little time to think . . ."

"Yes, by all means," he said at once. "I don't wish to hurry you."

But she felt he was disappointed in her, and found to her surprise that she minded this quite a lot.

Perhaps because his willingness to forgive his wife had revealed a generosity she had not expected. He crossed the breakfast-room and left her, without another glance or any attempt at persuasion.

Edith began to wander about, irresolute. She went to look out of the window, at the people strolling up and down in Green Park: children bowling hoops, nursemaids, saunterers enjoying the spring sun. There was an unfashionable group of sight-seers staring at the house. Did they know who lived here? Did they suppose that dukes and duchesses existed in a perpetual state of carefree pleasure?

I wish I knew what to do, she thought. She had one obvious way out, and she knew she could never bring herself to take it. She could not tell either of the Melfords that she did not want to go to Strenton because she herself was grieving for the loss of Are-thusa's lover. Imagine making such an admission to the Duke! It made her feel hot and cold all over. He obviously had no idea; why should he? To a man of his experience, her little ventures on the social scene must appear quite childish and insipid. And the Duchess? Two days ago, in her first anger, she had decided that the lovers had been using her to divert suspicion from themselves, but she believed enough of what Sam had said yesterday to acquit the Duchess, at least. And if she doesn't know, I can't tell her. It's too humiliating, thought Edith.

But how else could she go on refusing? Of course her parents' permission would have to be asked; could she pretend that they did not approve? That would sound ridiculous. It was not as though she were being expected to take any alarming respon-sibility for the Duchess's health. Unmarried girls were often given charge of a household where the wife was having a difficult pregnancy. Her elder sister Lizzie had gone to the help of a cousin in just such an emergency two years ago—yes, and now she

came to think of it, she remembered telling the
Duchess all about that and how mama had said it
was valuable experience. So no excuse was possible
on those lines.

If she turned down the Duke's suggestion, he
would think she was prudish and missish and strait-
laced, incapable of kindness to an unhappy woman
who, for all her faults, had been exceedingly kind
to her. He might also think that, in spite of the
many entertaining weeks she had spent in his town
house, she was not prepared to endure the tedium
of being buried alive in the country, where there
would be no society and no amusements.

The appearance of selfish ingratitude, on top of
everything else, was more than she could bear.

Making up her mind, and determined to act before she could change it, she went at once to the
Duchess's apartments. She would be there. She had
not left them since the dreadful scene two days earlier, though whether she remained a prisoner by
her own choice or the Duke's decree was not clear.

She was seated at the little escritoire, a pen in
her hand, though she was not writing, just staring
into space. It was extraordinary how her looks had
altered in the last two days. Her face had grown
thin with strain and her body heavier, as though
the admission that she was six months gone with
the child instead of four had defeated a heroic attempt to force nature into conforming with her desperate deception.

She greeted Edith with a smile that was pitifully
nervous, as though she was uncertain what terms
they were on.

"I hear you took Harriet and Bar to the Dampiers. I hope they were good."

"Yes, they behaved beautifully."

She was going to say more, but the Duchess hurried on.

"I am afraid you are very uncomfortably placed here at present. I dare say you want to leave."

"The Duke said that you would like me to go with you to this spa where you are to take the waters."

The Duchess looked more distressed than ever. "Oh dear, did he tell you that? I begged him not to, but he is so used to getting his own way that he does not always consider what he is asking. I ought not to have mentioned the idea. It slipped out when he said I ought to have someone to keep me company. For, of course, I know, dear Edith, that you do not—cannot—wish to stay with me, now you understand what a deceitful creature I am and how wicked I have been."

"But you are quite mistaken. I do want to come with you to Strenton," said Edith.

To her astonishment, she realised that this was true.

CHAPTER FIVE

Holly Lodge was an indifferent house, the kind that no one stayed in for long. Every neighbourhood had one; the Old Priory near Cotebury was just such another. Edith recognised the signs as soon as she stepped out of the carriage: the gaunt building that faced northwards into the side of a hill, the rooms that were too high and narrow, the slight pervading sense of damp. The Duchess was thankful to be at their journey's end, and hardly took in her surroundings.

Dr. James was there to meet them, full of apologies. He knew the house was not quite what her grace would like, but it had been difficult to find anything at short notice. This was true enough, for besides requiring a house reasonably near Strenton, the Duke had insisted that it must be extremely secluded, far from the gaze of regular passers-by or curious neighbours. Holly Lodge was at the end of a lane which led nowhere else; the parish church was two miles away; the vicar was a bachelor, and there was no village to speak of.

"I'm sure we shall be very comfortable," said the Duchess, making an effort to seem pleased.

Dr. James was gratified. He was a capable man of about fifty, who naturally knew all about his new patient's predicament but spoke of the necessary precautions without embarrassment.

"Your Grace will not wish to come to the bath-house, so I have obtained two empty wine-casks which will be filled every day with water drawn from our chalybeate spring and brought out here by the carrier. Your servants must draw off two pints of water for you to drink, and the rest must be heated and poured into a slipper-bath, so that you can bathe in tolerable comfort. That will alleviate any disagreeable symptoms."

When he had gone, the Duchess remarked, "He seems very attentive and practical. We all know that my most disagreeable symptom is the child that I ought not to be carrying, but there is nothing he can do about that!"

Edith noticed that she was learning to overcome her state of abject self-abasement. She was still acutely conscious of her situation, but was able to speak of it with a detached irony that made the whole subject less painful for them both.

She herself was growing accustomed to the knowledge which had seemed so horribly shocking ten days ago. She still felt a twinge of bitterness when she let her mind fasten on what the Duchess had done, but she knew in her heart that this was simply due to jealousy. It was no longer possible to go on thinking of Arethusa Melford as a monster of depravity. She was a very unhappy woman, now separated from everyone she loved, haunted by poor little Harriet's tears when they parted and blaming herself for everything.

Both children had clung to her, and wept and made a great outcry: Harriet because it was in her nature, and Bar, Edith thought, because he did not want to be left out. In contrast, the Duke had been cool, distant and correct, unbending just enough to hand his wife into the carriage and to hope her health would soon improve. All this had added to her load of remorse, and Edith had felt so sorry for her that she had stopped feeling sorry for herself.

She at once set about trying to make the house more habitable. Unpacking the books and games they had brought with them, moving the furniture about and discovering which of the drawing-room chairs was least uncomfortable, and going from room to room to make an ill-matched collection of candlesticks so that at least they would not have to spend their evenings in total gloom. She also explored the garden, which was pleasanter than the house, and being neglected had a sort of wild prettiness.

The Duchess's water cure began next day, and the day after that they drove into Strenton, the Duchess remaining in the carriage, while Edith bought a few items they had forgotten and also hunted out a piano-tuner. There was an instrument at Holly Lodge, which she hoped had not been quite ruined by damp. They gazed at the outside of the pump-house, an affair of classical white pillars dumped down incongruously among the weather-beaten buildings of an old market town. It was very inferior to Bath, the only spa Edith had ever visited, and she did not think they were going to miss much by never venturing inside.

There was no real reason at present why the Duchess should not walk about the town or visit the pump-house. Though it was plain she was expecting a child, no outsider could have forecast exactly when. But it would soon become obvious that she was due to be confined long before September. It would be pointless to hoodwink everybody in London, and then run the risk of some letter-writing busybody in Strenton spreading the news that the Duchess of Melford's lying-in was not, after all, premature. So it seemed wise that she should play the secluded invalid right from the start.

This had sounded a perfectly good plan in London, but they had overlooked the tendency of the country gentry to call on any person of title who appeared in their midst. A mere knight's widow would have done! The chance of visiting a duchess and talking about it afterwards was irresistible. The tenants of Holly Lodge spent their first fortnight more or less in a state of siege. Being at the end of a cul-de-sac, they luckily had some warning of approaching callers. So whenever the rumble of carriage-wheels was heard in the lane, the Duchess and Edith would retire into the morning-room at the back of the house, while Stodart, the butler, defended the front door, declaring impassively that her Grace was not at home. He was the under-butler from Melford House, and thus used to better things. He detested Holly Lodge, but stayed at his post out of devotion to the family.

After driving off the invaders, Stodart would present their cards to the Duchess, who was in two minds what to do about them. Failing to return a call was the simplest method of saying one did not desire the caller's acquaintance.

"But it seems so uncivil," she said to Edith. "Perhaps if you were to write on my behalf, explaining that I am not well . . ."

"If I do, they'll be encouraged, and they'll be sending constantly to enquire."

"Yes, that's true! What an awkward fix we are in. And if we are so very unsociable, don't you think people will begin to suspect something?"

"Yes," said Edith frankly. "But not the secret we are trying to keep. I'm afraid they will suspect that your Grace does not care to associate with the kinds of families who live around here, so you are pretending to be ill in order to avoid them."

"That is how it must look. I wish it were not so;
I hate to seem proud."

This was true. She would do anything to avoid
hurting people's feelings—unlike her husband and
some other members of the nobility, male and female, whom Edith had observed in London.

Without considering very carefully, she said,
"The accusation of pride won't stick. Whatever they
may be imagining now, when they hear you've lost
your baby, they will believe you were ill all the
time."

The Duchess gave a small gasp, and Edith was
horrified by her own heartless remark.

"What a dreadful thing to have said! How could
I have been so clumsy? I did not think . . ."

"It's not your fault, my dear. I am going to lose
my baby, and it's no more than I deserve. For I
have been hoping and hoping these last months that
I should miscarry. I suppose that's the worst of all
my sins, worse even than being unfaithful to Mel
and telling so many lies! But I have had three miscarriages before this, and I could not help thinking
it might be the best solution. And now, if the poor
creature does live, I am going to let them take it
from me without a struggle. What else can I do? It
is the only way I can return home to my dear little
Harriet and Bar."

The tears ran silently down her cheeks. She
brushed them aside, and sat gazing into the world
of her own unhappiness.

Edith sat down beside her on the sofa. "Do you
suppose, if the baby is a girl, the Duke might let
you keep her? I can understand that he does not
feel able to accept a boy, but a daughter . . ."

"No," said the Duchess with finality. "He has
made his sentiments quite plain. He could not bring
himself to love this child, so it is better the poor

innocent does not grow up in our house. Anything is better than living where you are not loved."

Edith did not think the Duchess could have much experience of such a sad condition. Her trouble seemed to be that she loved, and was loved, too easily.

Hoping to dispel her melancholy, Edith said, "Would your Grace care to take a turn in the garden before dinner?"

"Yes, if you like. And, by the way, I think you must stop addressing me so formally. It is quite unsuited to our situation now."

"Very well, Duchess," said Edith, trying out the last word a little uncertainly.

There was always a slight grammatical awkwardness in saying "your Grace", and although it was the proper way to speak to persons of the Melfords' rank, she had noticed that many of the London friends among whom they moved on more or less equal terms simply said "Duke" or "Duchess". Which sounded oddly unadorned, though she supposed it was no odder than hearing her father addressed as "Rector". But apparently it was not what the Duchess had in mind.

"That is a change without a difference. What I should like is for you to call me 'Arethusa'."

"Oh, but I could not—I mean, I don't think I ought. It does not sound at all respectful."

"Well, my dear, if you feel obliged to pay lip-service to my exalted station when we are in company, you are welcome to do so. When we are alone, it is your friendship I value. I have no particular craving for respect. Which is just as well, isn't it? For I'm certainly not entitled to any."

In spite of the deprecating note, Edith realised that she was being gently teased.

Time passed. Primroses in the lane gave place to bluebells in a nearby wood. The untidy rose bushes in the garden were covered with sugar-pink buds which uncurled in the sun.

Arethusa lay stretched on a garden seat in lazy contemplation. She no longer felt fit to walk anywhere. They kept themselves occupied with reading and sewing, chess, cards and backgammon, painting in water-colours and playing the piano, and Edith felt that in spite of everything, they had passed some happy hours in their strange exile, as remote as two heroines immured in one of those Gothic castles that featured in most of the new novels they received regularly from London.

"Though I do not think," said Arethusa critically, "that Holly Lodge is at all what one looks for in a romance. It is miserably un-Gothic, and if I were a proper heroine, I should write and complain to the author!"

Besides books and periodicals, there were letters from the outside world. One came each week from Melford House, and Arethusa would seize on it, pushing everything else aside, because there was sure to be a carefully-written letter from Harriet and a drawing from Bar. When she had studied these exhaustively, she would turn to her husband's letter, which Edith could not help noticing was always rather short. This did not prevent his wife reading them over and over with an anxious frown, as though she were looking for something that was not there.

"He hasn't forgiven me yet," she said sadly, one afternoon in June.

Edith had been diligently dead-heading the roses. She sat down in a garden chair.

"Surely that will come when you are together again, after all this is over? He is so much in love with you . . ."

"I'm afraid you are mistaken, my dear. He is not

in the least in love, and has not been for some years
now. I don't think he minded much my going to bed
with Sam. He isn't jealous in the ordinary way. It's
the lies I told him, trying to keep my poor little
cuckoo in the MountStephen nest: that is what I
have to live down, and I don't know whether he'll
ever relent."

One more illusion shattered, Edith stared at her
in dismay. Somehow she had come to assume that
the Duke adored his beautiful, faithless wife. This
must have been partly due to a misconception.
When she first met the Melfords, she had not liked
his caustic and unsympathetic manner, but because Arethusa took everything he said with such
sweet-tempered serenity, it had been easy to view
their marriage in a soft and sentimental light, to
imagine a tender devotion behind the façade. Then,
when the scandalous secret came out, and Melford
was at once so angry yet so ready to protect his wife
and ready to take her back, this had seemed so
much like the conduct of a man bitterly hurt, yet
still in love.

"Poor Edith!" said Arethusa, watching her. "I
keep forgetting how young you are and how un-
versed in the ways of married people. You are such
a tower of strength and so well educated, but your
experience of the world is still very limited, and
experience is the only useful guide through the
quicksands of anyone's marriage, one's own or other
people's."

"I suppose it is. I only thought—took it for
granted, perhaps . . ."

"That we were happily matched? Well, why not?
I thought so myself, once."

Arethusa fell silent. They could hear a cuckoo
giving its midsummer call, over and over, from the
wood where the bluebells had grown. Then she said,

"When I married Mel, I thought I was going to live happily ever after."

"How old were you? Had you known him long?"

"No. I saw him first at a ball, when I was seventeen. I was staying with my Aunt Moresby. You know, the one with the mad son, only he wasn't so mad then, only a trifle peculiar. Frank Bonham was there, too; he was a neighbour of ours at home and my childhood sweetheart, though my parents did not consider him a suitable match, for his estates were dreadfully encumbered. His father was a gamester. I paid very little attention to such dull scruples, and I was dancing with Frank when Mel first saw me. He was staying in Northamptonshire for the hunting, and he asked, 'Who is that ravishing girl?' His friends told him, 'That is Arethusa Woodruff, and they say she is going to marry Frank Bonham.' And Mel said, 'We'll see about that!'"
Arethusa gave a curt laugh.

"He went at once to speak to my aunt, so he was there, standing beside her, when Frank brought me back from the dance. The moment I caught sight of him, my heart turned over, and I wondered, Who can he be? He was twenty-two. Several years later, he was described as the handsomest man in England. To me, he has never been anything else."

Edith could believe her. You did not have to be in love with the Duke of Melford to recognise one inescapable fact about him: the magnetic quality of his good looks.

"We were introduced. We danced. Next day, the men were all going to hunt. Ladies aren't much liked in the hunting-field, especially in the shires. We are expected to fall off our horses and interfere with the sport—a shocking slander! So my cousin Margaret and I didn't attend the meet; we simply rode in the direction hounds were likely to draw and joined in at the second covert. Mel rode beside me all day, escorted us back to Wakeland, and got himself invited to dinner. Within the week, he had asked me to marry him. I didn't know what to do. I was well and truly in love, but I considered myself promised to Frank. My parents told me not to be so foolish. They wanted me to make this brilliant marriage, and they pointed out that I had no right to engage myself to anyone without their consent, so my promises could not be valid. And there was Mel, charming me out of my wits! I'm afraid I didn't put up much of a fight for my principles. I never have."

"What did Frank do?"

"Got over his disappointment, and married a splendid Irish girl who likes to live in the country all the year round and doesn't care that they never have any money. The last time we met, he said, 'It's lucky you didn't marry me, Tusie. I could never have kept you in white gloves.' Tusie is the name my brother gave me when we were children."

She spoke of the past with a pure enjoyment untouched by sad comparisons.

"We were married, and it was even better than I dreamed of, living at Rythorpe and in London, and being always with Mel. Even though I began so badly in one way, for I could not give him an heir. Two miscarriages and then a daughter. Mel was so good and patient, trying to raise my spirits. Never a word of reproach. At last our precious little boy was born. I shall never forget how happy we were then. I felt I had nothing left to wish for. Yet it was only five or six months later that Mel began to change. Everything I said or did seemed to annoy him. He became impatient, and then different. I have never understood what went wrong."

Perhaps he fell in love with someone else, thought Edith. She shifted a little in her chair, and Arethusa heard her.

"No, it wasn't that," she said, as though the

words had been spoken aloud. "Of course there have
been women; no one would expect otherwise. At
least you might, perhaps, because you have been so
very well brought up and your father is a clergyman. But it is not unusual for men to have mistresses, only Mel does not make a habit of falling
in love. I suppose we have just grown apart, as husbands and wives often do. It is hardly a subject for
tragedy, or has not been until now. We have both
been able to live very much as we chose; the heart
soon learns to accommodate itself."

There was a jarring note here. She had not mentioned Sam, but Edith thought of him, and of how
she had said of her husband: He is not jealous in
the ordinary way. Did this mean he had been given
cause for jealousy before, and that Sam was merely
the most recent in a line of lovers? Edith found this
a horrible idea, and thrust it out of her mind. She
was by now so fond of Arethusa that she did not
want to think ill of her.

All their preparations had been carefully made. The
discreet midwife, Mrs. Rigg, had arrived in Strenton. She could not come straight to Holly Lodge;
this would have had an odd appearance, since they
had to keep up the pretence that the baby was not
due until September. She had taken a room in the
town, announcing to anyone who was interested
that she had worked for Dr. James before, and
hoped he would find some further cases for her.

A method had been planned for the baby to be
smuggled away. As soon as Arethusa went into la-
bour, a groom would be sent to summon Dr. James
and then ride on immediately to Hereford, where
he was to deliver a cryptically worded note at the
house of an attorney, one Mr. Hemsley. Late that
evening a carriage was to stop outside in the lane,
and the baby was to be taken out and handed over

to a wet-nurse, who would be accompanied by either Mr. Hemsley or an agent acting on his behalf—Edith was not clear about this.

As soon as the child had been removed, it could be announced that the Duchess of Melford had been brought to bed prematurely, and that the infant had not survived.

Arethusa's pains began at breakfast time on the second of July. Edith sent Lawson, the groom, to warn the doctor and gave him the prepared note for the Hereford attorney.

"His Grace is away from home at present, and this gentleman will know how to get a message to him," she improvised, feeling that some explanation was needed.

"Yes, miss," said Lawson, who was so used to carrying out orders that he never queried them.

In due course Dr. James arrived with Mrs. Rigg, a grim-faced female who turned out to be much pleasanter than she looked. She retired with her patient to the large bedroom on the first floor. Dr. James sat down and read the newspaper until Arethusa's maid Barker came to summon him.

After this, Edith waited in a state of apprehension. It was three o'clock, and she was sitting in the hall with a clear view of the first-floor landing, when the door opened and the doctor looked out.

She ran up the single flight to join him.

"Is there any news?"

"Come in," he said in a low voice. "It's a girl, and they are both well. Her Grace wishes to see you."

Arethusa lay with her eyes closed, looking unbelievably fragile. The baby lay in a cradle beside the bed. Edith stared at the little flaxen doll, who gazed fixedly back at her. She did not look like either of her parents, which was a relief. There was a faint resemblance to her grandmother, Lady

Woodruff, but newborn babies often had curiously ancient faces for the first day or two.

Edith turned to Arethusa, who whispered, "Caroline . . ."

"It's Edith, my dear." She thought she had been mistaken for someone else.

"The child's name is Caroline. Will you make sure someone is told that, Edith, when they come, before she is sent away? She should have the little cap and dress I embroidered for her, and this." Her hand fumbled for a small leather case on the night table. Inside was a thin gold bracelet encircled by a garland of flowers and leaves worked in seed pearls, a charming ornament for a young girl.

"If she has something of mine when she is older," said Arethusa, "perhaps she will understand that I did love her."

Edith felt a shaft of pity like a physical pain. The nurse said that her Grace needed to sleep; she was drowsy from the effects of laudanum.

As Edith was leaving the room, Dr. James said to her, "I think you had better give the news to the servants, Miss Bruton, stressing that the child is not expected to live."

They had decided to carry out the deception in this way, in case the perfectly healthy baby was heard to cry during the remaining hours before it could be taken out of the house. It had not dawned on Edith that she was the obvious person to tell the servants, a task she very much disliked. She hated lying, she was unwilling to cause genuine distress (servants always adored Arethusa), and she had a superstitious dread of forecasting the child's death.

However, she managed somehow, and later she and Dr. James sat down and dined together. He was remaining at Holly Lodge, ostensibly to keep an eye on his patients.

At last it was late and dark enough to put the

plan into action. Edith had been up to a room on the second floor, from which it was possible to see, between the interlacing branches of the summer trees, the hard black hood of a closed carriage waiting at the end of the lane. The servants had gone to bed; the women up in the attic, Stodart the butler in a room behind the kitchen. None of them could get into the hall except through a baize door under the stairs. Dr. James stationed Edith outside this door to make sure the coast was clear at the most risky moment of the enterprise. Then he went and fetched the baby, carried her down the front stairs, across the hall and into the drawing-room. Edith followed him.

"When it came to the point," he said, "her Grace was very much overcome by her feelings, poor lady. It's a bad business. Will you open the window for me, Miss Bruton?"

The long drawing-room windows reached almost to the ground. Dr. James thought it would be quieter for him to go out this way and across the grass. This turned out to be a mistake.

He had just stepped out, the baby in his arms, when there came the sound of another window opening several floors above, and a shout of alarm. The doctor re-entered the house rather hastily. He and Edith stood petrified, waiting to see what would happen next. A few seconds later, and at ground level this time, there came a loud, piercing scream.

"Good God, what was that?"

"I'd better go and find out," said Edith.

She hurried towards the kitchen regions, led by the reiterated screams. Passing through the baize door and arriving in a short stone passage, she found several of the servants gathered at the foot of the back stairs. There was a moaning figure on the ground, her head bleeding copiously. This turned out to be Peggy, the under housemaid, in her night clothes. The screamer was the kitchen-maid, also dressed for bed, her hair down her back. Stodart in his nightshirt was kneeling beside Peggy, while the upper housemaid, Leah, chattered excitedly in the background.

" 'We'll all be murdered in our beds!' I said, so we come downstairs to find Mr. Stodart . . ."

"What is going on?" demanded Edith, eyeing the victim anxiously. "How did Peggy cut her head?"

"I was looking out of the window, miss," said Leah importantly, "and I saw a robber breaking into the drawing-room, so we came down to find Mr. Stodart, only Peggy tripped over the hem of her nightgown and fell. And the robber must be in the house, miss. Going to murder her Grace and the poor little baby!"

"Nonsense! There was no robber. What you saw was Dr. James looking out to see what kind of night it is."

"Is the doctor still here, miss?" asked Stodart. "Shall I fetch him to Peggy? She's losing a lot of blood."

"I'll go," said Edith hastily.

She sped back to the drawing-room, where Dr. James was walking up and down with the baby, who had been woken by the screams and was beginning to grizzle.

Edith explained the catastrophe. "If you would see her, sir—I know it is what the Duchess would wish. She is bleeding dreadfully."

"Of course. But I have to hand over the child."

"I'll do that. The sooner the better, don't you think, while everyone is occupied with Peggy? Only do please go, sir, or I fear Stodart will come to find us."

"Yes, very well."

Edith took the baby from him. She manoeuvred herself and the precious bundle of white shawls over the low sill on to the grass. At least she would not be overlooked. As she left the stone passage, she had heard the cook's agitated voice half-way down the stairs, wanting to know what was wrong. There was no one left to look out of a top-floor window and catch sight of a mysterious figure spiriting away the Lady Caroline MountStephen, legally a daughter of the Duke of Melford, who was to grow up anonymously, never knowing the mother and brother and sister she had lost.

It is a terrible thing I am helping to do, thought Edith, clasping the baby, who had stopped crying now and lay passive in her chrysalis of shawls, her face a faint blur of the dusk.

All the same, matters might have been worse. Edith had seen plenty of babies in the families of friends or when parish visiting, and she knew very well that Caroline's smallness was only relative. She was a healthy infant born of good strong stock, and no one, no woman at any rate, would ever have mistaken her for a seven-month child. If Maria Jarvis hadn't given the game away, if Arethusa had gone on trying to deceive her husband, he must have guessed the truth when the gossip started, and then there would have been the devil to pay.

Edith slipped through a side gate and began to walk along the lane. She knew where the carriage was, though it was hidden from her now. There was a movement ahead of her, a footfall and a darker shadow among the shadows. She shrank back as the shape of a man loomed out of the hedge.

A familiar voice said, *"Edith!"*

"Mr. Palgrave!" Panic was tempered with astonishment. "What are you doing here?"

"I've come to fetch my child."

"I don't understand. Does the Duke know?"

"Certainly he knows! I told him I wished to take

charge of my—son or daughter, is it? And he
agreed."

"Your daughter. Her name is Caroline."

He stared down at the tiny face in the engulfing
shawls. He did not make either of the usual mas-
culine comments, that the baby was very small or
very ugly, and she counted this to his credit.

"Caroline," he repeated gently. "Is that what her
mother wishes? How is she—Arethusa?"

There was no point in telling him how guilty Arethusa felt at parting with her child. She said, "The
doctor is satisfied with her condition. You have no
need to be anxious."

"Thank God for that! After doing so much harm already, I had a terrible fear that I might be the cause
of her death."

Edith felt a wave of sympathy towards him, the
sympathy of the young woman who had spent the
last eleven weeks with Arethusa at Holly Lodge,
not the prim, resentful, moralising girl who had
condemned him in London. It was odd to recall their
last two meetings. The day he had found her at the
pianoforte, when he had kissed her and she thought
she loved him, and that bitter interview the afternoon before his duel, when she was sure she hated
him. Now she felt no violent emotion, only a
friendly compassion.

"But, my dear Edith," he was saying, "I might
ask you what you are doing here? They should
never have sent you out alone at this hour. What
was the doctor thinking of?"

"There was an accident. One of the maids fell
and cut her head. The doctor was obliged to stay
behind, so I brought the baby instead."

"Well, I am glad you did, Swan. I hope you are
not still so angry with me?"

Edith did not answer. She was too busy transfer-
ring the sleeping Caroline into her father's arms,

making sure he knew how to hold her properly, and explaining about a packet which contained the embroidered baby clothes and the pearl bracelet.

As their hands brushed in the exchange, she said, "Where are you taking her?"

"Back to the home of her wet-nurse. She—Mrs. Brown—is waiting in the carriage. She is a very kind, good sort of woman. As soon as the child is old enough, she is going to someone Penelope Dampier has found for me. Her old governess, now a widow. I shall keep a very close eye on little Caroline, as her guardian and her godfather, for that is a role I can assume at her christening without causing any scandal. Which reminds me! You must not repeat any of this to Arethusa. I promised Melford I would do nothing to let her know that the child is in my care. He had a right to insist, and I could not refuse."

She supposed this promise had been given after the duel at which Sam's life had been spared. She agreed to keep silent, they said goodnight, and she stood alone in the lane, watching him retreat into the deepening dark with Arethusa's baby in his arms.

Then she went back to Holly Lodge.

CHAPTER SIX

Arethusa travelled up to Rythorpe towards the end of August, and Edith went with her. She had expected and intended to go home when the period of exile at Strenton was over, but Arethusa seemed so lacking in confidence, so pathetically nervous about rejoining her husband and her legitimate children, that when she begged Edith to accompany her, it was hard to refuse.

Her parents had, of course, been told, like everyone else, that the Duchess's baby was not due until September, so they were not expecting her back until the autumn. When they heard that the premature baby had died, they made no objection to Edith's paying a visit to the Duke of Melford's country house.

"I hope the children will not have forgotten me," said Arethusa, as they drove through a series of green upland valleys on the last afternoon of their journey.

"How could they forget? They have been writing to you regularly. At least Harriet has been writing and reading your letters in return, and Bar has sent you all those drawings of horses and dogs with bold faces like his own."

"You are right, of course. And they don't know why I was sent away, poor lambs. If only I could be

sure that Melford does not regret his great generosity in promising to take me back! It is so much
more than I deserve." Her lip trembled.

Edith knew her friend was still very unhappy.
She thought that a good many of these fears about
the Duke and the children were due to an abiding
sense of guilt because she believed her baby had
been given away to strangers. It seemed cruel not
to tell her the truth, but Edith felt she could not
break her word to Sam. Arethusa had heard about
the housemaid Peggy's accident and shown much
concern, but no one had gone into details, and she
did not realise that it was Edith who had handed
over the baby.

They were following the course of a young, bubbling river. The valley was filled with trees, the
surrounding grassy slopes were smooth and bare,
broken every now and then by clefts in the forma-
tion of the hills where tributary streams ran down
to join the waters of the Ryre. The road took a sudden sweep away from the river-bank and into a new
panorama, greener and wider than the last. Almost
immediately they passed through a pair of enormous iron gates. Edith was vaguely aware of a
lodge and a party of bobbing cottagers. Her attention was fixed on a horseman in the Melford livery
who, on seeing the carriage, set out ahead of them
at full gallop, no doubt to carry the news of their
arrival.

The avenue ran as straight as an arrow. No im-
prover had been allowed to introduce natural curves
here. The house was so far away they could not see
it properly at first. Isolated buildings sprang up in
the park.

"That's the family mausoleum," said Arethusa,
"up there on the right. And you can just see the
observatory beyond the Arch of Diana."

She was sitting erect, her cheeks faintly flushed.

The house itself was becoming clear. It was built of grey stone, the size of a palace. Edith remembered Sam saying that the first Duke of Melford had designed it after getting drunk in the company of Sir John Vanbrugh. At the time, she had been mystified. Since then, she had seen prints of Blenheim and Castle Howard and was able to appreciate the joke. The skyline of Rythorpe was a forest of domes, cupolas, turrets and peaks of crenellated stonework. Three tiers of windows lined the grand façade, those on the middle floor, the *piano nobile*, much larger than the rest. A flight of steps about fifty feet wide swept down from this level with a flourish of ceremonial splendour.

"Is that the way in?" asked Edith, awestruck.

"It was supposed to be. The first Duke liked everyone to enter the house by way of the marble hall and see at once how important he was. We use a door at the side, on the ground floor."

Not today, however. The horsemen had brought news of them, and as the carriage approached, two long glass doors opened at the upper level and three figures appeared at the top of the steps: the Duke and his two children. He came down at a leisurely pace, Harriet and Bar hopping and jumping on each side of him.

He reached the forecourt just as his wife stepped out of the carriage. He kissed her cheek, and said gravely, "Welcome home, my dear Arethusa."

She whispered something inaudible.

Harriet came up and clung to her mother. It was Bar, surprisingly, who hung back.

"Why, what a big boy you've grown," said Arethusa. "Aren't you coming to give me a kiss?"

"No!" said Bar.

Whether this was said through shyness (most unlikely), pique, or a simple desire to show off, his father was having none of it.

"Barlington!" he said sternly. "Go to your mother at once. You know what happens to boys who are disobedient."

Arethusa began to tremble. "Please, Mel? Don't frighten him. He's only young."

Bar did not seem unduly frightened. He cast his father a calculating glance, decided not to goad him any further, then rushed at his mother and hugged her.

The Duke turned to Edith with a civil question about their journey.

"It was very comfortable, your Grace."

She felt the old symptoms of clumsiness stealing over her, but was determined not to give way to them.

They climbed the steps, the Duke saying to his wife, "We are very quiet at present; there is no one here but the family."

They entered an imposing hall in the shape of a double cube, the wall and floor being faced with marble in various delicate colours and sinuous patterns. Some of the upper servants were there to greet their returning mistress. In a large drawing-room or saloon beyond were assembled fifteen persons aged between eight and eighty, all unknown to Edith except for Colonel Waters. She retired willingly into the background, but was approached almost at once by a good-looking boy perhaps a little younger than herself, who said, "How do you do, Miss Bruton. I am Harry MountStephen, Melford's cousin. One of his many cousins! You can see what a pack of us there are."

She knew from Arethusa that Harry was the eldest son of Melford's uncle Lord Robert MountStephen, and that he had just completed his first year at Oxford. He pointed out his parents to her, his brother Ralph, his sister Kitty, and the three much younger children.

"And the old lady my cousin Arethusa is shouting at is our great-aunt Sarah—Lady Sarah Man-
nering. She's as deaf as a post! The lady beside her
is her companion."

"And who is that gentleman?" asked Edith, sin-
gling out one of a small group who stood on the
outskirts of the party of relations. They puzzled her
a little, for the Duke had implied there were no
visitors at Rythorpe at present.

"Oh, that's Dr. Ballard. He's a celebrated historian, and he's writing a history of the Mount-
Stephens. The men with him are the chaplain and
the librarian, and Mr. Purbeck, our astronomer.
They all live here."

"Does the Duke need an astronomer?" asked
Edith, astonished.

"Well, I suppose he must. He's built an observatory in the park. And Purbeck needs a patron. He's
always hoping to find a new planet or comet or
something of the sort."

Presently they all separated to dress for dinner.
Edith was still feeling slightly at a loss, but was
not sure why. Rythorpe was certainly much grander
than Seddon Park or even Melford House, but she
was no longer as inexperienced or frightened of social pitfalls as she had been seven months ago. After a little thought, she realised that she had
become so used to caring for Arethusa that she felt
strange without the responsibility, while at the
same time acutely conscious of her friend's anxi-
eties, wondering how she was faring, now that she
was perhaps alone with her husband.

She watched her closely at dinner. They sat down
fifteen, for although Ralph was still at Eton and
Kitty in the schoolroom, they were allowed to dine
with their elders when there were no guests.

Arethusa faced Melford down the length of the
table. She was the centre of attention, talking and

laughing with a great deal of vivacity and giving a passable imitation of the beautiful Duchess who had seemed so light-hearted and carefree when Edith first met her. Seen for a moment in repose, however, there was a desperate sadness in her face, and it was still there even when Harriet and Bar and the three younger cousins came in with the dessert to be talked to and fed on sweetmeats and gooseberries. Perhaps, in this renewed domesticity, Arethusa was more than ever haunted by Caroline, the little outcast.

In due course the ladies left the men to drink their wine and retired to a room full of old-fashioned, heavily gilded sofas and chairs. They had scarcely sat down when a new ordeal confronted Arethusa, for Lady Robert MountStephen wanted to commiserate with her on the loss of her baby and to hear all the circumstances.

There was not a hint of malice or suspicion behind this curiosity. Lady Robert was a kind, motherly woman who wanted to show her genuine sympathy.

"Your little girl lived several hours, I think?"

"Yes."

"So you were able to have her baptised. I hope this was done?"

"Oh yes, certainly, my dear Aunt."

Arethusa caught Edith's eye. Now she would probably start blaming herself because Caroline's baptism had been left to strangers.

Well-meaning as ever, Lady Robert said gently, "At least you can rejoice, my dear, that your little daughter is safe forever with our blessed Redeemer."

For a horrid moment, Edith thought Arethusa was going to break down. She was twisting her handkerchief, and then got up, saying, "I ought to

go and talk to great-aunt Sarah. It is important not
to neglect her now that she is so deaf."

As she moved away, Lady Robert turned to Edith
in some agitation. "I'm afraid I have simply added
to her distress. I had no idea . . . It seems a dreadful
thing to say, but, after all, she has lost babies before, and it is nearly eight weeks. Has she been in
this melancholy state ever since, Miss Bruton? Is
there anything seriously wrong?"

"Nothing that time will not cure, ma'am." Edith
tried to invent a logical explanation. "She has been
living in seclusion so long, so that this may have
increased the final disappointment."

"That I can easily believe. I could not see any
point in her being sent down to that spa no one has
ever heard of. And as for Melford never going near
her, not even when the child died . . ." Lady Robert
broke off rather quickly, on the verge of criticising
the head of the family to someone who was not a
MountStephen.

The men came in from the dining-room, and in
the re-forming of groups Edith was able to make
her escape.

After a while, the Duke came over to her, and
said, "As this is your first visit here, Edith, I should
like to show you our famous view of the lake. The
light is particularly good this evening."

Edith noticed with interest his use of her Christian name. She went with him through the next
room and into the one beyond, which stood at a corner of the house. There was a window overlooking
a formal parterre, and another with a prospect more
in the style of Brown or Repton. A sweep of grass
ran down towards the edge of a lake. The pure opal
surface of the water shone pale in the softening
dusk against a background of dark dramatic woods
and the faint outline of the hills.

Edith gazed at the scene in wonder and pleasure. "Yes, it is ravishing," she agreed.

"I'm glad you like it," he said, with a casual, proprietary glance. "That is not the true reason I brought you in here. I want to thank you for the great care you have shown for my wife. You have been a good friend to her, she has said so constantly in her letters, and she has been singing your praises ever since she got home. We are both very grateful to you."

Rather overcome, Edith said, "I am sure I want no thanks. I am extremely attached to the Duchess, and it has been a pleasure to do anything I could for her."

"That may be. All the same, I ought not to have talked you into going to Strenton. It was not a fit undertaking for a young, unmarried girl. The truth is that I was so concerned with our family difficulties at the time, I was not able to think very clearly."

Edith was astounded. First by his recognising that he might have made an error of judgment, and then by admitting as much to someone like herself: young, inferior and female. There he stood, the immensely rich and powerful Duke of Melford, handsome, elegant and patrician, with his air of invincible self-confidence, but he must have moments of doubt like other men.

"Can I ask you something, sir?"

"Anything you like."

That was how monarchs talked in fairy-tales. Unto the half of my kingdom. What would he do if she said: I'd like that very pretty painting by Raphael in the red drawing-room? She pulled herself together.

"I was wondering if you would agree to let the Duchess know that Mr. Palgrave has taken charge of the baby."

The dark eyebrows came together in a formidable frown. "Who told you that?"

"I saw him. It was I who handed the child over, a few hours after she was born."

"Then you had no business to! What was the doctor doing? I gave strict instructions that no one else was to be involved."

"There was an accident, your Grace." She explained, adding, "It was lucky Dr. James was in the house, otherwise the maid might have bled to death. While he was attending her, I decided, on my own initiative, to carry the baby out into the lane. It seemed a good opportunity, with all the servants congregated round the back stairs."

"Yes, I see. But you have not told my wife? No, of course you haven't. Thank God for that! The sooner she forgets the wretched brat was ever born, the better."

Edith's sudden anger got the better of her feelings of awe and respect. "I think that is a cruel way to speak of an innocent child!"

"Perhaps you would prefer me to call it an unwanted bastard, which is an exactly truthful description?"

Edith did not reply. She was trying to control her temper, having noticed that all the easy charm and condescending gratitude had vanished the moment this arrogant egotist felt himself criticised.

"Your solicitude for the innocent child is very affecting," he continued sarcastically. "However, we need not become sentimental over the rather less innocent parents. Do not expect me to tell my wife that her child has gone to Palgrave. That is out of the question, and you must be a very silly little girl if you don't understand why. I won't have their association renewed, and it would be mad to give her an additional reason for wanting to meet him."

He turned away, impatient and contemptuous.

Edith might have seized her chance of slipping out of the room before he said anything else disagreeable, but a desire to help Arethusa made her persist.

Gazing at the broad shoulders and beautifully tailored back, she said in the most conciliatory tone she could manage, "I expect your Grace is right. I may be ignorant and silly, but I have spent the last four months shut up alone with the Duchess, so perhaps I do know what is in her mind at this moment better than anyone else. I am sure she has not thought of returning to the—the situation she was in with Mr. Palgrave. She has been terribly oppressed by guilt and by her sense of your generosity—that, and her longing to see Harriet and Bar. But she is anxious about the other little girl. Not wanting or expecting to keep in touch with her, but simply grieving at the thought of her growing up unloved with no one belonging to her. That's why I think that learning the truth might help her; not to forget, exactly, but to put the past behind her."

She waited for some sort of reply. When Melford turned, he had recovered his manners, or perhaps he had only remembered the need to behave in a way that befitted a great nobleman.

Distantly cool, he held open the door. "Shall we rejoin the rest of the party?"

Clearly she had done no good.

She woke in the night, wondering how she had been brave enough to stand up to him, and whether in the morning he would find some excuse to pack her off home. But in the morning she was asked to ride with the Duke and Duchess and the two elder MountStephen cousins.

"We should like to show you round," said Arethusa, "and we can go so much farther on horseback. I know you have your habit with you."

Edith had brought her riding-habit to London all those months ago, hoping she might have a chance to use it. Perhaps she had fancied herself exercising in the Row with Sam Palgrave. (Easy to see now why he had not asked her!) And as the Duchess was pregnant, she and Edith had always driven out in a carriage. All this was now changed, and the riding-habit would come into its own at last.

In spite of knowing that she looked rather fetching in bright russet with a stylishly military hat, she was a little daunted by the sight of her horse—a young liver chestnut with ears laid back and a somewhat excitable temper—and by realising that all the MountStephens, including Arethusa, rode like Centaurs and took it for granted that everyone else did the same. At home, she and her sisters had shared a safe, ladylike hack, and trotting along the country lanes, with an occasional canter on the grass, had hardly prepared her for the lively pace of her new companions or the sensation that the open space around Rythorpe stretched for miles in every direction in which a capricious animal might choose to bolt.

However, the cavalcade soon steadied down, the Duke pausing frequently to inspect a plantation of young trees or admire his thoroughbred yearlings in their paddock, pointing out various improvements to Arethusa.

Edith rode between the two brothers. Harry, she found, was made for every kind of sport. The sixteen-year-old Ralph, thin and slight, was probably the cleverer of the two.

They rode uphill for some distance, until they could look down on the enormous house below, sprawling and fantastic like a heraldic beast, couching rather than rampant. Several other buildings and follies were visible, including the observatory the Duke had put up two years before for his tame astronomer. Presently they came to a kind of plateau, and stopped again to look down at the River Ryre running like a silver thread through a patchwork of marsh and meadow and reed-beds far below.

The Duke said, "This is where I'm going to site my canal."

"Following the course of the river?" asked Arethusa doubtfully. "But it winds backwards and forwards for miles. Won't it take a very long time to get anywhere?"

"Far too long. That's why it's going straight across the valley at right-angles to make a direct link between the Ryre just below Hindley and the Barlington Canal beyond Garthside."

"But, Mel," objected Harry, "you can't take a canal up and down all those hills. You'd need hundreds of locks."

"Not if I build an aqueduct.

"An aqueduct! That would be an immense undertaking."

"Well, why not? It would add considerably to the landscape. A glimpse of a Roman aqueduct would set the seal on our ancestors' classical pretensions, don't you agree?"

As they rode on, Edith asked Harry, "Why does your cousin want a canal?"

"To link the towns of Hindley and Rysden with the outside world. They're in the next valley; you can't see them from here. They have several mills as well as the pottery, and they need a proper way to get their goods out and bring coal in."

"That's why the manufacturers want a canal," amended his younger brother. "Mel wants it because it is going to be such a problem to construct. He only likes to do things that are difficult. When life becomes tame, he gets restless and looks round for something new."

They kept to the high ground for some time, drawing a semicircle round the house and park. Presently they came down into the woods on the far side of the lake, entered a broad ride about two miles long, and settled into a steady canter.

Edith had forgotten her nervousness and was now enjoying herself. As they approached the sunny opening at the far end of the wood, there was an outcrop of rock which split the ride into two separate tracks. The Duke and Duchess were in front. She kept to the left of the boulder, he to the right. Harry went after Arethusa, with Ralph a little way behind them. Edith was level with Harry; it was automatic to follow the Duke. Indeed, he looked round as though to make sure she was still there. Arethusa, too, looked round and called out something Edith did not hear. It sounded like a warning. A moment later, she saw why.

Though the left-hand track ran straight on to the open turf, on her side, the way out was blocked by a fallen tree-trunk. She only grasped this as the Duke's horse jumped, about ten yards ahead of her. She saw him rise, and the glint of light on his metal shoes as he went neatly over.

Edith's heart came into her mouth. She had never jumped a fence in her life, and though this was a very small affair, it looked enormous to her, as it sprang up in a thick dark bar. But she couldn't—she wouldn't—pull up and go round the other way. She'd rather break her neck than show the white feather to the assembled MountStephens. Clinging on with every nerve and muscle, she felt her horse's back arch under her like the spine of a cat. She pitched forward, and then they landed on the other side with a tremendous jolt, and she lost her stirrup.

Arethusa, wheeling round on her chestnut mare, asked anxiously if she was safe.

"Perfectly safe, thank you," said Edith, trying surreptitiously to recover her stirrup and straighten her hat.

"Mel, you ought not to have led Edith over that jump," said Arethusa, speaking to her husband with more spirit than she had shown since her return.

"It was a very small jump, my dear. You could have taken it in your sleep!"

"I dare say. But Edith and I were brought up rather differently. She is not used to careering around the countryside as we do."

"Perhaps not." The Duke surveyed Edith with a mocking eye. "On the other hand, she likes tackling difficulties she does not properly understand. It suits her notion of independence. She is one of those who rush in where angels fear to jump."

He is deliberately trying to pay me out for last night, she thought. She ought to have been furious. Perhaps she would have been, if she had come unseated and found herself sitting on the ground, an object of ridicule.

As it was, she felt she had come off best in this encounter, so she gave him a saucy look, and said, "Your Grace has formed a very accurate view of my character."

Later that day she wrote to her parents, sitting at the table in her dressing-room, for at Rythorpe she had two prettily furnished rooms all to herself. There was plenty to tell and describe, quite enough to conceal what could not be told. Letter-writing at Rythorpe was going to be much easier than it had been at Holly Lodge. She had filled a page with details of the house, the pictures, the landscape and the MountStephen relations, when Arethusa came in, looking flushed and agitated.

"Am I disturbing you, Edith? I hope you are not too stiff after the ride." Then, without waiting for an answer, she sat down on the sofa, gazed at her guest, and said, "Who do you think is looking after Caroline?"

This was a tricky subject.

"Well, I suppose she has been put out to nurse."

"Oh yes, for the time being. But who do you think has taken charge of her upbringing and her future welfare? It is Sam. Her own father! Are you not astonished?"

"Yes, indeed," said Edith, aware that she must show as much surprise as possible, which was not very difficult because she *was* surprised, not by the news but by Arethusa's knowing it. "How did you find out?"

"My husband has just told me. He came to me and said, 'Are you pining for news of your child? Does it make you unhappy that you don't know where she has gone?' I don't know why he should have asked, for I hoped I had been able to hide my feelings, and I dreaded making him angry. I know I am a coward, but I find it so absolutely desolating when Melford is angry with me."

"I don't know why he should be," said Edith indignantly. "It is the most natural thing in the world that you should want to know your baby is in good hands. Any mother would."

"Yes, but he made it a condition that I must never ask. Before we left London in April, he said I could trust him to make proper arrangements, and of course I knew he would do what was right and spare no expense. Only that is not quite the same as finding someone who would love the poor little soul. When I tried to explain, he took my hands and said, very seriously, 'If I tell you the name of the person who has undertaken to care for your daughter, will you give me your sacred promise that you will never try to meet or question this person?' Of course I promised at once, and he said, 'Very well, then. She has gone to Palgrave. He wanted to take full responsibility for her and it seemed the best plan. He is going to board her out somewhere in the country, but he intends to visit her often, and she is to grow up believing he is her guardian. Now are you satisfied?' "

"And are you?"

"Oh, yes!" exclaimed Arethusa. "It has made all the difference. If Caroline has Sam there in the background, he will be good to her, I know. I can't imagine why I never thought of such a solution, except that I never told him I was carrying his child. He was as much deceived as everyone else, and after Melford found out the truth, I was not allowed to communicate with him. I suppose Melford did so. It must have been very disagreeable for them both."

Clearly she had not heard about the duel, and Edith did not intend to enlighten her. They talked a little of the baby's future, more cheerfully than they had ever been able to do before. After Arethusa left her, Edith wondered what had inspired the Duke to tell her the truth. Surely it could not have been her own suggestion, which had annoyed him so much last night. The whole episode was very strange.

She felt too restless to finish her letter, and presently wandered out into the garden. She walked to the end of the formal parterre and sat on a stone bench, looking back at the house. The people who lived in the seventeenth century must have been very odd, she reflected. They forced their flowers and plants to bloom in rigid lines and squares, yet when building a house, when geometry might have been considered a virtue, they burst out with every kind of Baroque extravagance.

As she studied the south façade of Rythorpe, a man came out of a side door and started walking towards her. It was the Duke, still in riding-dress with a spaniel trotting at his heels.

Edith felt a childish impulse to get up and run away, but that would be undignified. She stayed where she was and watched him drawing closer, the gravel crackling under his feet.

As he reached her, he asked, "Am I forgiven?"

She did not know what he meant, but made a rapid guess. "For making me jump that tree? My pride and I might both have taken a fall. I dare say that is what you hoped."

"No. I simply wanted to see whether you would come on or turn back. You were not in the slightest danger of falling. If you had been, I should not have run such a risk. I had been watching you all the morning. You are a natural horsewoman."

Edith was so taken aback by this praise that she could not think of a proper answer. By the time she had recovered her tongue, he was sitting beside her on the bench.

"What needs forgiving," he said, "is the way I spoke to you last night. I am sorry I was so uncivil, and I hope I have made amends. Have you spoken to my wife within the last hour?"

"Yes, I have. I am so very glad you have told her that Caroline has gone to Sam Palgrave. What made you change your mind?"

"You did," he said, looking at her intently.

"But surely," she said, her heart thumping oddly, "you cannot have been influenced . . . Why should you take advice from someone like me?"

"Well, it was what you wanted, wasn't it? My dear Edith, it is rather late to assume an appearance of bashful humility, and it doesn't suit you!"

He spoke with the astringent manner and the cool glance she had once disliked. Now they affected her differently, and certainly he was no longer treating her as though she was not there or did not matter.

Behind his habitual calm poise she sensed a concentrated power, and felt as though she had been touched by something cold and burning at the same time, like a piece of ice.

She looked away from him and heard him say, "I was obliged to admit that a woman, even a very young woman, might understand better than I could what fears and regrets were passing through Arethusa's mind. And I think you were right. Now that she feels sure that her child is going to receive a proper amount of affection, she seems more comfortable already, and I hope her spirits will soon revive. I've said all along that I would not have another man's child brought up in my house, and I dare say you think me heartless. But I am not a brute, and I don't want her to go on suffering for something that is over and done with."

Edith did not remember afterwards what she said, or if she said anything at all. When she went in to dress for dinner, she was in a strangely exhilarated state. Lady Robert MountStephen said she must have caught the sun, and scolded her mildly for not taking care of her complexion.

She did not exchange another word with the Duke that evening, but every now and then she looked at him, and thought how extraordinary it was that she had been able to influence the judgement of such a man. Once he caught her eye and looked steadily back at her. He was standing at the end of the long drawing-room, graceful and assured, his dark head outlined against the carving of the white marble overmantel, his dark eyes grave and considering.

The idle thought slipped into her mind: I could fall in love with that man.

CHAPTER SEVEN

Of course it was out of the question. No well-brought-up girl could fall in love with a married man. It was not only unthinkable, it was in some way actually impossible; she had held that assumption all her life and never wavered from it.

Until a few months ago, it was true, she had held another assumption: that no fastidious, well-conducted married woman could be unfaithful to her husband. She had found out she was wrong there, found out too that in every other respect Arethusa was as loyal, sensitive and religious as she had always supposed. Misjudging another person's principles was less serious than altering one's own. All the same, one mistake had made a crack in the fabric of complacency, and she was less inclined to be dogmatic. It could not be wrong, she decided, for Melford to inspire her secret devotion, to allow herself an innocent emotion which expected no return. Silent worship, there could be no harm in that. She went about in a private cloud.

"You are feeling quite well, my love?" enquired Arethusa as they strolled beside the lake.

"Yes—why do you ask?"

"She's afraid you are going into a decline," said the Duke. "You have not spoken a word for nearly forty-five seconds."

Edith blushed. This was the kind of barbed remark she used to hate him for making. Now she welcomed such an attention as though it was an endearment.

During the next week she was never alone with him, rather to her relief. She spent a good deal of time with Arethusa and the children; sometimes she went for rides with Harry and Ralph and their fourteen-year-old sister Kitty. In the evening the family usually played games, but the Duke did not always join them. Sometimes she felt a great need to be alone.

One afternoon she decided to explore the stream which flowed into the lake, tracing its passage through a gorge in the green surrounding hills, though she did not expect to reach the source, for the ground was uneven and steep, and the path, if you could call it that, was very much overgrown. Bushes and saplings hung thirstily forward, tender ferns and cushions of emerald moss clung to the bank, each with its glistening drops of water in a transparent veil.

Edith climbed slowly upwards, enjoying the sound and movement of the stream, which soothed the irritation of her mind and its constant preoccupation with the strange thing that had happened to her. She compared her present sensations with what she had felt for Sam in the early spring, right up to the moment when she had discovered that he was Arethusa's lover. That was all make-believe, she told herself. I enjoyed flirting with him and I wanted to be married so that I could stay in London, living a life I knew I should enjoy. She felt a slight pang of regret when she thought of Sam. She had valued his companionship, she thought she would still like him as a friend. She had liked him when she had met him in the dusk of a July evening and she had placed his daughter in his arms.

But as for love, that was another element, she was certain of it now.

She pressed on a little further. The sound of rushing water was louder than ever, and to her delight she came on a natural cascade, a sparkling torrent that plunged into the stream over the towering rocks which rose vertically ahead of her. She stood and gazed at the sword of light piercing the dark chasm. Such masses of water, travelling at such a speed, gave a curious illusion of stillness and solidity. It was both beautiful and mysterious.

"Romantic, is it not?" said a voice almost in her ear.

She spun round, and found Melford standing a few inches away from her.

"Good God, you gave me a fright!" she exclaimed, not very politely. "What are you doing here?"

"I followed you. I was afraid you might try to go on beyond the waterfall, and it isn't very safe walking."

They were standing extremely close; she had never seen the shape and colour of a man's eyes so clearly before, and there was something in his expression, at once private and challenging, which disconcerted her.

She said quickly, "I was not going on. I must return to the house."

As she backed away from him too hastily, her foot slipped on a wet stone. She heard him speak a word of warning and reach out his hand, but it was too late. She came down, sprawling. For a moment she stayed where she was, badly shaken by the fall.

The Duke bent over her, asking, "Are you hurt?"

"No," said Edith, untruthfully.

He helped her up and remained supporting her, his arm round her waist.

"I am perfectly able to stand," she said with dignity, "if your Grace will let me go."

He did so at once, but when she tried to put some weight on her right foot, the pain was so excruciating that she nearly fainted, and he was obliged to catch hold of her again. She clung to him until the vertigo cleared. It was humiliating.

"What is the matter?"

"I seem to have ricked my ankle."

"Then you had better sit down."

There was a large rock overhanging the stream, and he took off his coat and laid it on the damp surface. Then he bundled her into a sitting position with her leg stretched out in front of her.

"That comes of not looking where you were going," he said. "Whatever made you move so suddenly?"

"I don't know," muttered Edith.

She could hardly say: I thought you were going to kiss me. It would be insulting to suggest that a man of his character might behave so improperly towards an unmarried girl who was a guest in his house. Worse still, he would think her presumptuous and vain. And he would be right, she decided, wondering at the madness which for a second had misled her. There was nothing enigmatic in his expression now. He was lecturing her in a cross voice for being so careless, and sounded just like her elder brother.

She shivered. Though it was a hot day, the verge of the stream was always moist and cool.

"You are getting cold," he said. "Do you think you could walk back as far as the lake, if we went very slowly and I supported you?"

"I'm sure I could. I'm sorry to cause your Grace so much inconvenience."

"Don't be silly." He spoke crisply, looked her over, and added, "You've got mud on your face."

"Oh, have I?" she said, mortified.

She felt with her fingers where the splash had dried on her skin. There was nothing she could do about it here. Really, he was a hateful man! She could have hit him.

However, she was glad to take his arm and limp along as best she could, wincing at every step. He was very patient and thoughtful.

After a while he said, "I can see you are suffering a good deal—I dare say your ankle has swollen inside the boot. I think it might help if I were to undo the lace. Will you let me do that?"

Edith agreed thankfully. It was odd to see him kneeling at her feet. He unknotted her bootlace and tied it again more loosely, so that the relief from pressure made it much easier for her to walk. His manner was entirely unromantic, yet when he stood up again, she had a horrid idea that he had seen through her moment of panic at the waterfall and was slightly amused.

After this, she was almost too embarrassed to speak, but he behaved so kindly and talked so naturally that by the time they reached the Temple of the Sirens at the edge of the lake, she had recovered her self-possession. He left her there while he went to fetch a phaeton so that he could drive her back across the grass. She did not have to walk another step.

Edith's return to the house caused quite a stir. No one was surprised to hear that she had fallen on that slippery, treacherous path, though the older members of the party maintained that she ought not to have gone roaming about by herself. The younger people thought this very tame.

"The cascade is so romantic," said Kitty. "When I am in the woods, I always hope I shall meet some spirit from the past—a pilgrim on his way to the abbey, or a handsome cavalier."

Her brothers told her not to be a goose.

"Did you meet a handsome cavalier, Edith?" enquired Melford.

"I'm afraid not, Duke." She was determined by now that she would not give way to a fit of wilting self-consciousness. "But then I did not expect Cavaliers. I thought all your family fought for the Parliament."

"Such a dismal thing to have done," complained Kitty. "I can't think what possessed them! And don't try to tell me, Ralph, because you know I hate politics. No one would want to meet a Roundhead at the waterfall. Horrid, uncivil creatures."

Edith resisted the temptation to glance at Melford.

Lady Robert told her daughter not to talk so much, and said it was high time Edith was taken to her room so that she could bathe her ankle and have it bandaged with cold compresses.

By the morning, the swelling had gone down a good deal, but the ankle was still painful and needed rest. Edith was established on a sofa at the end of the library, a friendly room in spite of its imposing size and length, for it was divided into separate bays, and the book-lined walls seemed more comfortable and less overwhelming than many of the Rythorpe interiors. She was provided with plenty to read, and visited by a succession of grown-ups, children and dogs.

Towards the end of the morning she was alone, reading *The Lay of the Last Minstrel*, when Melford came in.

"I hear the ankle is improving," he said. "I hope you are not in much pain."

"Hardly any, thank you."

He sat down beside her and glanced at her book. "Do you admire Scott?"

"Yes, very much. Don't you, sir?"

"Some of his verse is extremely fine, but I am not a romantic myself."

This mystified Edith, who thought he was the most romantic person she had ever met. It began to dawn on her that a man of his type would not necessarily feel any preference for the glories of the Romantic style in art; his own life might supply all he needed.

He was asking her whether she read a great deal. What sorts of books?

"Anything I can get hold of. Mostly novels, I suppose."

"Ah, Mrs. Radcliffe."

"No, not Mrs. Radcliffe!" she retorted. "Well, I do read hers, of course. Everyone does, and I think her mysteries are very exciting. But it is extraordinary how gentlemen always think that if a woman reads a novel, it is sure to be Mrs. Radcliffe."

"I beg your pardon. I did not mean to sound patronising. Who is your favourite novelist?"

"Fielding. And my favourite book is *Tom Jones*."

The dark, patrician eyebrows lifted a little.

"You have received a liberal education!"

Edith bit her lip. She was afraid she had been ill-mannered. She also knew that many young women's reading was more restricted than her own, and she wondered if he was criticising her parents.

She said, "My sisters and I have always been allowed to read every book in the house. My father thinks . . ." She wondered if it would sound pompous, "that ignorance is no protector of innocence."

"I salute your father. He sounds a sensible man. Tell me what else you have read. Sterne, too? And Richardson?"

They discussed the great novels of the last century, finding they had many views in common.

Presently he asked, "Have you read *Clarissa* as well as *Pamela*?"

"Yes."

"What did you think of it?"

"It is very sad," she said inadequately.

This was a difficult topic. While the impropriety of *Tom Jones* was boisterous and diverting, *Clarissa* was a tragedy describing the sufferings of a virtuous woman at the hands of a wicked but fascinating man.

"It's a masterpiece," he said, "though decidedly farfetched. But then it was written a long time ago, and some of our ancestors were a racketty, devil-may-care set. (I know mine were!) But no man today would treat a girl so. I suppose such myths have to be perpetuated for the sake of morality, but I have never seen why men and women cannot feel friendship, or affection even, for each other, without risking their immortal souls!"

Something new had come into the calm, reassuring atmosphere of the library, something almost tangible in the air, audible in the silence. Edith said nothing. Innocent friendship, that was just what she longed for. It did just cross her mind that these lofty emotions might once have deceived Sam and Arethusa, and led them into the situation that had ended with the birth of poor little Caroline, but she thought this was a narrow, intolerant attitude and pushed it away.

Melford picked up *The Lady of the Lake*. "Shall I read aloud to you? I believe it is what one does for invalids."

His voice deepened, he gave great clarity and rhythm to the verse. She lay back on her sofa and watched him devouringly, this dark and brilliant demi-god whose influence over her heart was growing stronger every minute.

Edith's ankle soon recovered and life at Rythorpe

continued to exhilarate her. She saw a great deal of Melford, generally in company, but sometimes they were alone. There would be gallops through the park when they became separated from his cousins, or an occasional half-hour spent examining the family collections of Roman coins or Renaissance jewels. He took her on a comprehensive tour of the library, and introduced her to many books that had not come her way. There was nothing furtive about any of these encounters, nothing obviously contrived, though it did strike her that he was keeping a fairly close eye on her comings and goings.

She was sitting one afternoon in the Temple of the Sirens, trying to sketch the view across the lake where there was a particularly satisfying stand of noble trees, their rounded shapes perfectly mirrored in the glassy surface of the water.

She heard a step on the grass and knew it was Melford, even before he turned the corner.

"I thought I'd come and see how you were getting on." He looked over her shoulder at the pencil sketch propped on the small easel. "You've caught the sense of heat and stillness. There's something wrong with the reflection, though."

"Yes, I know. I shall have to start again. How did you know I was here?"

"I observed you from the observatory."

"I thought that was meant for looking at stars."

"Heavenly bodies," he murmured, sitting down on the steps of the temple. "And they need not be too far distant."

Edith thought she would be wise to ignore this remark, but she could not resist looking at him. Their glances met and locked. She recognised the expression in his eyes that had disconcerted her at the waterfall. This time she did not try to run away.

After a long moment he said, "You know what's happened to us, don't you?"

"I—I think so."

"Dearest Edith, I do love you so very much."

"I love you too," she whispered. "But I ought not to say so. This is terrible! What are we to do?"

"Do? We can't *do* anything. We shall simply have to *be*. Remain as we are, and take what happiness we can."

"How do you mean?" she asked frowning. "I don't understand."

"I mean, dear heart, that I cannot marry you, and I cannot make love to you on any other terms. You know that. There is no road forward for us to take. But if we stay where we are, we can still be friends, kindred spirits, constant and faithful companions, sharing the intimacy that goes with love— and ought to go with marriage, though too often it fails. Can you be my loving friend, Edith?"

"Oh yes," she said, her heart melted by the extraordinary tenderness in his voice which she had never heard before. "It is more than I ever hoped or dreamed of. Only I don't want to do anything that is wrong. We must not hurt Arethusa."

"There is no question of that. I shall give you nothing that belongs to her, or that she values. And to tell you the truth, I am not chiefly concerned with Arethusa. It is you I don't want to hurt. Do you think such an Ideal Passion can make you happy?"

The familiar note of mockery had come back into his voice with the words Ideal Passion, spoken in capitals, as they would be in some high-sounding play or novel. As though he was amused at himself for entertaining such an exalted concept. Yet she was sure he meant what he said, and as she had been living in a state of unrequited love without a hope of any return, what he was offering seemed to her a prospect of wonder and delight, and she said so.

"Though I cannot imagine why you should ever have looked at me. I'm not beautiful."

She meant, not like Arethusa.

"You are not a classical beauty." He leant back against one of the stone pillars and studied her thoughtfully. "But that sort soon grows tedious. Like those Palladian mansions so many of my friends live in, scattered all across England, each one so like the last that you know, as soon as you step inside, which way the dining-room faces and what the pattern will be on the ceiling. But then, you see, I grew up here at Rythorpe, a house of unrelated beauties and surprises, and those are what I saw in you, my dear. Your beautiful eyes (they are the blue of harebells, did you know?), your smallness, your sweet voice and your fiery courage, which is always putting me to flight."

"How can you say so?" she protested.

Yet she could not doubt he was in love, for surely a man would have to be, to see these things in her which she had never suspected.

He got up and moved towards her, and for a second she did just wonder whether their good resolutions were going to be proof against too hard a test. But all he did was to lift her left hand (the one that wasn't still clutching the pencil), stroke the back of it gently against his cheek, and lightly kiss the fingers.

"You mustn't be afraid," he said. "I'll take good care of you."

The Ideal Passion, loving friendship, whatever it was to be called, was having a good effect on Melford's temper. Edith had never seen him in such even spirits, so easy-going and ready to be pleased. Arethusa noticed it, too.

"It is so pleasant to have him in this light-hearted mood," she said, "and spending all his evenings with us. He would not do that if he was still angry with me."

Edith felt guilty. She could not bear the idea that she was somehow cheating Arethusa, whatever Melford might say. Yet if her innocent affection was making him easier for his wife to live with, wasn't that all to the good?

So she went on rejoicing in her unreasonable happiness. It was unreasonable, for they both knew they could not go on as they were indefinitely. In a month or two she would have to go home. But she was in that early stage of love when time stood still. She was living entirely in the present.

One day they set out in a large family party to inspect the proposed route of the new canal. Everyone rode except Lady Robert and the younger children, who travelled in an open barouche. Horses and carriage were left at a remote farmhouse, and they went the last quarter-mile on foot, to the site where an opinionated Scotsman was taking measurements and writing them down in a little book. Explanations were given, Melford and his engineer speaking more or less in chorus. Presently they wandered away, still measuring, respectfully followed by Ralph, who was fascinated by the whole enterprise. Lord Robert did not share his son's enthusiasm.

"It's madness," he said gloomily, staring after his nephew. "Wanting to build an aqueduct! He'll ruin himself with his wild schemes."

"Oh, I do hope not, Uncle Robert," said Arethusa. "It would be dreadful to end in a sponging-house."

"They can't arrest a peer for debt!" Lord Robert realised she was laughing at him, and grinned reluctantly. "Well, you won't be ruined, precisely, but it seems such a wanton extravagance. Look at that observatory he built a couple of years ago. Never goes near the place now."

"Not very often, perhaps. But Mr. Purbeck has the great new telescope and is doing valuable work, I believe. Will it matter, once the people of Hindley have their canal, if Melford soon tires of watching the boats go by? He will have achieved what he set out to do, and others will profit by it."

When the whole party had found out all they wanted to know, or in some cases didn't want to know, about the aqueduct, they moved over to the shady side of the hill, where several servants had arrived with a wagon and laid out a picnic on the grass. There were pies and chickens and bowls of salad on the white cloth, bottles of wine in buckets of ice, and baskets of fruit, peaches and plums, nectarines, pears and grapes, their warm skins glowing with the concentrated essence of the summer sun in which they had ripened. The summer was over now and it was autumn; there was a clear amber transparency in the light, but it was still hot, and they ate a leisurely meal, gazing out across the valley, and occasionally waving a wasp away from the fruit.

Edith had Bar next to her; she was cutting up his luncheon for him and trying to save him from getting too sticky.

"I do love you, Seedif," he said suddenly. "I'm going to marry you when I'm a man."

"That is a very handsome offer, my lord. You will have to ask your papa's permission first."

"Why?" enquired Bar. "You don't belong to papa."

"Certainly not!" She had not foreseen this response. "You do, however. That is, you must always do what he says."

Bar stared at his father and back at Edith.

"I'll ask him then. If he says No, I'll run away with you. On a horse."

All his relations burst out laughing. Bar was not at all abashed as most children would have been. He liked holding the centre of the stage.

When it was time to walk back to the farm, Melford offered Edith his arm. "I feel it is my duty to escort the future Lady Barlington."

She looked doubtfully towards the older ladies, but Arethusa was walking between Lord Robert and Harry, while Colonel Waters was taking good care of Lady Robert. Ralph and Kitty were shepherding the younger children.

As they fell a little behind the rest, Melford said, "I'm glad my son has such good taste."

"Dear Bar, he is very like you, isn't he? Or, on second thoughts, you are very like him. You both say clever things to show off."

"There is no call to be impertinent," he said coldly. "It doesn't suit you, and it certainly doesn't charm me."

He was plainly displeased. That was one of the disconcerting things about Melford, she could never be sure how he would react. She let go of his arm.

"And for God's sake don't let us have a parade of wounded sensibility. I have enough of that from Arethusa."

"That is very unkind!"

"Perhaps it was," he admitted after a moment. "I didn't mean to hurt you."

"Not unkind to me," said Edith, whose temper was rising. "It was extremely unkind about Arethusa. If you must think of her in that way, you ought not to say so to me. Your Grace."

Now she really had been impertinent! She wondered with trepidation what he would say next, and

whether the ground would open and swallow her
up.

To her astonishment, he laughed. "My dear love,
is that how I'm to be punished? Called *your Grace*
in such a disrespectful, revolutionary voice, as
though you were sharpening the blade of the guil-
lotine!"

His hand closed round her wrist as he gave her
an affectionate shake. She felt a surge of sensual
pleasure at the contact and a certain triumph, too,
because she had stood up to him and in the end he
had rather liked it.

All the same she felt obliged to say, "You must
be careful, Mel. If anyone had happened to look
round just then and seen us, they would have begun to suspect we were carrying on a flirtation."

"Very well, I will be discreet. But, I assure you,
no one is going to entertain such an idea."

He was right. No one had the faintest suspicion.
There were reasons for this. Melford had not been
in the habit of making love to unmarried girls. His
chosen mistresses had all been ladies of quality or
beauties of the stage. He had never pursued an intrigue inside his own house or on his own estates,
even among women who might have been considered fair game. He disliked squalor and confusion,
and kept his life in compartments. None of his family could imagine him making a cynical and heartless assault on the virtue of a girl like Edith Bruton
while she was living under his wife's protection.
How he might behave if he fell seriously in love
with her was such an unlikely contingency that it
never entered their heads.

CHAPTER EIGHT

Guests now began arriving at Rythorpe, among them Arethusa's sister Mrs. Gordon, and her family. She brought news of Lady Woodruff, now recovered from her accident and staying with their brother in Sussex.

Most of the friends who came had been invited weeks or months before, but in this vast house there was always room for an extra guest. One morning Melford announced casually, "Sam Palgrave will be here in time for dinner. He is on his way to visit his constituents, and will spend a few days with us as usual."

"Mr. Palgrave!" exclaimed Edith.

She sounded so astonished that everyone looked at her, which was embarrassing, though at least it meant that no one looked at Arethusa. Melford neatly explained away her surprise.

"You find it extraordinary that any Member of Parliament should travel so far, merely to humour his constituents. You must remember, however, that his seat is no pocket borough, as he likes to remind us whenever there is talk of Reform. The good burgesses of Aysby are free to vote as they please, so it pays him to keep on the right side of them. He's been coming up here for the past eight years."

Edith knew this already. The ancient borough of Aysby had prospered in the modern world on account of some local coal mines, and those citizens entitled to vote in a parliamentary election were successful men in their own right, indifferent to the whims of any aristocratic patron. Sam had told her this when they were in London. He was proud of representing such people, but what surprised her was his coming to Rythorpe this year, however often he had come in the past.

She glanced at Arethusa, who looked perfectly composed, and decided that she had probably heard the news already. But when, a little later, they were able to have a word in private, she found that she was wrong.

"No," said Arethusa in a colourless voice. "I did not know that he was coming. Melford chose that way of telling me to avoid the possibility of my giving way and making some sort of scene. He detests that."

Much as she loved Melford, Edith could not escape the knowledge that he was sometimes very unkind to his wife. Considering how generous he had been over the great trouble of Caroline's birth, the small cruelties jarred. She wanted to say so, to ask: Do you mind? Are you afraid of meeting Sam again? She was sure she would be in similar circumstances. But she knew it would be an intrusion; in any case there was no opportunity. They were standing at the head of the stairs on their way to put hats on before going for a drive in the park. She had no chance of speaking to Melford, either. He had gone off to shoot partridges.

Sam's arrival was public but informal. The shooters had just returned, and they were assembled in the saloon, telling Arethusa and the rest of the party about the day's sport.

Mr. Palgrave was announced. He paused for an

instant in the doorway, surveying the company, then crossed the room to his hostess.

"How do you do, Duchess. It is so very kind of you to put me up at such short notice. I'm afraid you must think I am treating your house like a posting-inn!"

"That is talking nonsense," said Arethusa with her sweet smile. "You know how glad we always are to see you."

Sam then turned to Melford, who shook his hand as though they had never ceased to be the greatest of friends.

Edith felt she could not hope to emulate such good manners or such good acting. Oddly enough, it was the sight of her which Sam did seem to find a little disconcerting.

"Miss Bruton—I did not know I was to have the pleasure of meeting you."

He did not sound as though it was altogether a pleasure.

Someone asked about the latest despatches from Spain. What was being said at the Horse Guards when he left town? The group in the saloon settled for some comfortable talk. Nothing could have gone more easily. Until, all of a sudden, a dangerous topic came into view.

Among the latest gossip from London there had been rumours of a duel between a member of the Government and a high-ranking Army officer. The quarrel was political; the General had called the Minister a liar, but it was likely to cause a great scandal. So what did Palgrave know about it? What had really happened? Edith wondered if she alone could hear the tension in his voice as he answered.

"There was no duel. The magistrates got wind of the affair and stopped it. Horton and Fraser were arrested, though it is not certain whether they will be charged."

This caused a good deal of comment. Most people felt strongly about duelling. It was a barbarous custom, the women insisted. It ought to be abolished.

"It has been abolished," one of the men pointed out. "It has been made a crime. Even wounding a man in a duel has been made a capital offence."

Edith had not known this.

"That does not stop men fighting," said a young soldier. "Hardly anyone is ever prosecuted. And the law is brought into disrepute."

"So it ought to be," declared Harry Mount-Stephen. "Gentlemen ought to be able to settle their quarrels in the honourable way, as they always have. What right has the law to interfere?"

He was the youngest person in the room, and his father told him to be quiet. He did not know what he was talking about.

Harry blushed, but looked for support towards his much-admired cousin, who had been keeping unusually silent.

"What do you think, Mel? There is nothing unacceptable in duelling, is there? Why should it be stopped?"

Melford was fond of Harry, who would be back at Christ Church in a week or two, living in a set of wealthy undergraduates, all trying out their new manhood, drinking a little too much and often getting into scrapes. Perhaps this compelled him to answer as he did.

"Times change. The old satisfaction of fighting out your differences is more complicated than it used to be. A friend of mine told me once that he'd called a man out—a man who had done him an injury—and had resolved to kill him if he could. At the very last minute, when they were facing each other in the cold light of dawn, he realised, from the way his adversary was holding his pistol, that he meant to delope. My friend said that if he'd killed that man he would have felt like a murderer."

"So what happened?" asked Harry.

"Oh, he just grazed the fellow's arm. He was such a bad shot, he probably couldn't have done any better if he'd tried. But that doesn't alter the case. Once moral scruples set in, nothing can be solved by duelling."

He had falsified the end of the story, to lull suspicion, Edith thought, for she knew he was an exceptionally good shot. She saw Sam's face of stone, and that he and Melford avoided looking at each other. Arethusa was so pale that she might be going to faint.

Edith wanted to go to her, but felt this would attract curiosity. She wondered how long they would all be imprisoned in this room full of people. Then a clock chimed and there was a rustle of movement. It was time to go and dress for dinner.

Later, in the dining-room, Edith watched Arethusa give a display of charming frivolity which was a travesty of her usual manner. There was a false, hectic gaiety about her, and her eyes were haunted. Yet no one else seemed to perceive anything wrong.

Edith wondered how often she herself had been deceived by that façade at Melford House in the spring, as Arethusa struggled to maintain the lie she had been forced to tell about the date of her baby's conception, knowing all the time that the odds were against her succeeding. Edith ate her dinner almost in silence. Her neighbours must have found her poor company.

There was a vapid interval in the drawing-room while the men were drinking their port, and then the guests were offered a choice of entertainment: an evening of cards or a game of hide-and-seek. This

was for the younger members of the party, and
Edith knew she would be expected to play.

She cast a glance of appeal at Melford, saying
with her eyes, I must speak to you. He made no
sign. Reluctantly she followed the other players into
an imposing stone corridor known as the parade.
They were all chattering about hiding-places. She
lagged behind, and only then realised that Melford
had come after her.

Putting a hand on her arm, he said, "We'll go
into the library."

As soon as they were in there and alone, he said,
"You need not be so anxious. She won't give herself
away. She has been on a public stage all her life,
you know, being who she is and what she is. She is
far better at keeping up appearances than you are,
my poor innocent."

"But aren't you sorry for placing her in such a
situation?" asked Edith. "I cannot believe you wish
to cause her pain."

She did half believe it, that was the trouble.

Melford frowned. "I didn't set out to frighten her.
It wasn't I who brought up the subject of duels."

"You invited Mr. Palgrave to Rythorpe. Surely
that was not necessary?"

"You think not?" His voice hardened. "Then let
me open your eyes to what goes on in the world
around you. This very public affray in London has
started people talking; all the encounters and suspected encounters of the last year are being discussed once again, as well as every supposed
quarrel and its possible cause. There was always a
faint risk someone might have noticed a certain
coolness between Palgrave and myself just about
the time he had his arm in a sling, and Arethusa
left town for the sake of her health. If he had failed
to come to Rythorpe this summer, that might have
started a line of speculation leading straight back

to her. So I wrote and asked him to pay us a brief visit to discourage gossip, and he agreed. Now do you understand?"

"Yes," she said, subdued and a little apologetic. "I had not realised. I suppose it was the wisest thing to do."

There were shrieks and running footsteps coming from the direction of the marble hall. The game of hide-and-seek was warming up. The door-handle rattled at the far end of the library.

"Heaven preserve us from these pestilential ya-hoos!" said Melford irritably. "Come in here."

They were still standing just inside the library under a little gallery supported by four Corinthian pillars. Melford reached out as though to remove a book from a nearby shelf. As he touched it, a whole section of the walled bookshelf swung forward: it was a hidden door, and the books were no more than leather spines stuck on the wooden panel in neat rows. Behind the panel was a small staircase leading up to the gallery.

Melford whisked Edith into the cavity, and closed the sham bookcase behind them just as a crowd of boisterous men and girls burst into the library at the far end, hotly pursued by the two seekers, hal-looing and making hunting noises. They rushed full tilt along the whole length of the room and out again by the door under the gallery, the sound of their stampede gradually dying away in the hollow echoes of the parade.

Melford and Edith were left in their hiding-place. There was a dim aura of light coming down from a lamp in the gallery above, just enough for Edith to make out Melford's expression as he stood gazing down at her. She could hear his quickened breath-ing. She was sure he could sense the beating of her heart under the thin rose-coloured silk of her dress as they stood close together in this intimate place.

Then they heard the click of a door, and a man's footsteps. Someone else had come into the library.

Edith and Melford exchanged glances of exasperation and mock alarm. They could not see the intruder, but they could hear him walk some way down the room and then stop. So long as he was there, they could neither move nor speak, for if they could hear him, he could certainly hear them. They were now in a ridiculous situation. It would look very odd if they stepped out together from their curious refuge. Of course there was the game of hide-and-seek which they could use as an excuse, but it might still seem strange that Melford and Edith should have paired off together, or indeed that he was playing at all. It really depended who was the unknown occupant of the library.

Then someone else came in—a woman this time—walking past them under the gallery. They could hear her light steps change as she reached the carpet.

"Sam," said Arethusa's voice. "I thought you might have come in here."

Edith felt Melford stiffen. Apprehension gripped her like a cramp in the stomach.

"My dear Arethusa, we mustn't be caught in here!" Sam sounded thoroughly put out. "If you want to ask about Caroline, she's perfectly well, and that's all I can tell you. I can't break my word to Melford."

"I know. I wouldn't want you to. But there's something else I think I have a right to ask. The story he told before dinner—was that true? Did he call you out?"

"Well, yes. But we neither of us came to any harm . . . You've heard what he said. Don't cry, Tusie. You know I would never have hurt him. Not that I could have done," said Sam frankly.

"He nearly killed you! He said so, and they would

have called him a murderer. Your death and his
ruin, it would have been all my fault." The last
words came out between choking sobs.

Melford whispered very softly to Edith, "I shall
have to go to them. You stay here."

He slipped out of the sham bookcase, gently closing the panel behind him. A moment later, she
heard the noisy opening and shutting of the library
door, as though he had just entered from the parade. There was a gasp of fright from Arethusa and
a sound like someone knocking over a chair.

"Melford!" exclaimed Sam. "I'm very glad to see
you, and I hope you don't think you have interrupted an assignation, for I assure you it's no such
thing!"

"What have you done to make my wife cry?" demanded Melford, obliged to pretend that he did not
know.

"It wasn't his fault," said Arethusa, husky and
defensive. "I asked him whether you had fought a
duel . . ."

"And the fool told you. My dear Sam, I should
have expected you to have more sense!"

"You were such good friends until I came between you," faltered Arethusa, her voice breaking
in a fresh access of tears.

"And we can be good friends again if you don't
keep reminding us of events we should all prefer to
forget! So do stop reproaching yourself, there's a
good girl."

There were indeterminate sounds: Sam picking
up whatever it was that had fallen over, Arethusa
trying to stifle her emotions, Melford comforting
her, kind if a little impatient. She had better go
and bathe her eyes. He would make some excuse
for her, say she had been called to the nursery, one
of the children had woken from a bad dream . . .

Edith heard them all go out together. After a

brief pause, she pushed open the panel and emerged
into the empty library. She felt uneasy, without
knowing exactly why. She had not meant to spy,
and she had learnt nothing about those three she
did not know already. Yet she felt a kind of weari-
ness, a dislike of subterfuge. How pleasant it would
be to live in a world where everything was honest
and open, and there was no need for secrets! Well,
that was a luxury they had all learnt to do without,
and she was learning fast.

She made her way back to the saloon. The game
of hide-and-seek had degenerated into an argument
about which rooms were out of bounds. There were
resentful murmurs and accusations of cheating. Several of the party were looking rather dishevelled.

The first person to notice Edith was Sam. "Where
have you been all this time?" he asked, smiling and
coming towards her.

"I was so well hidden that I didn't know the game
was over."

He studied her carefully and she had a moment's
panic, thinking he might ask her where her good
hiding-place was. Or even that he guessed. Stupid
to feel guilty! He of all people could have been told
why she and Melford had felt the need for a private
conversation.

But he didn't ask any awkward questions. They
sat down together in a corner of the saloon, and she
asked how he had escaped from the serious business of cards.

"I know you are a famous whist-player."

"I wanted to talk to you. To hear all you have
been doing since we last met."

This was something he was not going to hear, but
she obliged with a recital of all the outward pleasures of Rythorpe and how much she was enjoying
herself. He listened gravely, still watching her.

Presently he said, "You've changed."

Edith knew she had changed. Plenty of people besides Melford had told her she was prettier. She had gained in poise simply through living with Arethusa. She glowed with happiness through being in love. Yet she did not think Sam was paying her a compliment.

"I'm older," she said.

"You've grown up too quickly, Swan. You shouldn't have had to bear the burden of Arethusa's troubles, and the Melfords' marriage is hardly an inspiring model. As for my own part in this sorry story—well, you shouldn't know anything about that, either. Don't let the world become distorted for you."

Why was he talking like this? Perhaps it was just his own guilty conscience. She remembered once thinking that she had hardly ever seen him serious, but he too had changed, or at least revealed a different side of his character. She looked at him, the light glinting on his thick, close-cropped curls, the colour of light brass—or perhaps pinchbeck was more accurate—his features so irregular after Mel's. She was amazed to remember she had once thought herself in love with him. Yet there was a sadness in feeling that they were now so far apart.

"You seem to take a gloomy view of my future," she said lightly. "Can't we find a more cheerful topic? Tell me, how is Caroline?"

He brightened at once. Caroline was a most satisfactory baby; he had excellent reports of her. He was just beginning to explain his plans for her future, when they were approached by Harry.

"These running-about games seem to upset people, so we're going to play commerce instead. Do come and join us, Edith." He glanced at Sam, hesitating. "I don't know if you care for such childish amusements, sir? I thought you'd be in there with the grandees."

He glanced through the open doorway of the white drawing-room, where the serious card-players were seated at their small baize-covered tables.

"I'd far sooner stay in here," declared Sam.

He proceeded to become the life and soul of the commerce party, speculating wildly and amassing a huge pile of the little mother-of-pearl fish they used for counters. He made everyone laugh, and Edith, sitting beside him, had an unexpected memory of schoolroom games at Seddon Park.

When the tea-table was carried into the drawing-room, she went to preside behind the silver spirit kettle, which was now her nightly task. Arethusa was in there, talking to some of the older guests, her serenity quite restored. Sam helped to hand round the cups and saucers. Presently Melford came across to the tea-table. He had been playing whist.

"Will your Grace have tea or coffee?" Edith asked.

"Coffee, if you please." He added in a low voice, "I'm sorry I was obliged to desert you. All is well now, however."

She gazed after him as he went to join the group round his wife.

Sam's voice at her elbow said, "Don't lose your heart in *that* direction."

She spun round on him, angry because this went too near the bone.

"That is a monstrous suggestion!"

"I'm sorry. It was not meant to be. I'm not accusing you of anything improper, you are far too good and sensible. But he is a man who fascinates women without trying to. I don't want to see you waste your life playing Patience on a Monument."

This speech made her more conscious than ever of the change Sam had seen in her but could not define. Much as she liked him, she was glad he was staying such a short time at Rythorpe. He made her feel uncomfortable.

The continued presence of visitors made it necessary for Melford and Edith to find a place where they could meet in private, if only to talk and enjoy the innocent pleasure of being together, quiet and undisturbed. Edith had already volunteered to transcribe some documents that Dr. Ballard, the historian, was studying in the muniment-room. She wrote a very good hand, and was used to copying her father's sermons for publication. Dr. Ballard was delighted to have such a helper, but the muniment-room was so full of rent-rolls, leases, wills, marriage contracts, pedigrees, heralds' visitations, letters and journals dating back over four centuries, all the written records of a great family, that there was hardly room for one person to work there, let alone two.

So Melford suggested that Miss Bruton should have the use of the nearest available room where she could spread out her papers on a large table and work in comfort. Of course Dr. Ballard was entitled to go in and talk to her as often as he chose, but the room was up a few stairs, the old man was heavy and breathless, and his approach was always quite audible. If he found his employer there, explaining historical details to the young amanuensis, he was innocently pleased that the Duke should show such an interest in the projected history of the MountStephen family.

Edith's writing-room was no extravagant bower of delight. Intended for conversation only, it smelt of ink and old parchment, but there was a bright fire lit every day and besides the single upright chair at the table, there were two rather shabby armchairs where she and Melford could sit and talk about anything that came into their heads.

They did talk about history a good deal, and on one particular afternoon he had been telling her how the various family properties had been acquired. A grant of land in East Anglia to a Norman follower of Henry I, a certain Sir Roger de Mont St. Etienne, whose name had been anglicised over the centuries, a string of Midlands manor houses accumulated through marriage, vast acres of church property bought by the Earl of Melford in the reign of Henry VIII, an Elizabethan castle in Ireland. All these places still existed, together with the London property and a villa on the Thames. Not a house had ever been sold. All had been surpassed by Rythorpe, built by the first Duke on the site of a Cistercian abbey.

"You must feel very strange to have come into such an inheritance," said Edith seriously.

"As to that, I could not say, my love. I never inherited so much as a penny piece."

"Whatever do you mean?" she demanded, brushing aside a mad idea that he was going to reveal himself as an impostor and not the Duke of Melford after all.

He laughed at her bewildered expression, and reached across to take her hand.

"Dear Seedif, it's a shame to tease you! But it is perfectly true that I did not inherit in the usual way. I became possessed of Rythorpe and the title and everything else the instant I was born. I was a post-humous child. My father died of a rheumatic fever at twenty-six, and my mother lived less than a week after my birth. I think the shock of losing him contributed to her death."

"Who brought you up? Was it Lord Robert?"

"He was only a boy himself. He'd been summoned back from the Grand Tour and kept hanging around waiting to see whether he was the seventh Duke of Melford or not. In the event, he wasn't.

He's never held that against me—except when I threaten to build an aqueduct, or something he considers equally irresponsible!"

"Then who did take care of you, if your uncle was too young?"

"Oh, I was surrounded by a tribe of worthy protectors: nurses, governesses, tutors, chaplains, riding-masters, controllers—not all at once, of course. They came and went in succession, but there were seldom less that four at any one time. They had violent rivalries, and I used to play them off against each other."

"But were they kind to you?"

"Kind? They were certainly not unkind. To tell the truth, they were a pack of toadies, far too easily satisfied with my accomplishments and eager to tell me so. All except one fellow: Captain Lennard. He was called my military tutor, and he was supposed to instruct me in manly pursuits: shooting, fencing and boxing. There was no pleasing him! He was as strict as a Prussian, and never missed a chance to give me what he called a salutary thrashing, however flimsy the excuse."

"How infamous!" she exclaimed. "He must have been a wicked brute."

"Well, he prepared me for the horrors of Eton," said Melford without rancour, "and I don't think his motives were entirely evil. He saw that the others punished me too little and he tried to redress the balance. Only he was a stupid man. When I struggled to gain his approval, which at the time I should have valued, he remained implacable. And a man who will never be pleased has no more influence in the end than a man who is pleased too easily. I learnt to compete against myself, to be the judge of my own achievements. I've been doing it ever since, and it isn't a bad method for a rich man, who has an advantage over most of his friends."

Edith remembered Ralph saying that Melford only liked doing things that were difficult, and admired his determination. The rest of the story sickened her. She could imagine a little boy who looked very like Bar, not cherished as Bar was by a loving father and mother and sister, but solitary and isolated. Fed and taught and flattered by a constantly changing group of people who did their duty without showing any real affection for him. Her eyes filled with tears.

"Why, what's the matter?" he asked, watching her.

"I cannot bear to think of your being so lonely and neglected!"

"My sweet girl, what a tender heart you have!"

They were still holding hands. He crushed her fingers even closer as they sat on their separate chairs, both caught in what seemed to her an irresistible current. He half rose as though he meant to take her in his arms, but she pulled her hand away.

"No, Mel. We must not. You know what we agreed—a loving friendship, nothing more."

"I was a damned fool," he said, scowling, but he sat down again and pushed his chair a little further from her. "I should never have suggested such a charade. I'm being torn in pieces, and you sit there looking angelic and serene—don't you care?"

"Mel, you know I care," she whispered, the tears brimming over now, for she ached with longing for the kind of love she knew she must refuse.

"Yes, I know you do. Forgive me. The whole thing is iniquitous. If only I could marry you!"

"That's impossible," she said steadily. "And you ought not to think of it."

"Why not? I can't help wishing I were free."

She stared at him. How could he be free, except

through Arethusa's death? The idea shocked her deeply.

Perhaps he understood the look in her eyes, for he said quickly, "If I had divorced her when I had the chance, I should be able to marry again."

Edith had not considered this. Nor did it strike her until much later that if he had disowned his wife when he found out she was Sam Palgrave's mistress, they themselves would never have fallen in love. She would have returned to her family, and ten to one she would never have set eyes on the Duke of Melford again.

It was easy to forget common sense with the sudden bitter realisation that he could have been able to marry again. She had no wish to hurt Arethusa, her dear friend, and she was determined not to fall into the same trap, to commit the same sin. But she could not help feeling that she now had more justification for loving Melford, so long as that love looked for fulfilment only in their hearts and minds.

He had been brooding in silence. She glanced at him nervously. Was he going to make difficulties?

He gave her his old, mocking smile. "Don't look so anxious, sweetheart. I've said my say. I'm back on the chain. No need to shoot the mad dog!"

The constant stream of visitors came and went. The Oxenhams were expected.

"You will be glad to see Fanny again," said Arethusa, in whose mind Fanny Oxenham had been assigned the role of Edith's particular friend.

It was true the girls had seen a good deal of each other in London, but Edith had never quite got over her first impression of Fanny: a silly, affected creature in a London ballroom, her eyes rolling ceaselessly in search of young men. One of the young men in that ballroom had been Richard Weare, whom Edith had found dreadfully conceited and patronising. He too was due at Rythorpe for the shooting. She hadn't the smallest desire to see either of them. So it made her feel awkward and ungracious to discover how pleased Fanny was to see her.

"How delightful it is to be reunited with you, dearest Edith," she declared, as they strolled up and down the length of the library. She said she needed exercise after sitting so many hours in the carriage. "I have missed you dreadfully all these months in London. It was a shame you had to go off to that watering-place just before the start of the season. And then the Duchess's poor little baby died after all, which was so sad."

"Yes, it was very sad. But I should not have been in London during the season. If the Duchess had not taken me to Strenton, I should have gone home."

"Well, I am very glad to find you here, for I have a great deal to tell you."

In spite of this, Fanny did not tell her anything. She grew rather silent, almost reserved. Edith thought she seemed less giddy, and had lost her inclination to giggle. Richard Weare, too, when she sat next to him at dinner, seemed much less of a puppy. He did not boast of his own exploits but talked in a perfectly rational way and listened to what Edith said in return. She was agreeably surprised. It took her another twenty-four hours to understand the change that had come over Fanny and Richard. The explanation was perfectly simple. They had fallen in love.

"I'm so glad," she said when the news was broken to her the following evening. Fanny had come to pay her a bedtime visit in her dressing-room. "Can I wish you joy? Are you engaged?"

"Yes, we are," said Fanny, a little defiantly. "That is to say, we are determined to get married, but our families are being quite horrid."

"Oh? I'm sorry to hear it. Richard is quite eligible, is he not?"

"He will become Lord Sandlease in about a hundred years' time, but that is no use to us now. Everyone says he is too unsteady to marry at present. Just because he got through rather a lot of money last year! Poor Richard, he was only kicking up a few larks. How was he to know that he wouldn't want to make any more stupid bets or get drunk, once everything began to change. It does, you see, when you discover the one person in the world you can truly love. I must say it does seem very odd, because we used to detest each other when we were children."

Fanny poured out the whole romantic history, which had begun at a race ball in July when Richard had rescued her from the tipsy advances of a captain of militia. He had then surprised both Fanny and himself by giving her a stern lecture on the folly of flirting with a man she scarcely knew. They had gone on from there, and there were many incidents to describe, many allusions to Richard's good looks and devotion. Edith listened with interest and an underlying touch of envy. However ill-used they felt at present, with their families considering them too young and irresponsible to settle, she was pretty sure they would be able to marry in the end if they stayed the course. They would live happily ever after, their love honourably acknowledged before the world—something that could never happen to her.

When Fanny had talked about herself for about an hour, it struck her that she ought to make some return.

"Are you not in love with anyone, Edith? I wish you were. It is such a charming state to be in!"

"Perhaps I have not met the right person yet."

"It isn't easy to recognise the right person. I'm

sure I never thought that mine would be Richard!
You are so pretty—everyone says so. And then, of
course, you are clever."

"Well, if everyone says that, too, it is no wonder
I have no suitors," said Edith, laughing.

"Oh, stuff! It isn't true that men dislike clever
women. My mama says older men often prefer wives
who have read a great many books and can talk
about politics. And then they have one great advantage: men of over thirty are not likely to be subject to family pressure."

"They are also likely to be married already,
which is a corresponding disadvantage!"

"That's true," Fanny admitted. "Still, I shall try
to think of a husband for you. I wish there was
someone at Rythorpe, but there don't seem to be
any fascinating charmers here at present, married
or single. Apart from the Sun King himself."

"Who?"

"That is Richard's name for the Duke. I was only
joking!"

Edith felt a flash of anger at Richard's imperti-
nence, followed by a quick acknowledgment that it
really was rather a good name for Melford in his
moments of grandeur. She made an involuntary
movement, and Fanny caught her change of expression.

"Edith—you haven't formed an attachment
there?"

"No, no—of course not! How could I do anything
so ridiculous? It would be quite improper."

"I dare say." Fanny continued to stare at her.
"He is the handsomest man I ever saw, but I could
not love him myself. That cold, sarcastic manner—
I've always been a little frightened of him."

"Oh, but he can be so very different when you
come to know him well," protested Edith. And then
she stopped, realising she had given herself away.

Fanny was the kind of girl who recognised different shades of feeling by instinct, and her love for Richard Weare had made her even more perceptive. In the end, Edith gave her a brief account of her relationship with Melford.

"You won't tell anyone, will you?" she begged. "Nothing can come of these sentiments. He won't ask me to do anything seriously wrong, and if he did, I shouldn't agree."

"I won't breathe a word, I promise. Or try to give you good advice. Who am I to moralise? I'm sure you intend nothing wrong. Only once one gets into a scrape, it is so hard to get out again. My dear Edith, do be very, very careful."

When they parted for the night, Edith was left wondering whether she could trust Fanny to keep her secret. Fanny wouldn't gossip deliberately, but she might let slip something by mistake. After a day or two, she decided she had nothing to fear. The young lovers had learnt to be discreet; they wouldn't betray a friend in a careless moment.

She saw a good deal of them, because Lady Jane Oxenham, determined to preserve her daughter's reputation, insisted that she should always have a female companion with her whenever Richard was in the offing, and Edith, tactful and sympathetic, was the obvious choice. They sat and talked, or sauntered in the pleasure grounds, sometimes as a trio, sometimes accompanied by another of the bachelor guests, Captain Stuart Bruce, a heavy dragoon, whose conversation was weighty rather that spritely.

Melford observed all this from a distance, and questioned Edith at one of their meetings in the writing-room.

"What the devil are you up to, my treasure? Am I to regard Bruce as a rival? Not a very flattering choice."

"Poor Captain Bruce! He will follow us about like a large dog. You must know I am playing gooseberry to Fanny and Richard."

"Good God, why?"

She gave him the history of the love affair, which she herself found rather touching, so that she was inspired to ask if he could help. Both the Oxenhams and the Weares might pay attention to him.

Melford was not impressed. He said, "Richard's too young to marry."

"He's twenty-two! You were married at the same age."

"That was different," he said, a little sententiously. "I had a duty to my family. My parents were dead, and I needed a wife. Richard's father and grandfather are both living; he has no responsibilities yet. And a very young man does not often make the right choice."

"Were you not in love with Arethusa?" she asked, remembering how Arethusa herself had described their first meeting.

"I thought I was. She was a great beauty—she still is. Very sweet and gentle and willing to be pleased. But she is no companion to me now. She does not share my interests in the way you do. She is essentially light-minded."

Edith considered this. Arethusa was certainly not stupid, and she always stood up for Melford most loyally if anyone—his Uncle Robert, for instance— was criticising his tendency to build aqueducts or undertake other eccentric schemes. Yet she never played any part in encouraging these schemes, never came up to the muniment-room to see how the family history was getting on. (Just as well, in the circumstances!) But the other charge was quite unfounded.

"You would not accuse her of being frivolous if you had been with her at Strenton as I was. She thought seriously about her past actions and really did suffer a great deal of remorse."

He looked a little uncomfortable. "I know that. I'm not saying she can't tell the difference between right and wrong. Only that she is too shallow to recognise which of two wrongs is the worst. When I found out what had gone on between her and Palgrave, she cried a great deal and kept insisting, in extenuation, that she'd never been in love with him. As though this reduced the whole matter to a minor peccadillo, I thought it made her conduct a great deal harder to forgive. If you were married, Edith, could you betray your husband simply to gratify your senses with a man you did not love?"

"No, never."

She gazed at him adoringly. His dark, stern beauty, his brilliant glance drew her like a magnet. How could Arethusa ever have looked at another man, she wondered, even if they had worn out their passion and he was away in Ireland. I shall be faithful to him for the rest of my life, without his ever becoming my lover.

She sat down at the table, shaking so much that she could hardly pick up the pen. Melford had gone to stare out of the window.

It is criminal folly to go on like this, she thought. I ought to stop meeting him in private. The danger was growing more intense because, in spite of all her good resolutions, she could not help thinking how unreasonable it was that they could not do, with a deep and sincere love, what Arethusa had done out of mere self-indulgence.

CHAPTER NINE

It was November. Melford and his friends shot pheasants and hunted foxes on alternative days. He kept his own pack of foxhounds and they hunted across a wild, hilly country that was largely unenclosed, and since there were very few fences to jump, the ladies of the house-party were made welcome by the sportsmen, provided they rode well enough not to get in the way.

Edith was by now a confident rider. She loved these days in the bright tingling air, the hushed, covertside waiting, the music of hounds in full cry. The pulsating speed of a gallop across open country, broken by downhill scrambles and sudden checks, the excitement of never knowing what was going to happen next. It was only during these hours in the saddle that she could temporarily forget the problem of her love for Melford, which was now beginning to haunt her night and day to an uncomfortable degree. She was reminded, of course, whenever she caught sight of him, of a splendid horseman in a scarlet coat, hunting his own hounds. But this was simply an immediate pleasure, not connected with all the worry and self-questioning that filled her mind when she was away from him, or the growing desire that possessed her when they were together. Hunting was an escape.

Fanny was also a keen follower, eager to show Richard that she could keep up with him, but the most daring of all the women was Arethusa.

So Edith was very much surprised, at the end of the second week when she told her regretfully that she thought she had better not hunt any more this season.

"Not hunt?" repeated Edith, stopping in the middle of Arethusa's dressing-room with a watering-pot in her hand. She was attending to some plants in an elegant jardinière. "I hope there is nothing wrong—you are not ill?"

Arethusa certainly did not look ill. She had recovered her slender figure, and a peaceful autumn in the country had given her a renewed glow of health. It was hard to realise that she was nearly twenty-eight years old.

She looked up from her embroidery and smiled. "No, I'm not ill. In fact, it will be a real deprivation not to hunt, but I think I must make the sacrifice. You see, I am very anxious to to have another child, and I know that is what Mel wants, too. I think he feels it would somehow close a door on the past, and I expect he is right."

Edith felt as though she had been winded, and her mouth went dry.

"Do you mean . . ." She stammered. "Are you . . ."

"Am I in what is called a delicate situation? No, my love, not yet. But they say women are far less likely to conceive if they are continually jolting over rough country on horseback or leading too active a life. So I feel I must do what I can to reduce the odds." She broke off, noticing Edith's frozen expression. "Have I shocked you? I'm so sorry; I ought not to have mentioned such a matter. The trouble is, dearest Edith, you have been such a rock of strength to me in all my difficulties, that I am apt to forget you have never been married yourself. Do forgive me?"

Edith managed some sort of protest: of course she had not been shocked, she was not such a prude. She was then able to go on watering the plants, her back to Arethusa while she struggled with her emotions. Here and at Melford House the Duke and Duchess had separate bedrooms, each with a large canopied bed, and a dressing-room adjoining. She knew by now that this was the usual arrangement among the high aristocracy, even those with a great number of children. It had surprised her at first, because among the families of the landed gentry from which she came, a husband and wife were accustomed to share one matrimonial bed. Somehow she had convinced herself that in the Melfords' case the existence of different rooms was a proof of their continued estrangement. From the way Melford had talked about loving her and not loving Arethusa, she had taken it granted that their private lives were now quite separate. Yet here was Arethusa blithely hoping that they would soon have another child as a kind of peace-offering between them. Edith felt cheated, confused and acutely, shamingly, jealous.

She was still wondering how to hide her feelings when Lady Jane Oxenham came in, wanting a chat with her hostess. Edith was able to slip away.

It was Sunday. The house was full of people, not one of whom she wanted to encounter. She needed to be alone to think. Fetching a pelisse and bonnet, she decided to go for a walk. She was heading across the parterre towards the park when she heard her name called and caught sight of Captain Stuart Bruce, dogged in pursuit.

This was the last straw! Pretending not to hear, she took refuge behind the massive statuary of one of the fountains and then doubled back round the next corner of the house. Following the outline of the first Duke's Baroque fantasy, she came to the orangery, paused, and went in.

The high glass-fronted pavilion was filled with plants and shrubs that would have astonished the original builder. Brought from China and other exotic places, they lived in a hot, scented world of their own. Some of the more portable were brought indoors to make small, pretty gardens carefully arranged in jardinières, like the one she had been watering in Arethusa's dressing-room. She stood by the great stove, gazing at the many shapes and textures of the lush greenery, spiked and fringed, cushioned like velvet, sleek as polished leather. The air smelt peppery, yet sweet.

There was the sound of an opening door and a man's footsteps. She thought it was Captain Bruce, and did not look round.

"What are you doing, skulking here by yourself?" asked a quite different voice.

"Oh, it's you!" She still kept her face averted.

"No need to be so discreet, my love," said Melford. "We are quite alone."

He laid a hand on her arm, and she shook it off.

"What's the matter?" he asked in surprise.

"Nothing. Why should there be?"

"You are not very friendly."

"I don't feel inclined to talk to you at present. Is that so extraordinary?"

"Yes, it is. You're hardly a silent sphinx as a rule. What is the matter, Edith?"

He pulled her round to face him. Just seeing him so near made her almost sick with love and anger. She would not meet his eyes.

"Well, what's wrong?" he repeated impatiently.

"Your wife tells me you are hoping to increase your family," she mumbled.

"Well, that's counting our chickens. She is not

yet with child, but she has this idea that she will be, much sooner, if she avoids strenuous exercise. I think it's nonsense myself but I don't care to discourage her."

"I did not know—that is, I did not understand that you had given Arethusa any reason to expect . . ."

She broke off, unable to continue.

"Need we be so prim? If you mean, have I been making love to Arethusa, of course I have. I'm her husband."

"And you keep telling me you wish you weren't."

"That's beside the point. She and I have to make the best life we can together, and it is no one's concern but our own."

"Isn't it? I thought—if you loved me, as you say you do—I thought you would not want anyone else. In fact I don't see how you can be so two-faced and cynical. False to us both."

"That's because you don't understand the difference between men and women."

Edith did not answer. She was dangerously near tears, and she hated the note of shrewish scolding she could not keep out of her own voice.

Melford stood back a little and said, "If I was able to be your lover, I could be perfectly faithful to you alone."

"But that is an abominable suggestion!" She felt the hot blood come pounding up under her skin. "To say you could exchange one of us for the other without caring, as though we were animals. It's altogether monstrous!"

"No, it isn't," he said coldly. "It's realistic. That's what you don't like. I love you with my whole heart and I know you love me. In order to enjoy as much of that love as we dare, we have always to meet as though there was a wall of glass between us. It has become a torment to us both, and if you, a sheltered innocent, have felt that, have you ever considered how it has been for me?"

He gave her his burning ice look. She was too stricken to answer.

"Men are by nature more passionate than women," he went on. "That's no excuse for the way we sometimes behave, but it is a fact which romantic girls like you ignore at your peril. Love and desire don't always keep in step. It is only because my love is so strong that I have never taken advantage of your weakness. If I am prepared to put this restraint on myself while we are together, you must let me live the rest of my life as I choose."

The painful, uncompromising words seemed to echo through her head. She thought she was going to break down completely, the final humiliation. Brushing past him, she ran along the path of wet flagstones between the swaths of tropical foliage and out of the orangery into the cold November afternoon.

She was utterly wretched. How could she have made such a vulgar scene? Melford was disgusted with her, and what was worse, he had shown her how stupid and rash and inconsiderate she had been during those secret encounters which had meant so much to her and had apparently been so unsatisfactory to him. She was further weighted down by her affection for Arethusa. It was dreadful to feel jealous of such a loving and trusting friend.

While she thought the Melfords were living entirely separate lives, she had not believed she was taking anything away from Arethusa. Now she was not so sure. Arethusa's feelings were a puzzle. According to her own statements, she had drifted away from Melford and become the mistress of a man she did not love. All the same, she must get some reassurance from the idea that Melford still needed her, and the arrival of a new baby would certainly help to compensate for the loss of Caroline.

I can't do anything to injure her, Edith thought. I ought to leave Rythorpe to put an end to the dangerous situation, once for all. Her parents' letters had become rather querulous lately, demanding to know when she was coming home. They had not seen her for more than eight months. Yet she could not tear herself away. It was something to be still under the same roof as her idol, even if it was such a large roof, and she spent the next two days deliberately avoiding him.

"You have not been to the muniment-room," said Dr. Ballard reproachfully, as they assembled in the saloon before dinner.

Edith had no intention of going anywhere near the muniment-room, or that little private study beyond. She said she had been suffering from eye-strain, and thought she must give the documents a rest.

"Of course you must not do anything to impair your sight," said the old historian immediately. "I fear I am apt to be a slave-driver! And there are other demands on your time, with so many young people in the house."

He glanced around him vaguely at the various guests, as though he was not quite certain of their ages or which of them qualified to be Edith's youthful companions.

She looked quickly at Melford to see if he had overheard the exchange, but he was talking about the news from the Continent and paid no attention. She had a miserable suspicion that all her efforts to avoid him had gone unnoticed, and that she had succeeded only because he had not troubled to seek her out. Glad to be rid of her, probably.

Lord Robert, complaining about the weather, said

he hoped it would be dry on the seventeenth. "The day we have our bonfire."

"Why the seventeenth?" enquired Mr. Oxenham. "Surely the fifth is the right day for a bonfire?"

"Not for us here. The seventeenth of November is Queen's Day—the anniversary of the accession of Queen Elizabeth. It was celebrated all over the country for more than a hundred years, and we keep up the tradition, though most people nowadays are more interested in burning an effigy of Guy Fawkes."

"I have never been able to see why," remarked Melford. "I cannot cherish an overwhelming hatred for a man who wanted to assassinate James I. To try to destroy the Lords and Commons was going a little far, perhaps, but only consider, if Guy Fawkes had succeeded, we should have been done with the House of Stuart, and England would have been spared one civil war, one revolution and three armed rebellions."

There was a murmur of protest from his guests. Whigs though most of them were, they could not quite accept this. Edith remembered the first time she had seen him, at Melford House, declaring that Macbeth was an abominable play and Mrs. Siddons ranted. She had thought him perfectly serious and taken an instant dislike to him. Now the provocative words and astringent irony touched a chord in her heart and only increased the desperate love she felt for him.

The seventeenth was fine and dry, though cold. An enormous stack of timber, brushwood and garden débris had been tangled into a gigantic tower on the grass between the house and the lake, far enough away to keep the smoke from discolouring the walls. As soon as it was dark, the carriages of the local gentry began to arrive, the mothers and children and the older ladies all going indoors to be received by Arethusa and comfortably seated in the windows all along the south façade so that they could watch the proceedings in safety. Their menfolk and the more stalwart girls and young women remained outside well wrapped up, mingling with the tenants and cottagers who had come from miles around. Later there would be an elegant supper in the house for the ladies and gentlemen, and a hearty meal for everyone else set out on trestles in the indoor riding-school. But the evening began with the bonfire.

Melford himself had to set the first faggot alight, taking a torch from the head gardener and manoeuvring it carefully so that little tongues of fire ran in among the dry twigs. There were rustlings and spurts of light and then the whole pyramid was ablaze, roaring and crackling, pale tongues of fire deepening to red at the heart as the heat grew greater.

It was awful yet fascinating, thought Edith as she stood beside Fanny and Richard, half mesmerised by the leaping waves of light. Everyone else seemed to feel the same, but after a while there came an urge for noise and movement. They joined hands and began to swing their way round in a great circle, singing songs they all knew: "Hearts of Oak," "Rule Britannia," "Lillibullero" . . .

Pewter jugs had been placed round the edge of the fire. Now the brew was hot enough to pour into tankards.

The first was given to Melford, who toasted in a ringing voice, "The Glorious Memory of Queen Elizabeth!"

Chestnuts, too had been roasting in the embers. They were drawn out on shovels, popping and sizzling, to be handed round for the more courageous to pick up among squeals of merriment. As the crowd sucked their burnt fingers and drank their punch, and the fire began to fall in on itself and diminish a little, a firework display began down by the lake.

Dazzling spirals shot out across the water, rockets whistled upwards, splinters of gold trailed across the night sky. The watchers stopped talking, their silence broken only by concerted gasps of pleasure.

Edith moved away from Fanny and Richard. She was not going to spoil their chance of a tête-à-tête, whatever Lady Jane might expect. Outside the ring of firelight, she walked across the dark grass alone. She was still warm from the dancing and singing, the chestnuts and the spiced wine. For a short time she had forgotten her unhappiness. It came back to her now as she watched the sparkling threads of silver and gold spread further and further apart against the immensity of the upper air. Nothing could be lonelier than that solitude.

There was suddenly a tall figure beside her in the darkness. "Edith."

She caught her breath and half turned, as though prepared for flight.

"No, don't run away, my dear love. I must talk to you. I can't bear to make you unhappy. Will you forgive me?"

"Oh, Mel!" She whispered as he fumbled for her hands through the thickness of her cloak.

"I've been a selfish brute, I see that now. I should never have inveigled you into this shabby game of pretence and deceit. You are worth so much more than I can give you here. I'd leave all this and go away with you tomorrow, if you would agree."

She was startled; presumably "all this" included the invisible palace of Rythorpe somewhere on the other side of the bonfire, his family, his tenants and all his responsibilities.

"You cannot be serious," she began.

"Why not? An ancestor of mine lived thirty years in Venice with a lady he was unable to marry. I can't take you to Italy—the Corsican brigand has barred the way—I could take you to my castle in Ireland, though, you'd be safe there. We'd hunt all day and make love all night. Eventually we could arrange to go abroad, to Portugal or Sicily perhaps, or even to America."

"But, Mel, consider. You can't desert Arethusa and the children, especially Bar. You cannot leave him to grow up here without a father, as you had to. And there are my parents. How could I involve them in so much pain and disgrace? It's impossible."

"Yes," he said sadly. "I suppose it is. What are we to do?"

"Go on as we are."

But, next day, she took her decision to go home. It was not difficult to arrange. The men were out shooting when the letters arrived, fetched as usual from the Post Office at Barlington. There was one for Edith from her mother, mentioning that Dr. Bruton had been suffering with a severe chill. He was well on the way to recovery, but it sounded just serious enough for her to explain that she was needed at home.

Arethusa was full of sympathy, conscious that they had kept Edith away from her parents much longer than they ought.

"Though we shall miss you dreadfully," she said. "I don't know what Bar will do without his dear Seedif. But of course you must go."

It was Friday and, as it happened, two of the guests, Mr. and Mrs. Dacre, were leaving on Monday. They could take Edith with them as far as Gloucester, less than a day's journey from Cotebury, so that she could safely finish the journey alone, travelling post. Mrs. Dacre made this offer of her own accord while her husband was still out with the guns. So everything was arranged by the time the men came home, and there was nothing Melford could do or say to keep Edith at Rythorpe.

"You're running away," he told her accusingly, having cornered her in the library.

"Yes," she admitted. "Don't be angry with me! I can't endure it."

But he was unhappy rather than angry. His face taut with strain, he gazed at her imploringly, and though she was almost ill with misery herself, she could not help feeling a sort of amazement that she could have reduced such a man to such a state.

"You don't love me enough," he said. "If you did, you wouldn't go."

"I love you too much. That's why I'm going."

CHAPTER TEN

Edith's parents were delighted to have her back, and speedily forgave her for staying away for so long. Friends and neighbours came to call, some remarking how pretty she had grown and how fashionable, others merely commenting that she was too thin. And everyone said she was bound to find local society dull, after associating so grandly with dukes and duchesses.

She had known when she parted from Melford that she would have to fight hard to conceal her deep unhappiness and to seem pleased with everything at home. Now her determination was stronger than ever, for she realised that any sign of drooping spirits would at once be put down to pride and discontent, the fatal result of having been spoilt and pampered and taught to think too well of herself. And really, she thought, that kind of affectation would be so disgusting, I should almost prefer to have it known that I wish I could form a forbidden attachment for a married man.

Her continual chatter and liveliness seemed quite a successful disguise, but it imposed a fearful strain. All the more so because she could not even stop acting at night. She and her sister Emma had always shared a bedroom. She was fond of Emma and wished she could confide in her, but it was impossible. Their elder sister Lizzie would have known how to listen to Edith's adventures without becoming censorious, but Lizzie was in the West Indies, and Emma was on the way to becoming a contented old maid. Never had she shown the smallest inclination to fall in love, never looked at men with the speculating interest usual among young girls. She said frankly that she could not imagine a home happier than the one she had already, and she never wanted to leave it. How could anyone so reserved and austere be expected to understand the sweetness and anguish that had filled Edith's life at Rythorpe? Living so close to her sister, Edith had to be on her guard all the time, and a dreadful moment came when she wondered if it was even safe to go to sleep.

"Who is Nell?" Emma enquired one morning when they were dressing.

"I don't know. Who should she be?"

"You were dreaming about her last night. You kept saying, 'Oh, Nell—you must not, you must not.'"

Edith turned hot and cold. Her dream came back to her now, and she could only be thankful that Emma had misheard her. She always spoke of the Melfords by their titles, knowing that even the use of Arethusa's Christian name would seem strangely impertinent to anyone who had not been told the secret of those months at Strenton which had led to such a close intimacy. And of course no one here knew what the Duke was called by his family and friends.

Improvising quickly, she said that the eldest Dampier girl, Elinor, was often called Nell or Nelly.

"Though why I should dream of her, I can't imagine."

"Oh, that is the way with dreams. I was dreaming last week of old Mrs. Martin. She was complaining about one of Papa's sermons. And she's been dead three years."

Emma was quite satisfied with Edith's explanation. Edith went on combing her hair. Watching herself in the glass, she thought she could actually see her heart thumping under the tightly-drawn material of her high-waisted dress.

Later in the morning, she asked her mother whether she could move into Lizzie's old room. She said she was afraid her restless moving about disturbed Emma's reading. Mrs. Bruton often wished that Emma would not read so much. However, she sympathised with her youngest daughter, and let her have the other room to herself. Edith was now able to lie awake for hours in a state of bleak despair, or bury her face in the pillows and sob her heart out. She had run away from Rythorpe at short notice because she had known she would not be able to make the break in any other way, but she had not realised how much her nerves and senses, as well as her emotions, would be affected by the separation from Melford.

There was one consolation. She had been at home ten days when she received a letter addressed to her in a strong well-known hand, with the signature "Melford" scrawled across the bottom left-hand corner. She caught her breath when she saw it lying on the table, torn between delight and embarrassment, for she thought her parents must be eyeing it with great astonishment. But they merely assumed that the letter was from the Duchess and that her husband had franked it for her.

They were right, of course. They did not know that, as well as Arethusa's friendly, affectionate bulletin of news, there was an extra sheet inside, a passionate love letter from Melford. After that, he wrote quite often. The franking system served him very well. Members of both houses of Parliament were entitled to send letters free through the post, and it was understood that others in their households might use the same privilege, provided the Member himself addressed and franked the cover in his own hand. So Melford was able to write to Edith with or without enclosures from his wife, while the Brutons went on thinking that all these letters came from Arethusa. They remarked that she was a very regular correspondent.

Edith dared not write back in case her handwriting or the postmark was noticed by someone at Rythorpe, for naturally she was already answering the letters she received from Arethusa. She could send only guarded messages to the Duke.

Melford writing to her direct, was totally unguarded.

. . . my precious love, I am still bereft without you and this place is a wilderness . . . It would be cruel to hope that you suffer as I do, so I won't make that selfish demand. At your age it is hard to realise how life stretches from year to year, how events are overtaken, friends come and go, and how very, very seldom can two people meet whose hearts are as perfectly united as ours . . . I think of you night and day, my sweet siren, and wonder how long you can go on loving me in a limbo where we are never to meet. I shall not change. I shall not recover from this death-blow that has struck me at thirty-two when I am no longer free to claim the only woman I ever really wanted.

If these letters did nothing to banish Melford's image or restore her peace of mind, at least they brought her some faint distillation of joy, the secret joy of being loved. So she was able to go through the Christmas festivities in fairly equable spirits, pleasant to everyone though quietly discouraging to a couple of young men who showed signs of becoming too attentive. It was not difficult. As far as she was concerned, they were practically invisible.

One evening towards the end of January, Edith went into the principal shop in Cotebury High Street to match some embroidery silk. She was waiting for her parcel when she noticed that she was being observed by another customer, a pleasant middle-aged lady who was having several yards of white flannel measured out for her. The lady's glance was so intent that Edith could not help feeling that this was someone she ought to know. She was about fifty and wore grey with lavender trimmings, as though she was in half-mourning, the style in good taste if a little dowdy.

By the time Edith had counted out her money, the grey lady had also paid for her purchase, and as they left the shop together she spoke, in an agreeable voice, although with a touch of diffidence.

"May I ask, are you not Miss Edith Bruton?"

"Yes, ma'am. I'm afraid it is very stupid of me, but I can't for the moment remember . . ."

"You have never seen me before. My name is Wells, Mrs. Wells. And that will mean nothing to you either, but I have heard of you from Mrs. Dampier. I used to be her governess."

It came back now: Seddon Park almost a year ago, and Mrs. Dampier speaking of this old friend who had taken a house near Cotebury.

"Where exactly are you living, ma'am?"

"I have a small house at Hinchdown. It has a well-fenced garden with no ponds or running water, which is just what I need, for I generally have several children living with me, children whose own families are not able to take care of them. And that is the real reason for my accosting you in the street,

Miss Bruton. The youngest and newest of my little flock is a child in whom I think you are interested. Caroline Miller."

"Caroline!" repeated Edith. "I do know of a little Caroline, but she is quite a baby. When I last heard of her, she was boarded with a wet-nurse. Surely this cannot be the same child?"

"Yes, the very same. You are right about the wet-nurse, but unfortunately the poor woman was taken ill, and as the baby had to be weaned, it was decided that she should come to me straight away, instead of waiting another year. I don't usually undertake the care of infants, but I have engaged a good nursemaid, and the older children are delighted to have such a pet in the house."

Arethusa's baby, thought Edith. And Sam's, too. She stood in the grey, windy street while women clattered past on pattens, bumping her with their baskets, and carts trundled over the cobbles, and she remembered crossing the grass at Holly Lodge in the quiet July dusk with the tiny Caroline in her arms.

"I must not keep you standing in the cold, ma'am," she said, pulling herself together. "But will you give me your direction? I should so very much like to call on you."

Edith's parents made no difficulty about her visiting Mrs. Wells, so a few days later she set out on the three-mile walk to Hinchdown, avoiding the turnpike road, but following some little lanes and taking a short cut over the fields.

Nutways was a small weathered house on the edge of the village, with little windows and low doors. There was a good strip of garden at the front, and as she closed the gate behind her and walked up the path, she saw three children playing round a swing: two girls aged about nine, and a small boy perhaps a year older than Bar. As soon as he caught sight of the visitor, the boy came running to meet her.

"Are you my aunt?"

"No, my dear, I'm afraid not."

"Of course she's not your aunt," said one of the girls, coming in pursuit. "You are silly, Ned!"

"Is he expecting his aunt?" asked Edith.

"He's always expecting her. She never comes."

The little boy's face fell, and Edith's heart contracted with pity.

"I'm sorry," she said, "that I am not the person you hoped for, but some people have more than one aunt; it is quite the usual thing. So shall we pretend that I am your Aunt Edith? Would you like that?"

Ned brightened at once. He was an ugly little boy and his ears stuck out, but he had a very appealing smile. By now Mrs. Wells had come to the door.

"How kind of you to visit us so soon," she said, ushering Edith inside. "Let me take your cloak. I can see that you are very good with children. The baby is asleep at present. She generally wakes around midday."

She took Edith into a room where the furniture was rather scuffed and shabby, but the feel of the house was homely and comfortable, a place where children were not always having to mind their hands and feet. They sat by a wood fire and Mrs. Wells talked about the trio in the garden, Mary and Susan and Ned. Mary's mother was dead and her father was serving with the Army in Spain. Mrs. Wells expanded on her history, but when she spoke of the other two children, she made no mention of their families, and Edith guessed that they, like Caroline, were illegitimate.

Presently the nursemaid carried in the baby. Caroline was now seven months old. She had small, delicate features, a rose-petal complexion and fronds of almost white hair peeping out from under her cap. She held up her head and gazed around her, her smoky grey eyes full of curiosity.

"She's beautiful!" Edith exclaimed.

Which sounded fatuous, but beyond her admiration for the pretty baby, she felt a kind of surprise. Caroline did not actually look like her mother, or her father either, come to that. Yet, in the carriage of her head, there was a fleeting reminder of Arc thusa, the ravishing beauty, the focus of a loving circle of family and friends. Edith held out her arms instinctively, and the nursemaid handed over Caroline for her to hold.

"I dare say you would like to give Caro her feed," suggested Mrs. Wells.

An oval feeding-cup, called a pap-boat, was brought in. Edith spooned tiny portions of bread and milk into the hungry little mouth. Caroline gurgled and laughed and sometimes tried to catch at the spoon, but on the whole seemed a very well conducted baby.

"She is good," said Mrs. Wells. "She hardly ever cries. I never knew a better-tempered child."

She takes after her mother, thought Edith, but she did not say so aloud, for she had no idea how much Mrs. Wells knew about Caroline's antecedents. Probably the woman felt the same uncertainty about herself which restricted their conversation a little.

Though she did say presently, "You are acquainted with Mrs. Dampier's cousin, I believe. Mr. Palgrave."

"Yes, I met him first at Seddon Park."

"So he told me. He is Caroline's guardian, you know. It was he who suggested that you might be interested to hear of her progress."

Edith was touched. She felt that Sam had chosen her to be a friend to his daughter, someone who lived near enough to become a familiar part of the world that was gradually opening around her. This provided her with an object. Since leaving Rythorpe, she had grown accustomed to the feeling that nothing would ever happen to her again.

The winter was over and past, the time of the singing of birds had come, as it said in the Bible. The disturbing new vitality of April, the fresh colours and the rising sap, all made the agony of frustrated love harder to bear. Edith no longer cried herself to sleep, but was just quietly and unobtrusively wretched, and the fact that she was able to conceal her unhappiness made her slightly resentful towards those she was deceiving. She had sacrificed her love for Melford to save her parents from sorrow and disgrace, and they had not even noticed. It was true she had not wanted them to notice. It was also true that she had not wanted to draw Melford away from his wife and children, and that her conscience had been oppressed by all the teaching of religion and morality. Just at this moment in mid-April she resented that, too. Virtue might be its own reward; she found it a very poor compensation for what she had forgone.

"Will you be going to Nutways this week, my dear?" asked her mother at the breakfast-table.

"On Thursday, I think, Mama."

She paid regular visits to Mrs. Wells, to see Caroline, and the other children too, for they had all become attached to her.

"Thursday will do very well," said Mrs. Bruton. "And I thought we might ask the Maidwells round tomorrow evening to drink tea. Would you write a note to Mrs. Maidwell? We can leave it when we go out."

"Very well, Mama."

"You will have to offer Edith's admirer something stronger than that," said Dr. Bruton from behind the *Morning Post.*

"Henry, I wish you will not tease the poor child," said his wife severely.

"I don't mind."

Edith was able to laugh at her father's well-worn joke. She was really rather glad that he and Emma were inclined to be critical of her mother's attempts at matchmaking. This made it easier for her to avoid situations which could only end in awkwardness.

Poor papa still thinks I am too young to fall in love, she thought guiltily, going into the drawing-room to write her note and seeing the glossy new pianoforte he had just bought for her. She practised hard every day, and it maddened her that even music had lost some of its magic.

She wondered when she would hear again from Melford. The family were back in London now and there had been a longer gap than usual since his last letter. Perhaps he was beginning to forget her. But surely he would not be so faithless after all his protestations, she told herself fiercely, as she sat down dutifully to write to Mrs. Maidwell, who lived in a large house on the outskirts of the town with her husband and their only son, Cotebury's most eligible bachelor. Later in the morning she and her mother set out together with various errands in view, social and charitable.

They had just left the house and were waiting to cross the street when a very smart curricle, sweeping round the corner by the church, came bowling towards them. Edith caught her breath.

Her mother did not hear. She was too busily engaged in speculating who the driver might be, a dark handsome stranger whose demeanour and carriage matched his own air of splendid accomplishment. His groom wore a livery she did not recognise. His curricle drew up outside the rectory.

The gentleman stepped down, handing the reins to the groom, and took off his hat.

"Good morning, Edith. I hoped I should catch you at home, and I see I am only just in time." As she was apparently struck dumb, he added, "Will you not present me to your mother?"

"The Duke of Melford, Mama," said Edith in a stiff little voice accompanied by a stiff little curtsy.

She hardly knew what happened next. Her mother was speaking, and they were all going into the house, into the drawing-room. Her father was sent for, and Emma was there, too, quite eager to meet a man who owned an observatory.

By the time they were all seated, Edith had recovered enough to say, "It is a surprise to see your Grace in this part of the world. Is the Duchess with you?"

"She is in Bath. We have taken a house in Lansdown Crescent for a few weeks, so that she can drink the waters."

"Oh. Does this mean she is not well? I am so very sorry."

She really was rather alarmed. The Bath season was nearly over, and in any case people like the Melfords no longer looked on Bath as a pleasure resort, but went to fashionable Brighton instead. If Arethusa had come to Bath, it must be for a medical reason.

"My wife has been out of sorts ever since we came south." Melford glanced at each of Edith's parents and spoke in a confiding tone. "It may be nothing—a slight nervous disorder—but to tell you the truth, I came over here on an impulse when I discovered how close we were to Cotebury. I have been wondering whether you would be kind enough to lend us your daughter for a short visit? I have not told my wife I was coming, in case there was to be a disappointment, but if you agree, we can send the carriage for her any day, and Arethusa will be delighted. The sight of Edith will probably do her more good than all that hot water she dislikes so much."

"It is very kind of your Grace to say so," said the rector, glancing at his wife. "I'm sure Edith will do anything she can to please the Duchess, who has been so very good to her. That is so, is it not, my love?"

"Yes, Papa."

Edith knew she was being treated like a child and behaving like one. She dared not look at Melford, much as she longed to. It had begun to dawn on her that all this talk about Arethusa's health and drinking the waters had been part of a plan to give him an excuse for arriving in Cotebury! And there he sat, charming her parents, who had no idea he was simply doing it to get his own way, and that his natural manner was often very disagreeable. It was deceitful and shocking, and she was so affected by his presence that her senses were swimming and she was hardly able to act rationally.

Though she did not know it, her unusual diffidence was serving her very well. The Brutons might live out of the world, but they were not simpleminded. They had made discreet enquiries about the Melfords when she first went to stay with them, at the time of Lady Woodruff's hurried journey to Northamptonshire. Their informant, a neighbour of the Woodruff family in Sussex, had reported that the Duchess was a model wife and mother, unspoilt by fashonable life, and that although the Duke had an uncertain temper and some of the failings of a man of his rank, he was scrupulous in keeping to the rules and his domestic life was exemplary.

When they actually met him, Mrs. Bruton had

been startled by his good looks, so much more re-
markable than anything she had expected, and if
Edith had glowed with pleasure or talked and
smiled a great deal, she would have seen him as a
positive danger; not an intending seducer, but a
man who would put in the shade the kind of suitor
who was likely to come her daughter's way.

But Edith had reverted to what she had been at
sixteen: modest, amenable and rather shy. She was
clearly over-awed by their visitor. In spite of the
lively way she wrote and talked about the Melfords
and their friends, her mother thought she was probably a great deal less forthcoming at Melford House
and Rythorpe than she was at home, and this was
a relief. Even the Duke's open use of her Christian
name fitted into the picture, for it sounded as
though he and his wife treated her like a favourite
niece, and she respected them accordingly.

By the time he rose to go, it had been arranged
that the carriage should come on Friday and convey her to Bath. She had got past staring at his
well-polished boots and could face him with moderate composure.

"I can now go back and tell the Duchess my good
news," he said as they shook hands.

"Please tell her Grace how much I look forward
to seeing her."

The touch of his fingers tingled in waves of excitement right up her arm.

CHAPTER ELEVEN

The carriage brought Edith to the house in Lansdown Crescent, and she was shown into the upstairs drawing-room where both the Melfords were waiting for her. Arethusa embraced her affectionately.

"How glad I am to see you again, dearest Edith! When Mel came back on Tuesday and said he had a surprise for me, I could not guess what it was going to be. He had to tell me in the end. He has been very sly."

Melford leant against the mantelshelf with his hands in his pockets, looking down his ducal nose and pretending indifference.

Arethusa enquired after Edith's parents and gave news of her own family. She had plenty to say, which was just as well, for her companions were both inclined to be rather silent.

"And your Christmas balls—these young men you mentioned in your letters, were they really so dull?"

"Deadly," said Edith cheerfully.

"What a pity. I was thinking the other day that I never made a proper effort on your behalf while you were with us. Practically the only bachelors you met at Rythorpe were Richard Weare, who is

in love with Fanny, and that blockhead Stuart
Bruce. I don't count dear Dr. Ballard."

"No, indeed," said Edith, laughing. "But please
don't put yourself to any trouble. I am in no hurry
to find a husband!"

"I shall take you to a ball at the upper rooms."

"No," said Melford, so forcibly that Edith was
alarmed. She thought he was on the verge of giving
himself away.

"Why not?" asked Arethusa.

"Because I refuse to escort you to anything so
absolutely Gothic. At the end of the season, too. A
ball where they still dance minuets, and where you
would have to sit on the peeresses' bench and be
gaped at by all the clodhoppers! Out of the question."

Arethusa giggled. "Perhaps you are right. I must
say Bath is the one place where I feel it is rather
stuffy to be a duchess. Only I should like to take
Edith somewhere she can be properly admired as
she deserves."

"Then Melford House will be her rightful setting.
We are giving a ball, Edith, as soon as we return
to town in about three weeks. It will be a great
trouble, because the Prince of Wales is coming and
he always upsets one's plans, besides wanting all
the rooms overheated, he is so afraid of catching
cold, silly fellow. But apart from having to put up
with him and George Brummell, I dare say it will
be quite an agreeable evening."

"I am sure it will, Duke." Edith was struggling
with several contradictory feelings at once. "Perhaps you have forgotten that I am only paying the
Duchess a short visit. That was what my parents
agreed to. I don't think they will let me go off again
to London."

"They will if I ask them," he said loftily.

She knew he was right, and almost hated him for

it. He was implying that they had been unduly flattered by his rank and condescension. He had drawn her back into his orbit, that was why he had brought Arethusa to Bath. She looked extremely well and as beautiful as ever. There was clearly nothing wrong with her health.

Edith had suspected this all along. She had known she ought not to come, but had kept telling herself it would be too awkward to explain. Mama would be horrified if she knew only a quarter of the things that had happened at Rythorpe. The truth was, of course, that she wanted to see Melford again, and was too weak to resist the temptation.

"Well, we will talk about London later," said Arethusa. "In the meantime, Edith and I are going to enjoy Bath."

She began to make plans for the rest of the day, and Edith gathered that there was no one else staying in the house, except, naturally, the servants. No relations, no Colonel Waters. They had brought with them the personal attendants—butler, housekeeper, dresser, valet and so on—who really cushioned their lives against discomfort and inconvenience, but sitting down to meals or conversing in the drawing-room, they would be a party of three. This made her feel a little awkward. It was odd how seldom the three of them had been together like this. She had so often been alone with Melford, but when they were both present there had nearly always been someone else there. She wondered whether she would be able to keep her feelings hidden, and when she would be able to see Melford alone.

It was nearly seven hours before she managed this, by which time she had been shown round the furnished house, eaten a delicious luncheon, and driven down into the town with Arethusa, who had bought her a charming spring bonnet and taken her to choose some new novels at one of the circulating libraries.

They were to dine early before going to a concert, so Edith changed hurriedly and entered the drawing-room at a quarter to six, hoping Arethusa would be late. She always was. Melford, too, must have calculated on this. He was there alone, looking austere and magnificent in the black and white of evening dress that suited him so well. She closed the door, and they stared at each other.

It was all she could do not to run into his arms.

"My dearest love," he said. "How I've longed and planned for this! Right up to the last moment I was afraid you might cry off."

"And so I ought! But you made it so awkward and difficult for me, Mel. Winning over my parents with your insinuating manners. It was a shockingly underhand way to behave."

"I liked them both so much, and your bluestocking sister. But, my dear Edith, you are quite a different creature in your home surroundings. So modest and retiring, hardly a word to say for yourself. I was quite astonished!"

His eyes were dancing, and she could not resist the laughter in them.

"You put me out of countenance, you wretch. I hardly knew what I was doing. And it is all very well," she added more seriously. "However glad I am to be with you again, I have let you entice me here under false pretences and I am determined I will not do anything to hurt Arethusa."

"I shan't ask you to."

"I'm glad to hear it. The last time we were alone together, you wanted me to go to Ireland and live in sin with you in the middle of a bog."

"That's my little firebrand!" he said approvingly. "It's amazing how soon you cast off the manners of the parsonage when it suits you."

"Yes, I'm afraid it is," said Edith, sitting down some distance away from him.

She knew very well that all this lively repartee, besides expressing their pleasure at being together once more, was also a disguise for dangerously quickening emotions.

Melford said, "I have a new plan for the future, but there is no time to discuss it now."

When Arethusa came in, he was telling Edith about the progress of the aqueduct.

Edith wondered about Melford's plan during the concert and the night that followed, all through Saturday and Sunday morning, when they attended the service at the Octagon Chapel. Between church and dinner, he announced he was going to take her for a walk, there being nothing more amusing they could do on a Sunday.

"I suppose it is no good pressing you to come?" he said to his wife.

Arethusa, who loved riding, never walked anywhere if she could help it. She had ordered the fire to be lit, for it was a chilly day, and she was settling down to read.

Melford looked over her shoulder. "Novels on a Sunday! What would your mother say? Come along, Edith, I must take you out before her Grace begins to undermine your morals."

As they left the house, Edith told him, "You should not have said that, when it is you who are undermining my morals! And you should not have private jokes with me in front of your wife. It is very bad form."

They turned right-handed along the broad pavement of the Crescent. It was like being on the top of a cliff, with the green valley of the Avon and the city of Bath taking the place of the sea.

He said seriously, "I think you refine too much

over Arethusa's sensibility. She was able to deceive
me with a light heart when it suited her."

"Surely you are not still angry with her?"

"No, but I see no reason to be over-punctilious.
You are my first consideration."

They were descending a flight of steps, and she
took his arm and felt the hardness of bone and muscle through the cloth of his coat.

As they walked on down Cavendish Road, he
asked, "Why did you take fright and desert me last
winter? Was it because of the brutal way I spoke to
you in the orangery, or because I asked you to go
to Ireland with me?"

"You don't need an answer. You know the whole
situation was getting out of hand."

"Yes, but Edith—if we went back to our good resolutions, if I promised never to make such demands
on you again, would you be happy to come back and
live in my house? Happier than you are now, at all
events?"

Edith felt an extraordinary tug of longing, sharp-
ened by uncertainty and fear.

"I don't see how it could be managed," she tem-
porised.

"I have been studying ways and means. This is
what I have worked out. We persuade your parents
to let you come to London with us for our ball; we
keep you there as long as they will allow; and when
you go home, it will be with an invitation to accompany us to Ireland in the autumn. I mean to take
Arethusa with me this year, no leaving her in London to get into mischief while I am away. Don't you
think we can gradually extend your long sojourns
in our family until they become a regular arrangement, one that your parents will be quite ready to
accept, especially as they realise how much your
company means to Arethusa? And it is true she does
need a friend like you."

"An unofficial maid of honour, in fact," said Edith.

He looked hard at her, trying to decide whether this was meant to be ironic, decided that it was, and said evenly, "Your position would be perfectly honourable, I assure you."

The temptation was strong, and she did not think it would be hard to obtain her parents' agreement, provided they were handled in the right way. Her life at Cotebury was not entirely satisfactory, even to her mother. With mama herself so active and Emma so good and dedicated, there was not enough for Edith to do, either at home or in the parish. If they believed she could make herself useful in some other household, and that household happened to be so interesting and privileged from every point of view, they were not likely to object. It struck her at once that her parents must meet Arethusa, who would impress and charm them at the same time, while removing all fears that she might exert a dangerous, worldly influence.

Edith and Melford had been walking very correctly down Cavendish Road. There were few people about on such a chilly Sunday afternoon, but any number might be looking out of the rows of sash windows above them, and he would be easily recognised.

Now they turned along a footpath towards Weston village.

"Well," he challenged her. "What have you to say to my plan?"

Still Edith hesitated. It would be shabby, she thought, to deceive Arethusa in such a way. Her parents, too. For there was one definite reason why mama, at any rate, would approve of her living for long periods with the Melfords: in such a circle she would meet plenty of eligible men. After she had spent four months at Rythorpe, she realised now, they had half expected her to come home and announce a serious attachment. This plan of Melford's, if it led to nothing worse, would effectively prevent her marrying anyone else. She cared nothing for that, but mama would care. And, besides, there were bound to be dangers ahead, and it was no good pretending otherwise.

"It must be wrong for us to continue in this way," she began, but he interrupted her fiercely.

"Why should it be wrong? We are not going to hurt anyone else or do anything to outrage your tender conscience. It would be wrong only if you became my mistress, and I told you I won't let that happen. I suppose the truth is you don't trust me."

He strode on ahead so that she had to run to keep up with him.

"I do trust you, Mel! I promise I do!"

And she certainly did trust his good intentions. So why agonise over difficulties that might never arise? All her fears and scruples were insubstantial beside that loving confidence.

His anger melted at once. He stopped and grasped her hands and they stood spellbound under a tree, held in the long, still rapture of foreseeing some kind of future together, however limited.

On Monday morning Arethusa announced that Edith must come with her to the Pump Room, where she had to drink the statutory glass of water.

"It is much nastier than the stuff I had to swallow at Strenton last year," she said as they were handed into the carriage and she took the place of honour on the right. "And not likely to do me any more good. But I may as well drink it as not."

"I think you are very well already."

"Oh yes, I am. It is Melford who has the fidgets. He has been so restless lately, always wanting to be somewhere else. But he seems better since we came to Bath; that is why I must pretend to take the cure."

This guileless remark struck home uncomfortably to Edith, and she was wondering what to say when there was a diversion.

They had reached the end of Lansdown Place and were about to turn into the main road when a sporting tilbury came charging down the hill, the driver blowing his horn. Their own coachman, half across the road, was obliged to swerve in order to let the tilbury pass them on the near side. They were now on the wrong side of the road, facing a wagon that was lumbering up from the city. The coachman tried to get over to the left, but unfortunately the horses had been frightened or excited by the careering tilbury. They began to bolt themselves, and this on the steep Lansdown hill was fatal.

Everything happened very quickly. The two women were pitched over inside their padded enclosure. Edith saw the great dray-horse shave past the window beyond Arethusa and tried to drag her across the carriage, but it was too late. The vehicles collided, and the light town carriage, going full tilt, was virtually sliced in two.

The violence of the impact was frightful, though it seemed at first to be made up entirely of noise. Rending wood, splintering glass, horses shrieking with pain, people screaming. Edith was screaming herself as she clung to the up-ended seat of the carriage, engulfed in dust, holding on with her fingernails to stop herself falling into the road several feet below where Arethusa was lying perfectly still with her eyes closed, in the débris of smashed coachwork and tortured iron.

Edith never remembered how she got out of the carriage. Somehow she found herself kneeling in the road among all the flotsam of the accident, trying to make out whether Arethusa was still breath-ing. She ought to be able to tell, but it was impossible to make anything out in all the commotion.

"Can you move a little, miss? We'll soon have the lady out," said a large, kind stranger holding a broken door-panel.

She realised that a sharp, heavy object, perhaps the snapped-off step of the carriage, was wedged under Arethusa's back, and that if the rescuers were not careful, their efforts to move her might make matters worse.

Ignoring everything else, oblivious of the crowd that had now assembled, she set herself to protect Arethusa from further injury, and as she leant over her, saw her lips part and caught a faint moan. A moment later she heard a familiar voice saying forcefully, "Let me get near!"

She looked up, and saw Melford towering over her.

"Edith, are you hurt? Where's Arethusa? Oh, my God!"

"She's alive," said Edith. "She's alive."

"Tusie, can you hear me? We'll soon have you out of this."

Much later Edith realised that this was the first time she had heard Melford use the intimate shortening of his wife's name. For the present, she was incapable of thought.

She watched while Arethusa was delicately removed from the shambles of wood and metal that threatened to cave in and crush her. She was carried to the house in Lansdown Crescent on an improvised stretcher and laid on her bed. Her maid wanted to take off her clothes, but Melford said they had better wait for a medical opinion.

He had already sent for the leading physician in Bath, who soon arrived bringing with him a colleague, a well-known surgeon. They were admitted to the bedroom. Barker remained with her mistress, who was now semi-conscious and showing signs of distress. Melford and Edith were excluded. They went into the drawing-room, where he raged up and down in an effort to relieve his feelings.

"I'll have those damned horses shot! And as for Green, I'll turn him off tomorrow! I'll see he never gets another place."

"Don't say that. Your coachman was not to blame. Or the horses." Edith described the accident as best she could. "It was the fault of that stupid oaf in the tilbury rushing past us, not caring what havoc he left behind. Even now I suppose he does not know what he has done."

As she spoke, trying to determine cause and effect, a much more horrifying thought struck her. "If it's anybody's fault, it's mine."

"My dear girl, what do you mean?"

"You only made her come to Bath because I was living near. If it hadn't been for me, Arethusa would not have been driving down the Lansdown Road this morning."

He stared at her in growing comprehension.

"That's nonsense! You did nothing. I am the one who thought of the whole scheme. Edith, don't try to blame yourself."

He put an arm around her, and they pressed close together for comfort. There was no hint of lovemaking between them; neither of them had ever felt less amorous.

The butler had thoughtfully placed the brandy decanter on a side-table. Melford forced her to drink a little before pouring some for himself.

The doctors reappeared, looking grave. The Duchess had received a severe injury to the spine . . . It was hard to tell for certain . . . Too early to diagnose exactly . . . Wrap it up how they might, they had to admit the fear that her back was broken.

"Is her life in danger?" Melford asked in a curiously empty voice.

"I'm afraid we cannot preclude the possibility, your Grace. But the case is not hopeless."

Melford drew a hand across his eyes as though to brush away invisible tears. Edith made a private vow: O God, if you'll only let her recover, I'll go away, I swear it. I'll never see or think of him again.

There was some more medical talk. The surgeon, a younger man than his colleague, scrutinised Edith in her stained and crumpled dress, her face as white as chalk.

"Were you also in the accident, ma'am? Are you feeling faint?"

"Good heavens, Edith," exclaimed Melford in sudden concern. "I ought to have asked these gentlemen to treat you as a patient, too. I never thought—I'm so sorry."

Edith insisted there was nothing the matter with her. She was feeling rather dizzy, but she put that down to the brandy. She had no thought to spare for her own minor bruises.

The pleasant easy-going life of the Lansdown Crescent house had now turned into a nightmare. Time became so distorted that she hardly knew what hour of the day it was. Meals appeared at intervals, anonymous and tasteless. At least there were things to be done. Nurses had to be engaged and installed, servants sent to fetch drugs and other necessities, letters despatched to London by express post. The doctors paid constant visits; two more had now been called in for consultation. All this time Arethusa lay unconscious in the darkened bedroom, stupefied by laudanum.

At nine in the evening, Melford announced that

he meant to spend the night at his wife's bedside. This annoyed the nurse, but there was nothing she could do about it. Edith wanted to sit up in case she was needed, only he would not hear of it.

"You're dead on your feet," he said. "You were in the accident, too, as the doctors keep reminding me. If you go on being heroic, you'll end by collapsing, and we don't want another invalid on our hands."

It was almost reassuring to hear him talking in his old caustic manner. So she want to bed for a few hours, and did actually sleep in spite of everything, worn out by the most terrible day in her life.

In the morning, Arethusa seemed a little better. She was conscious and perfectly clear in her mind, Melford told Edith. He himself looked haggard and haunted, walking about the breakfast-room and drinking black coffee.

Edith said, "I'm afraid the pain must be much worse if the effects of the laudanum have worn off."

"No, I believe it is not too severe. She speaks of a numbing sensation."

Edith looked up quickly and caught his eye. He glanced away. She wondered if he realised what that numbing sensation might mean. Almost certainly he did; a man who had ridden to hounds all his life must know the possible results of a broken back.

It was deadly quiet in the breakfast-room. Melford and Edith, who had so often longed to be alone, now hadn't a word to say to each other. I suppose it serves us right, she thought.

Presently she asked, "Can I see her? Would she like that?"

"Yes, I'm sure it would do her good. But wait till the doctors have been."

Edith waited until they had come and gone. Soon

afterwards she saw the nurse hurrying downstairs on some errand. She thought Melford was by now in the hands of his valet, who had been lying in wait, hoping to persuade him into having a bath and a short sleep.

She went quietly into the sickroom. There was a screen round the door, so she could not see the bed. She paused, wondering in the silence whether Arethusa was asleep, and was surprised by the words that reached her, low but perfectly audible.

". . . you were in Ireland and I was lonely. I know I was weak and wrong, but there was no other reason. I never loved anyone but you."

And the second voice, very gentle. "Don't let it trouble you any more, sweetheart. I've been very much to blame; I was often careless and unfeeling. You know my talent for hurting people. You will have to forgive me as well, Tusie."

Edith got out of the room as fast as she could without making a noise. She had received a revelation. Why had she never understood that Arethusa was still in love with Melford and had been all along? Probably, she decided after some thought, because Arethusa had misled her deliberately when they were at Strenton, implying that she and her husband had become estranged through their mutual indifference. She was too generous to complain that the indifference was all on his side, and that he had neglected her without any good reason.

Now he is sorry for it, thought Edith, and she was sorry for them both. She could only be thankful that she had not encouraged him to be flagrantly unfaithful. As for their private infidelity, as far as it had gone, she did not believe that had touched Arethusa, and it never would now.

She dreaded further tête-à-tête encounters with Melford at this juncture, but the risk diminished that evening when Lady Woodruff and Mrs. Gordon arrived from London.

There was not room for them and their attendants in the furnished house, with two nurses already in residence, but there were other houses vacant so near the end of the season, and Lady Woodruff was able to rent one only a couple of doors away. It was then decided that Valeria Gordon should move into Edith's room and that Edith should join Lady Woodruff in the new house.

"If you are sure you want me to remain," said Edith, addressing herself half to Melford and half to Mrs. Gordon.

They were holding a conference on the landing. She was acutely conscious of not being a member of the family, and did not wish to intrude.

"Of course you must stay," said Melford, almost roughly. "Arethusa wished it. She said so."

Valeria Gordon had never liked Edith very much, since they had got off the wrong foot at their first meeting. However, she had been forced to admit that little Miss Bruton had proved invaluable in the crisis last year—for she herself was one of the few people who knew the secret history of Arethusa's baby. And now distrss at the sight of her sister had melted her usual ungracious manner.

She said, "Do please stay, Edith. I don't think I can manage without you."

Lady Woodruff came out of the sick-room, looking terribly aged since Edith had seen her last, fourteen months ago. She had driven off from her house in Hertford Street, saying she would be back in a fortnight, and what an extraordinary succession of things had happened to Edith as a consequence.

She soon found she was able to justify her presence by taking on various chores. In particular she was kept busy answering notes of enquiry, thanking for gifts of fruit and flowers, and receiving callers whom Arethusa's relations did not want to see. She took her turn at watching by the bedside, but only when she was sure that those with a greater claim were not available, or needed rest.

For Arethusa's condition was growing steadily worse. The threat of paralysis, at first so alarming, was now irrelevant. Apparently some vital organ had been pierced, and nothing could be done. The numbing sensation in the lower part of her body did at least obliterate a great deal of the pain, so that she could exist on moderate doses of laudanum and was conscious a great deal of the time.

On the sixth day after the accident, Edith was sitting beside her, talking at intervals, mostly about the children. Arethusa lay gazing upwards; her lovely complexion had changed to the colour of old parchment, her eyes were clouded, but she still had her enchanting smile, and she smiled now.

"Dear little Bar, what an imp he is! And Harriet so good. I wonder what my other poor baby is like now."

Edith suddenly realised there was something she could still do for Arethusa. There could no longer be any need for secrecy.

"Your Caroline is a pretty little girl," she said. "I saw her the day before I came here. She is living with a Mrs. Wells, Penelope Dampier's former governess, in a village three miles from my home."

Arethusa turned her head a little. "Edith, is it true? Do tell me more."

Edith described the baby in detail, the character of Mrs. Wells, the house they lived in and all the other inhabitants. Arethusa's face lit up. For a moment she forgot the pain of her imprisoning body.

Someone had come into the room.

Arethusa said, "Edith is telling me about Caroline."

"Oh?" Melford shot a rather dubious glance at

Edith. Perhaps he thought she had been trying to raise Arethusa's spirits with some fairy-tale.

She got up to give him her place by the bed, saying in a low voice, "It is quite true. She is in the care of a woman who lives near Cotebury, and I see her constantly. You don't mind Arethusa knowing?"

"Of course not." He kissed his wife's forehead, saying, "This is good news for you, isn't it, my love? Edith has been watching over Caroline."

"Watching over Caroline," repeated Arethusa. She closed her eyes, and remained silent so long that they thought she had fallen asleep. Then she said, "The other children too. Edith will care for Harriet and Bar."

"Yes, to be sure," said Melford.

It seemed as though she had become confused.

Then she opened her eyes, looked straight at her husband and said, "You will be able to marry Edith when I am dead."

Edith was struck dumb by this thunderbolt. Melford, equally shaken, reacted in the opposite way.

"Don't talk nonsense, Tusie," he exclaimed violently. "You are not going to die! I won't let you go."

He did not look at Edith, and she slipped out of the room before they were forced to recognise each other's self-questioning remorse.

She shut herself in her room and tried to wrestle with her guilt. How long had Arethusa known, and how much? I'm sure she never guessed while I was at Rythorpe, she decided, but after I left and he became difficult and restless, perhaps she began to suspect. And when he manoeuvred their visit to Bath and fetched me from Cotebury, of course she guessed. And she must have minded, much more than I thought she would, loving him still. That last Sunday, when she sat by the fire and saw us go out together, and I dare say was secretly longing to come too . . . Oh God, how could I have been so wicked?

It would have been easy to break down entirely, only she could not make an exhibition of herself while Arethusa's mother and sister were keeping such a command over their emotions. Any hysterical behaviour might arouse their curiosity. So she stifled her grief and went back to the other house, not knowing how she was to meet Melford.

Yet when they did meet, it was in the presence of his mother-in-law, and they were all so affected by the artificial atmosphere, the unnatural stiffness and meaningless phrases, that no one could have seen any other kind of constraint in the demeanour of those two who were trying so hard to forget their memories.

Arethusa was sinking fast. A clergyman friend of Lady Woodruff came to the house every day and gave far more comfort than the doctors.

Melford stayed with her all the time now. On the tenth day, she sank into a trance and died a few hours later in his arms. He shut himself in his room and would speak to no one.

Lord Robert MountStephen and Colonel Waters had arrived in Bath, and they arranged for the conveyance of the coffin to Rythorpe. The Duchess would of course be buried in that classical mausoleum on the hill above the great house where she had been, at different times, so happy and so lonely.

Among other messages, one was sent to Cotebury, and a note arrived back saying that Edith's father would fetch her at noon the following day. She passed on the information to Colonel Waters, the only person, apart from his valet, that Melford was willing to see.

Colonel Waters immediately said that of course the Duke would wish to see her, though Edith was not at all sure he was right, and felt strangely nervous, late that afternoon, when she entered the darkened study. All the windows overlooking the Crescent had their shutters closed because this was a house of death, and the pair of candles on the mantelshelf seemed very dim in contrast to the spring sunlight outside.

"I have come to say goodbye. I hope I am not disturbing you."

She thought how ridiculous this sounded, for clearly she was disturbing him. He was doing absolutely nothing, just sitting in a chair, with not so much as a book or newspaper within reach.

He stood up without answering, and she brought herself to look at him, seeing him as a stranger, altered by Arethusa's death, as though something in him had died also.

"I am glad you have come," he said. His voice sounded husky and unnatural. "I wanted to thank you for all you have done for us. She was so much attached to you, and you have been so good . . ."

"Oh, please don't say so," she burst out. "It's bad enough hearing such things from Lady Woodruff and Mrs. Gordon, who believe them to be true. But you know what a false friend I was, and very far from good. If only . . . I wish . . ."

"Yes," he said quietly. "I wish it, too."

What was it exactly that he wished? That Arethusa had not guessed the truth? That there had been nothing for her to guess? Or even that they had never met? Though plunged in the depths of remorse, Edith could not go so far as to wish that, but she thought perhaps he did.

They were still both standing in the little study, three feet apart and divided by an infinity of space. She thought she detected a kind of resentment in his remote formality as he drew out a chair and asked her to sit down.

"I don't know how I'm going to manage without her," he said, "but that's not the worst of it. I never valued her as I ought. I was the chief cause of all her unhappiness."

Edith made an involuntary movement, and this must have reminded him whom he was speaking to, for he said at once, "Don't distress yourself. You were not to blame for my constant acts of unkindness. So often I thought myself justified when I was being perfectly heartless. Forcing her to part with her child—how could I have been so barbarous? Thank God I told her that Sam had taken charge of their daughter. That was your doing, Edith. You must let me thank you for that, if nothing else."

"Perhaps it may help you to know," said Edith diffidently, "that she never for one moment thought you heartless or ungenerous. From the way she talked of you when we were at Strenton . . ."

"What did she say?" he asked eagerly. "Tell me."

The barrier was down. The trace of hostility had gone, if it had ever existed. Perhaps it had been merely a shadow in her own mind, because she, too, resented the accusing memories that would intrude. But memories of Arethusa could be shared, and she stayed with him for nearly half an hour, talking or listening, while he talked of his wife and the early days of their marriage.

She did see him once more on the following day, when her father arrived to fetch her. Melford accepted the rector's condolences with a stoical self-command, and praised Edith's unfailing kindness—this time she was not able to protest. He accompanied them to the front door and shook hands with them both. His hand was cold and lifeless.

As they were turning to go, an idea seemed to strike him, for he leant forward and murmured a few words to Dr. Bruton. Edith took a last look at the house in Lansdown Crescent, with the shutters closed and the straw still lying in the road outside. It had been laid down freshly every day to deaden the sound of traffic during Arethusa's illness. She saw Melford go back indoors.

"What did the Duke say to you, Papa?" she asked, as the horses drew away.

"He suggested that we should drive slowly. He reminded me that you have not been in a carriage since the accident."

So he had been able to spare a thought for her. It was something to cling to in the desolation.

CHAPTER TWELVE

A year ago this month, thought Edith, picking daffodils in the rectory garden, Melford arrived out of the blue and invited me to Lansdown Crescent, and in less than three weeks, Arethusa was dead. Two years ago there was the terrible scene in the Grecian room at Melford House. Arethusa was banished to Strenton, and I went with her.

All the while she had been living quietly in Cotebury, her mind had been fixed on a series of anniversaries. Caroline's first birthday, celebrated by a nursery feast at Nutways. The date of her own arrival at Rythorpe, the encounter with Melford at the waterfall, the bonfire on the seventeenth of November. And so round to January, Seddon Park in the snow, and Lady Woodruff inviting her to London. She was still bound to the revolving wheel of past events as though she were on a treadmill.

In one way the return from Bath had been less difficult than her homecoming from Rythorpe. There had been no need to act. She was not expected to be happy and smiling. Everyone understood and sympathised with her grief for the loss of her friend in such dreadful circumstances, and because she had learnt to control her feelings, her distress had never seemed excessive. No one had been able to detect her acute bouts of pain at the separation from Melford.

If her parents thought she took a long time to recover her energy and her appetite, they reminded each other that she too had been in the accident, and that some of her symptoms probably had a physical origin.

Eventually she had recovered, secretly ashamed of her own resilience, yet unable at twenty to remain frozen in an attitude of perpetual mourning.

She still missed Arethusa, thought of her every day with affection and some compunction, but she had accepted her death and the fact that everyone else had to go on living, whatever the consequences. And of course it was the still unknown shape of these consequences that left her so confused, a prey to hope, despair and apprehension by turns.

She picked three more daffodils in the deep grass at the edge of the lawn and stood gazing absently across the glebe, as she considered for the thousandth time the situation that existed between herself and Melford now that he was a widower. She still loved him as deeply as ever, but was it possible that he still loved and wanted her?

When she remembered his renewed love for Arethusa, the violence of his grief, the hidden resentment she had sensed at their last meeting, her heart sank. Yet his acute remorse had not much to do with her, he had made that plain, not wanting her to feel guilty; and after that they had been able to talk easily and frankly about Arethusa. (At that moment, they could hardly have talked about anything else.) So how would he be thinking of her now? She had no means of telling.

When she re-read his old letters, she was convinced he must still be in love with her. Surely such an intense and urgent passion could not die out so tamely. Yet these letters had been written over a year ago, and if, during that time, he had been learning to forget Arethusa, perhaps he had forgotten her as well.

He no longer wrote to her, but that proved nothing, for of course they were unable to carry on even a one-sided correspondence, as they had when he was franking letters that were supposed to have come from his wife. Now he had no such excuse.

He had written once last summer, sending certain mementoes he wanted her to keep: some of Arethusa's books and music, as well as a pendant of sapphires and rose diamonds, with earrings to match.

"I know she would have wanted you to have these," he had written.

Mrs. Bruton had exclaimed at their value. "They are almost too good! However, you must accept them; to the Duke, I suppose, they are nothing out of the way. What a pity you will not be able to wear them until you are married. Gentlemen never consider these things."

Edith thought that this particular gentleman would have known quite well that such jewels were suitable only for a married woman. She also noted that he had chosen sapphires to match her eyes, which he had always admired. She allowed herself to think that he was trying to convey a message in the only way he could, for although his letter was warm and unaffected, it was addressed to the intimate friend of his dead wife, and he must have known that it would have to be shown to her parents. She had replied in the same vein, her letter too had been overseen, and there had been a long silence ever since.

Whenever she took out those sapphires and looked at them, she was conscious of wild secret hopes, but then the pendulum swung, and doubts assailed her. Not only her own guilty conscience and the long separation, but the immeasurable distance between them. In the old days it had hardly concerned her at all that the man who said he loved her was a very rich duke. His marriage had been the great, impassable barrier. Now that was gone, it seemed presumptuous to suppose that the Duke of Melford should choose his second wife from a provincial parsonage. And yet there were so many memories to suggest that he might. Altogether she grew more and more unsettled as the anniversary of Arethusa's death approached and he would be free to come and look for her, if that was what he wanted.

She had been too long day-dreaming in the garden. She crossed the lawn, swinging her basket, and entered the rectory by a side door. Here she met one of the maids, who had come to close the shutters against the strong sunlight.

"Why, Miss Edith, where have you been? Madam's been wanting you this age. There's a gentleman called—a gentleman from London."

Edith stood still. Her heart seemed to swell so that she could hardly breathe.

"From London? Who? No, never mind, Betty. It doesn't matter."

He's come, she thought, with a mixture of triumph and relief. She put down the basket and looked at herself in a convenient glass. Should she try to improve her appearance, or walk in on them just as she was? She knew the rustic straw hat suited her. She made straight for the drawing-room, treading on air. There was a gentleman sitting with her mother. He stood up as she came in. It was Sam Palgrave.

Edith checked. She heard them both speaking, as from a long way off. Sam's pleasant, half-forgotten voice greeted her. She hoped he had not caught any change in her expression.

"Mr. Palgrave—what a charming surprise!"

She had managed that all right. It was stupid to be disappointed. She ought to have realised that it was still too soon for Melford to come; the year was not yet over.

"Mr. Palgrave has been visiting his little goddaughter," said Mrs. Bruton, who had heard of his interest in the orphan Caroline, and thought well of him for it. "I have persuaded him to stay and dine with us."

"I am so glad."

"Perhaps in the meantime, Miss Edith, you would care for a drive in my curricle."

Edith accepted after a glance at her mother. In an open carriage, an unchaperoned drive was perfectly proper. She had recovered her composure and was genuinely pleased to see Sam, who was such a very good friend.

Sitting in his well-sprung curricle high above the hedge-tops, she piloted him away from the turnpike road into some quiet lanes where they could dawdle along, talking happily.

"How long is it since you have seen Caroline?" she asked him.

"I was here in August. I meant to call on you then, but Mrs. Wells told me you were staying with your uncle in Dorset."

"Yes, it was an honour to be invited. He is a recluse, you know. Hates visitors. But he was very kind to me."

"I hope everyone is kind to you, Swan," said Palgrave, looking down at her.

His hat was set at a rakish angle, his fair hair glinted in the sun. She had never thought him handsome, compared to Melford he was almost ugly, but there was a bond between them, perhaps because they had shared the strange and secret moment when she had placed his daughter in his arms.

They talked about Caroline's progress, then she enquired about friends in London. Fanny and Richard had been married just after Christmas, and she was longing to know how they went on.

"Very well," said Sam. "They live in a little dolls' house just off St. James's Square. Richard's grandfather didn't care for the match and was niggardly over the settlements. Richard goes every day to the Foreign Office, where he is trying to make a career, and Fanny goes to unfashionable shops to practise economy. In the evening they dress up in all their finery to attend the grandest parties in London."

"I can just imagine," she said, laughing. "You describe them exactly."

After a few more enquiries, she asked, "Have you seen Melford?"

"Yes. I met him at the club last week."

"How is he?"

"In better spirits, I think. He shut himself up at Rythorpe for several months, wouldn't see anyone. Now he goes about very much as he used to. Doesn't entertain—well, he's still in mourning. The children are with him in London, and Penelope tells me they have an excellent governess found by Lady Robert. But I should think Melford House must be a sad place without Arethusa."

Edith agreed, only too conscious that Arethusa would be hard to follow, impossible to imitate.

Mention of her brought them back full circle to Caroline.

"She is a beautiful child," he said, "and I simply cannot wish she had never existed, in spite of all the trouble and misery I brought on her mother. I shall never forgive myself for that."

"She forgave you," said Edith, "and I think he

did, too. You must have realised that, the last time
we were all together at Rythorpe."

They were driving along a shady, unfrequented
road, and he drew up on the wide verge.

"I want to talk to you, Swan. Do you remember
my saying, two years ago, that I would come to
Cotebury and call on you?"

She remembered very well. She had been playing
the pianoforte and he had kissed her. No need to go
into that!

"I meant that I would come and ask you to marry
me. I'm not sure whether you guessed."

Edith had guessed. More to the point, she guessed
where he was heading now, and said hastily, "That
all happened a long time ago. No need to drag up
the past."

But Sam had begun what he wanted to say, and,
like a good House of Commons man, he did not attend to interruptions.

"When I fell in love with you, which I did within
half an hour of our first meeting, I had no idea there
was any impediment, legal or otherwise, to prevent
my offering you my whole heart and a promise of
fidelity. I had been Arethusa's lover very briefly,
and we had separated by mutual consent. She never
told me the child she was carrying was mine, and
all the time I was getting to know you, and trying
to fix my interest with you, I thought myself perfectly free from that entanglement. It was Arethusa, even more than I, who had wanted the whole
affair forgotten. But of course you could not understand all that, and when that damned woman betrayed Arethusa's confidence you saw me as a
two-faced monster, completely detestable. I don't
blame you. Any girl would have felt the same. But
I did love you truly. I love you still, and I've been
waiting ever since in the hope that you can overcome your distrust and overlook my past follies.

Have I waited long enough, Swan? Could you consider marrying me now?"

Edith had been taught that if you meant to refuse a man, you should never let him get to the point of actually proposing. She had felt obliged to let him go on talking, however, because she was sorry for him. She knew what it was to carry a secret load of guilt. And she wanted him to know that she took a more charitable view of the whole episode than the provincial girl of eighteen who had been so shocked and disgusted.

"I gave up distrusting you a long time ago," she said. "I am better able to understand what happened between you and Arethusa. I grew very close to her while we were at Strenton and I could never condemn either of you. So I hope you will believe that it is not on her account—nothing to do with your past life—I am deeply sensible of the compliment you have paid me, and I hope we may always remain fast friends."

She had an idea she had left something out of this speech, but wasn't sure what, until he asked, with what sounded like a trace of amusement,

"Are you refusing me, Swan?"

"Oh. Yes. Didn't I say so? I'm sorry."

"I'm sorry, too!" He no longer sounded amused. "Could you not come round to the idea in time? Think it over. I've always felt we should be well suited."

"There's no point in raising your hopes."

They sat silent in the curricle, side by side, gazing through the dark green shadows while the horses cropped the grass. It was a ridiculous place he had chosen for a love scene, but they could not leave the horses unattended, and if he had brought a groom with him, they could not have held any private conversation at all.

She was getting ready to suggest they might now

drive on, when he asked, "Are you expecting to marry someone else?"

Edith flushed. "I am not engaged, if that is what you mean. And in any case, I don't think you have the right to enquire."

"Of course I haven't. If it's some neighbour of yours down here whom you like better than me, then I must grin and bear it. So long as it isn't Melford. That's why I asked."

Edith was already so flushed under her milkmaid hat that she could hardly give herself away. She merely said, with repressive dignity, "I don't know what you mean."

"You were in love with him at Rythorpe. He's a fascinating devil, but he won't marry you, so don't delude yourself."

"He isn't a devil! And why shouldn't he marry me?" Discretion and dignity vanished pretty quickly. Then she recalled a little of her long-practised caution, and said loftily, "I don't see why you should imagine I'm in love with the Duke, but supposing I was, what reason have you for asserting that he wouldn't marry me? I suppose you think I'm not grand enough."

"Don't be silly, Swan."

"And don't call me Swan!"

"Then don't be silly, Edith. Your family is as old as the Woodruffs and a good deal more respectable than the MountStephens. And in justice to Mel, he is not unduly concerned with rank. His trouble is something quite different, and you don't understand it."

"And you do, I suppose?"

"I think so. I've known him since we were both twelve years old. He had a very odd childhood. Born a duke, brought up in that Baroque palace by people who cared nothing for his welfare or his happiness but only for his importance, their own importance, and living well at his expense. The way they treated him would have ruined most boys, and it is much to his credit that he survived. He wasn't content to be toadied and flattered, allowed to win every contest or succeed in pastimes where a rich man can always excel. When we were at Eton, he was already taking up any genuine challenge to his mind or skill. You must have come across all those monuments to his energy: the observatory, the family history, the aqueduct."

"Yes, I know," she said impatiently. "He only likes doing things that are difficult. For a man in his position, it is a trait to be admired. I don't see what it has to do with . . ."

"With his choosing a second wife? Don't you? How do you think he came to choose his first? He saw her in a ballroom and asked who she was in a tone of idle curiosity. (I was there, I heard him.) He was told she was already engaged to someone else. From then on, nothing would do but he must capture her himself. He got her away from her first love: no great achievement, I dare say. Still, the rival must have provided a spur."

"They weren't properly engaged," said Edith, determined to defend Melford. "Arethusa told me that story. And they were very happy together for some years."

"Oh yes, he was a good husband. Kinder than many would have been, especially men with titles to pass on, when she had two miscarriages and then a daughter. It was another problem, you see— Arethusa's difficulty in giving him an heir. Once Bar had arrived, he soon lost interest in his marriage."

"I think you are being spiteful and unjust!" Edith burst out angrily. Arethusa had given much the same account of her marriage, though without drawing any disagreeable conclusions. Sam's view was obviously distorted by jealousy. "In any case, I can't see what your theories have to do with me. Are you under the impression that the Duke seduced me while we were at Rythorpe, because I can assure you that he didn't. Perhaps you think he is the sort of man who ruins lovelorn girls just for the sport of it. And catalogues them all in his game-book, I dare say! Pheasants, fifty. Hares, five. Housemaids, two. Visiting young ladies, one."

Normally this would have made Sam laugh, but by this time he was flushed and angry too, and he told her sharply not to be a little fool.

"Mel's a gentleman. He doesn't go round seducing innocent virgins. In most most cases he'd find it too tame. On the other hand, he might imagine himself seriously in love with a girl like you—a virtuous, well-brought-up girl with religious principles and great strength of character. You are the kind of precious, unspoilt creature who is entirely inaccessible to a married man. And you didn't like him when you first knew him, which must have added to your inaccessibility. I can see him becoming your slave! And if he did, if he swore he'd love you for ever, it wasn't just a lure to get you into his bed. No doubt he believed it at the time. So long as Arethusa lived, you were out of his reach, and that was enough to make him desire you to the point of madness. So if he's ever spoken of love or marriage, I do beg you not to set your hopes too high. When Arethusa died, you lost your strongest weapon. He's a widower, and he can marry you without the slightest hindrance. So he won't want to."

She found herself unable to speak. Not because of his verdict on Melford's character, which she discounted at once as a pack of malicious lies, but because of the way he had spoken to her resisting temptation with qualities she did not possess. It just showed how stupid he was and how little he understood either of them. All the same, she felt ashamed.

"Please would you take me home," she whispered.

They drove back to Cotebury without speaking.

Having been invited to dine at the rectory, Sam could not escape without making the Brutons wonder what was wrong. He bore the social awkwardness better than Edith. Her parents found him intelligent and agreeable, and after he left, they said several times how very much they liked him.

Edith did not rise to the bait. She remembered thinking two years ago that if he called on her at home, everyone would assume he had come as a suitor. Luckily, circumstances had changed. Sam was known to be the guardian and godfather of little Caroline, and when he went to see her at Nutways, it was natural enough that he should visit a friend who lived so near. He might be suspected of admiring Edith, but he had not committed either of them by this civility.

Thinking along these lines, she was faced by a new anxiety. Her confidence had not been shaken, or hardly at all, by Sam's dark prophecies, for she simply could not—would not—believe that Melford bore any likeness to the feeble creature he had described, capricious and indecisive. But she did now begin to wonder how, if he really loved her, he was going to pay his addresses. She had somehow settled it in her mind that if he came at all he would arrive unannounced, as he had last year, and ask her to marry him. She had visualised scenes in the garden, in the drawing-room, invented heart-searching dialogues, imagined embraces that could now be enjoyed without fear, yet she had quite failed to see one tremendous obstacle. How could he come here and make her an offer without scandalising her parents?

It would have been different if she had accepted
Sam this afternoon. They had known each other for
some time, both were unmarried and free to fall in
love, and if Sam had been rather slow in coming to
the point, there was nothing unusual in that. But
all the while she had lived in the house of the Duke
of Melford *he* had been a married man, the husband
of her friend. She had last seen him two days after
the death of his wife, and they had not been able to
correspond. How could he come to Cotebury and de-
clare, in a matter of hours, that he wanted to marry
her? It would be perfectly obvious that something
improper had been going on while his wife was
alive. In spite of his well-known preference for difficulties, she did not think he would care for this
one.

It would be different if she were in London. There
would be plenty of opportunities for meeting; seem-
ingly casual encounters could easily be contrived.
And if it was soon noticed that he was paying her
a good deal of attention, people would only say that
he was doing what many another bereaved widower had done before him: finding consolation with
a friend of his first wife. Not very flattering, but
what did that matter if it would enable them to
marry without any unpleasant gossip?

As for the alternative, that he might not want to
marry her after all, she would never know the answer unless she put her fortune to the test. Since
he, clearly, couldn't come to Cotebury, she would
have to get herself to town.

She unlocked her writing desk and sat down to
compose a letter to Fanny Weare.

CHAPTER THIRTEEN

"I should like to hold a reception for you," said Fanny, "only I'm afraid this house isn't suitable. One could hardly invite Melford—he would think it very odd."

Since the Weares' London house would have fitted comfortably into one of the smaller follies at Rythorpe, this was probably true. Fanny's tiny drawing-room was garnished with wedding presents. The actual furniture consisted of a sofa, two chairs and a folding tea-table. There was no room for anything more. Her harp stood in the window embrasure, and Edith quite expected the strings to twang in the breeze.

"And we don't give dinners," her hostess added, "because we have a very bad cook. I thought I should run across Melford somewhere before you arrived, but I haven't managed it."

"Never mind," said Edith. "I have brought some presents for the children. I plan to go to Melford House and ask to see them, which I want to do anyway. That will be quite proper, won't it, if you are with me? And once Melford knows where I am, it will be for him to make the next move."

"Yes, and we can borrow mama's carriage and go in style."

It was May. Melford's year of mourning was over.

Edith had just reached London in answer to a pressing invitation from Fanny, and was trying to keep her private hopes and fears decently suppressed. She was amused to see her flighty friend playing the part of a married lady, and presently Richard came back from the Foreign Office, talking as if he ran the place, and basking in his wife's devotion. They spent a happy evening, and all three laughed a great deal.

Next day, having borrowed Lady Jane Oxenham's town carriage, Edith and Fanny set out for Melford House. Edith had spent a good deal of thought on the presents that were to gain her an entrance. It was hard to think of new toys for children who had so much. But Harriet and Bar loved dressing up, so she had made them each a fancy costume. Harriet was to be a little pedlar woman, with a black bonnet and scarlet cloak, and a tray with many small items to sell. Bar's costume was Puss in Boots, his cat's fur made from cunningly contrived strips of black, brown and grey velvet.

She sat with the parcels on her knees, feeling very nervous as they turned off St. James's Street and through the archway into the quadrangle. She was excited and apprehensive at the prospect of meeting Melford, but returning to this old haunt brought back the memory of Arethusa more clearly than anyone else. Of their driving off to Strenton with Arethusa beside her, silently weeping.

The carriage drew up under the porte-cochère. Edith got a hearty welcome from the porter, but then there was a disappointment. The children were not in the house. They had been taken to spend the day with their grandmother.

"Is his Grace at home?" asked Edith rather uncertainly.

"His Grace has driven down to Richmond, miss."

This was a setback. They would leave the parcels

for the children, but it was impossible for two ladies to leave cards on the Duke, and if no one in the nursery thought of mentioning Edith's visit, he might never know that she had called.

Fanny now took a hand, saying they would like to see the Duke's secretary. They were ushered into a room Edith had never entered before, and the secretary was fetched.

Unfortunately he was a newcomer since Edith's time, and though very polite, he was obviously puzzled and could not make out what the Honourable Mrs. Weare and her friend wanted from him.

Edith had lost her nerve and did not know what to say, but Fanny spoke up.

"You may not know it, but this is the lady who was with the Duchess in Bath at the time of the accident. She has not seen any of the family since, and she is particularly anxious for news of Lady Harriet and Lord Barlington."

The man looked at Edith with respect and commiseration, and said that Lady Harriet and the young Marquess both appeared to be in good health and spirits, as far as he could judge.

"I am glad to hear it," said Edith, recovering her tongue. "I should very much like to see them again. Perhaps you would be so kind as to ask the Duke if I might call at some time when it is convenient. I am staying with Mr. and Mrs. Weare."

"I will inform his Grace as soon as he returns," promised the secretary.

"Well, we've accomplished what we came for," said Fanny, when they were back in the carriage. "He'll hear that you're in town, and with us, and he'll come to call on you. Probably tomorrow."

But when tomorrow came, he did not come.

They both stayed in; Fanny saying that she would be there to receive the Duke, and would then produce a convincing reason why she was urgently needed in some other part of the house. Edith thought that in view of the Weares' domestic arrangements and their rather inefficient servants, it was only too likely that she might be needed. Though the Duke himself lived in such a very different style, he would hardly understand. She amused herself with these thoughts for about an hour, with intermissions of hurrying to the window every time she heard a carriage in the street. It would not matter how Fanny got out of the room and left them alone, Melford would not care.

Gradually her mood changed. Why hadn't he come to her immediately, at the first opportunity? Could it be true that he did not love her any more? She crushed down this insistent dread. It was the secretary's fault. He'd forgotten the message. He looked a stupid fellow. And the excellent governess would probably see that the children thanked her for their presents without bothering their papa.

So he would never know she was in London, unless they ran across him by chance, and this did not seem nearly so likely as she had imagined at home in Cotebury, for he had never really enjoyed large fashionable gatherings of mixed society. When he went to such parties, it was chiefly to escort Arethusa. Fanny said very sensibly that he probably had an engagement that morning which he could not break.

In the evening they went to the play. Edith gazed round in hope and desperation, but he was not there. She saw plenty of other acquaintances, including Sam Palgrave. She was not very pleased to see him. She did not wish to be reminded of their recent conversation, and she knew that he would guess, if no one else did, why she had come to London. However, he greeted her without mockery or rancour, and most of the time he was in their box he spent talking to Fanny.

Next day, Fanny herself had an engagement she could not break. It happened to everyone, she pointed out. She had promised to support her mother through the horrid ordeal of an appointment with the dentist.

Edith was left in possession of the miniature drawing-room. She sat embroidering a rose on a tapestry chair-seat, wearing a blue muslin dress she had hoped Melford would like, wondering if her arms were too thin and whether she was losing her looks, and playing ridiculous games. If he doesn't come by the time I've counted fifty, he won't come today. If he doesn't come by the time I've counted two hundred, he won't come at all. But two hundred was giving herself no proper chance. Make it five hundred. A thousand.

When she did hear the rap of the knocker on the front door, she assured herself calmly that this was only some acquaintance of Fanny's. There was a short pause. Then the drawing-room door opened, and Fanny's footman announced with a satisfied grin,

"The Duke of Melford, miss."

He came in, towering in this small space, and as usual his dark romantic splendour was a little daunting at first. In all her day-dreams, she could never quite call up the effect of his actual presence.

"My dear Edith." He held out his hand. As their fingers met, she felt almost faint with love. He glanced round. "Where's Fanny?"

Presumably the footman had been too overawed to say that his mistress was out.

Edith said, "Fanny is with her mother. Won't you sit down, Duke."

The servant had gone and they were alone, yet she felt obliged to address him formally. The year of separation had left a barrier.

He took the chair opposite her, saying, "It was so

kind of you to bring presents for the children. They
are delighted with them. I found a large tabby cat
under my breakfast table yesterday morning. They
will both be writing to you."

"I should so much like to see them. I expect they
have grown a great deal."

"Yes. Harriet is quite tall. She is very much
calmer and more contained than she used to be. We
had a good deal of trouble with Bar last year. He
could not understand what had happened, kept expecting his mother to return, as she did before,
when she had been away at Strenton. He began
to have violent tantrums. However, Madame Villerond is very good with him, and I think we are over
the worst."

"Poor little boy," said Edith, remembering Bar
as he stood on the steps at Rythorpe, refusing to
kiss his mother after her long absence.

She looked at Bar's father. He did not look at her,
but sat gazing absently at a china vase with a bird
painted on it.

She asked, "Who is Madame Villerond?"

"The children's governess. She is a French émigrée, a widow, and very talented. I'm thankful to
say that both the children have become attached to
her."

"I'm so glad," said Edith, not altogether sin-
cerely.

Everything was going wrong, all her worst fears
were being realised. She even wondered whether
she had been supplanted by the elegant émigrée.
At all events, the change in him was unmistakable.
The loving tenderness had gone, so had the painful
honesty of their last meeting, and he was not even
being caustic and scornful. He was treating her
with a ceremonious politeness, as though she were
a stranger.

He enquired about her own parents, and her own

health: he hoped she was quite recovered? No ill-effects from the disastrous accident? He spoke of Fanny and Richard, and was sure she must be enjoying her stay in town. She answered as best she could. She had never had such an insipid conversation with him, even in the days when she first arrived in his house, a timid country mouse. It was dreadful.

There was a pause, as though they had both run out of conversation. Trying to escape from the silence that was so much more revealing than words, she asked again about Harriet.

"You must see her for yourself. Call any time you like. She said I was to extract a promise from you." He managed a smile, which seemed to Edith quite artificial. "I think you will find her greatly improved. She will never be her mother's equal for beauty."

"That would hardly be possible."

"No. However, she may surprise us. She is not quite nine; it will be another six or seven years before she can take her place as hostess and the mistress of Rythorpe."

"As your hostess?" repeated Edith, rather astonished by the dragging of such an idea into this trivial chat.

"That is what she will have to become. I shall not marry again."

Their eyes met as he said this and hers fled away, unable to bear what they saw. Contempt, or merely dislike, was it? She felt sick with humiliation. He thought she was running after him, and so she had been. He was telling her in no uncertain terms that she had nothing to hope for.

When he stood up to go, she had just enough presence of mind to pull the bellrope for the footman to show him out. She did not actually remember their saying goodbye, only the door closing behind them.

Then she began to cry with a shuddering violence
that went on and on until she was exhausted and
lay on the sofa, her hot temples throbbing against
the silk cushions. Her whole body ached as though
she had been physically beaten.

What a fool I am! she thought, when she was capable of thinking at all. What else could I expect?
I was wicked, and I'm being punished for it. It's
what I should have been prepared for, all along.
And looking back now, wise after the event, she
wondered how she could ever have been so presumptuous and silly as to hope that his love might
have survived the shock of Arethusa's death. The
accident had not only revived all his old love for his
wife, it was peculiarly horrible because it had come
about as a direct result of his intrigue with Edith.
It was hardly surprising that he wanted nothing
more to do with her. Perhaps he even hated her
now. She did wonder for a moment whether the loss
was too recent, whether he would feel differently in
another year's time. It was hardly likely that he
would stick to his resolution never to re-marry. But
it would make no odds. I am the one woman he will
never marry, she thought.

She began to cry again, so did not hear another
visitor arrive, and was taken by surprise when Sam
Palgrave walked into the room unannounced.

"My poor girl, what's he done to you?"

"Go away!"

He stood watching her compassionately. "You're
making yourself ill. I wonder where Richard keeps
his brandy."

"I hate brandy," she said, remembering the glass
Melford had made her drink on the day of the accident.

Sam handed her a handkerchief, and she mopped
her face, still huddled on the sofa. He pulled up a

chair and sat down close to her, holding one of her hands.

"Would you like to tell me what's happened?"

"I should think you might guess. He isn't in love with me any more, and now you can say you told me so."

"I don't think that's very kind. I should never say anything so shabby."

He had chosen the right note to take with Edith, who said, "I beg your pardon. I am sure you did not come here to triumph over me. I don't know why you did come."

If her wits had been working better, she might have remembered Sam's long conversation with Fanny at the theatre, and guessed that he had been watching the house to see whether Melford called. He had seen him come and go, noted the shortness of his visit and arrived after a decent interval to offer any comfort he could give. Edith did not realise any of this; luckily, perhaps.

She blew her nose and said, "I must look a fright. Not fit to be called on. Though since you are here, I owe it to Melford to say that you were quite mistaken about him. He hasn't tired of me and taken up with a new love. It is something different and far more serious, and he is not to blame. At least he is—we both are. What we did was very wrong, and now I think it over, I cannot wonder at his not wishing to marry me. I have only got what I deserve."

Looking slightly grim, but speaking patiently as though to a child, Sam asked, "May I know why you think you deserve to be so unhappy?"

She said simply, "I was responsible for Arethusa's death."

"Come, that cannot be true!"

"Well, it is. I suppose I had better tell you."

And she did tell him the whole story, including

her hasty flight after the night of the bonfire, her weak capitulation in Cotebury and the plans they had made in Bath. Sam sat listening, frowning a little, but showing no other sign of disapproval.

When the recital was over, he said, "My poor Edith, you have had a rough passage, haven't you? As for that damned philanderer, I'd like to break his neck."

"You must not say so! He wasn't philandering. And he is truly sorry."

"So he should be. He must have been out of his mind—playing such games with an innocent young woman whose virtue he was under an obligation to respect."

"That's rich, coming from you," she retorted with unladylike frankness. "At least he didn't get me with child, which is what you did to his wife."

"*Touché!* What a ramshackle pair we are."

She gave a small gasp and then, to her own surprise, actually laughed. It was not a very confident laugh, though better than renewed tears. I don't think I could cry any more, she thought dispassionately. Later it would all begin again. The anguish and loneliness, the dreadful sense of failure and despair. For the present, there was a faint relief in sitting here with Sam's strong fingers clasping her hand.

"What will you do now?" he asked.

"I don't know. I shall be a dismal sort of visitor for Fanny and Richard. Only, if I go home at once, they will guess there is something wrong and my mother will talk and talk at me, trying to find out what it is. I have been deceiving them ever since I came back from Rythorpe more than a year ago. Now I shall have to keep up the deceit for the rest of my life. It is terrible, not daring to be truthful with your own family. I knew I could never be quite frank about what happened between me and Melford while Arethusa was alive, but I did not think that would signify if everything was put right. And, besides, I did not expect to be living always in Cotebury. I was imagining . . . hoping . . ."

"You were hoping to be married," he said in a matter-of-fact voice. "And that I think will still be your best plan of action. If you can admit that the past is over and done with, and marry me."

"Good God, you don't have to make me an offer," she said, pulling her hand away. "And after I've refused you once already. My dear Sam, you are very good, but I could not take advantage of your chivalry."

"It's no such thing. I still mean everything I said to you the last time we met."

He got up and went to stand in front of the fireplace, making the little drawing-room look smaller than ever. He was not so tall as Melford, but more angular and less graceful.

"I know this is the worst possible time to put myself forward, when you are breaking your heart for Melford. No man with an ounce of sensibility would start plaguing you now, but I must speak while I can. I have just visited Caroline, and I can hardly return to Cotebury without making you an object of speculation. So just consider this. We are good friends, I hope, and I can offer you a life for which you are well suited. You enjoy society, and you also have a well-trained mind, you like to think and read. I think you would soon come to understand the serious side of my career as well as sharing its advantages. This must all seem dead sea fruit to you now, but many happy marriages have been founded on less. Would you have accepted me two years ago, before you fell in love with Melford?"

"Yes, I believe I should, but I did fall in love with him, so what is that to the purpose?"

"It proves that you don't hold me in aversion."

"Aversion? Good gracious, no—of course I don't! What a horrible idea . . . But Sam, how could I let you throw away your freedom to get so little in return? I have nothing left, don't you see? Nothing to give."

"You are wrong. There is one very particular happiness you could give me that you may not have thought of. You are the very person Arethusa would have chosen to bring up her daughter."

Edith had been staring moodily ahead of her, smoothing out the creases in her dress. She looked up, roused out of her apathy.

"You mean to adopt Caroline?"

"I have always hoped to do so when I marry. And if you would agree to become her mother, that would seem the perfect solution." He came to sit beside her on the sofa. "It was the inconvenient arrival of Caroline that drove us apart. Could she not also be the means of drawing us together? Think it over, my dear little Swan."

The idea was curiously appealing. She already loved Caroline, and through her she could repay her debt to Arethusa. Utterly free from bitterness or jealousy, Arethusa had wanted her to marry Melford and bring up their two legitimate children. Her generosity had been in vain, but now instead, Edith was being offered Caroline, the little outcast, the one who perhaps needed her most. And she was already fond of Sam. She was leaning against his shoulder, feeling faintly comforted. All the same, she knew she was in no fit state to make a serious decision.

"I can't make up my mind yet. You must give me time to think it over."

"As long as you like," he said quickly. "I shouldn't dream of pressing you. At least you know that you have two alternatives to choose from, and that may make the future seem a little less bleak.

In the meantime, if you are not anxious to go home and face a lot of questions, why don't you stay out your full month with Fanny? There will be more distractions here than you would find in Cotebury, and we could meet very often, as we used to when you first came to town. I promise not to make a nuisance of myself."

"Dear Sam, I am sure you would never do that."

She was so grateful for his kindness and consideration that she did not feel able to argue about the wisdom of this arrangement. In any case, she was past arguing. Exhausted by so many conflicting emotions, she simply agreed with everything he suggested.

CHAPTER FOURTEEN

For the next ten days Edith endured the pleasures of London with gritted teeth. She was increasingly unhappy, but felt obliged to hide her feelings from Fanny, Richard and, above all, Sam, who were trying so hard to amuse her and raise her spirits. Rides, drives, theatres, ices at Gunters', visits to the Royal Academy were all offered with touching solicitude, and only proved to her that the weight of misery was even greater if, all the time, you were struggling to smile and look agreeable. She really would have done better to go home where she could have moped in decent privacy, no matter how much mama scolded. But she could not say this to her well-meaning friends.

Fanny was as angry with Melford as Sam, and much more vocal.

"He has treated you disgracefully," she said. "After making up to you like that and insinuating his way into your affections. Duke or no duke, he's a heartless villain, and I wonder you don't hate him. It would be better for you if you did."

"Well, I don't, so please stop abusing him, Fanny."

"I'm sorry. Of course he is unbelievably handsome."

Edith's passion for Melford had long passed the

stage when she cared whether he was handsome or
not, and she could not hate him because she did not
believe he had behaved so very badly, at least not
to her. There had been a great deal wrong with his
marriage, but he was sorry for that, and if she was
one of the victims of his remorse, she did not think
she had any right to complain. So she still pined
for him in lonely secrecy.

Luckily Fanny had too much knowledge of the
world to go round telling people that Melford was
a villain and why. If it got about that Edith Bruton
had hoped to catch him, she would be made to look
a scheming fool, or worse. So Fanny set herself to
forwarding the match with Sam. Very few jilted
young ladies had such an eligible understudy waiting in the wings. If only Edith didn't let him drift
away while she was feeling low and lackadaisical—
perhaps it was to prevent such a disaster that
Fanny allowed herself to be a little indiscreet.
Within a week, Edith discovered that several of
their friends thought she and Sam were already, if
unofficially, engaged. She was extremely annoyed
and at first puzzled, for she was sure Sam would
not try to force her hand. Then she guessed who
was responsible.

"You haven't been telling people we're engaged,
have you, Fanny?" she said, pretty sure that Fanny
had, but not wishing to make a direct attack.

Fanny looked a little self-conscious. "You know
how rumours travel! Dick's sister did say she supposed you were only waiting until you had your
parents' approval before making the engagement
public. All I said was that you would not do so without their blessing, which I am sure is true."

"I had Mrs. Dampier practically offering me Seddon Park for our honeymoon, because that is where
we first met."

"Well, I have never discussed you with Mrs. Dampier," said Fanny virtuously.

She would hardly need to, thought Edith, considering that all the Weares, Oxenhams and Dampiers lived in each other's pockets, long-standing members of the Melford House set.

"Are you going to wear your new white and silver gauze tonight?" asked Fanny, changing the subject. "I shall wear my pink. Not that anyone will see us properly. The parties at Ingatestone House are always a terrible squeeze."

"Well, I shall be very grateful for a few inches of floor," replied Edith, quick and bright. "I have never been there before. It was so kind of your mother to get me an invitation."

Ingatestone House, like Melford House, was one of the great London mansions which everyone wanted to be asked to, and in the ordinary way she would have been delighted to have the chance of going there. Today, all hopes of enjoyment were overshadowed by the knowledge that Melford would probably be there, too. They had not run across him once in the last ten days, but their social engagements had been small private affairs. Now there was this grand party tonight, and tomorrow an al fresco breakfast at the Birketts' villa at Roehampton. The Birketts were frequent visitors at Rythorpe; Edith had met them there two years ago. It was pretty certain Melford would attend both these occasions now he was out of mourning. Edith dreaded meeting him again, yet at the same time longed for a sight of him with the perverse craving, she told herself angrily, of a ruined gamester who cannot keep away from the card-table.

Edith put on her new dress, which did something to restore her confidence. Mr. Oxenham and Lady Jane picked them up in their carriage. It was rather a crowded drive, but everyone was cheerful, and

she began to hope she would get through the evening quite creditably. Arrived at Ingatestone
House, they had to join a queue on the grand staircase. They caught sight of Sam a little way ahead.
He waited at the top, and joined them after they
had been formally received by their host and hostess.

They now entered a very large oval saloon,
crowded with expensively dressed persons, all apparently endowed with perfect self-assurance and
all competing to be heard. Edith looked around her,
but could see not a sign of Melford. Fanny's parents
had stopped to talk to some older friends. The young
quartet were swept slowly on by the movement of
the crowd. The place was like a furnace—heat as
well as light radiated from the chandeliers.

"It's far too hot for this kind of mob," grumbled
Richard.

"But ideal for the Birketts' breakfast tomorrow,"
said Fanny.

"That reminds me," Sam glanced at Edith. "May
I drive you to Roehampton?"

Before she could reply, Fanny said this would be
most improper.

"Good God, Fanny," said Sam, amused, "I never
thought I should hear you preaching propriety!
Edith's mother has no objection to my driving her
in an open carriage."

"That's all very well, but I don't suppose she
would like you to arrive at the party alone, as a
solitary couple. Even if you are going to be married.
I am Edith's chaperon. For some reason, engaged
girls have to be guarded more carefully than anyone else; I know I was practically kept in purdah."

She had raised her voice, and Edith thought people were beginning to look at them. She was acutely
uncomfortable. She was not engaged to Sam,
though it would be difficult to say so without ap-

pearing ungracious. She was just about to try, when
she became aware of a dark, brooding presence at
her left shoulder and was instantly struck dumb.

Had he overheard what Fanny was saying? He
gave no sign of it, but greeted them all with his
usual composure. Small talk was exchanged. Was
he going to Roehampton tomorrow? Yes, he was.

Edith remained rigid with embarrassment. She
knew what silly, loyal Fanny had been doing: she
had caught sight of Melford before the rest of them,
and seized the opportunity to let him know that the
girl he had rejected was triumphantly engaged to
someone else. Which was not at all what she
wanted, for she was convinced that Melford had
seen through her very indifferent acting at their
last meeting—which was why he had said so posi-
tively that he was not going to marry again. Now
he would see her as a determined husband-hunter
who, having lost the greater prize, had wasted no
time in securing the best offer she could get.

Could she proclaim, loud and clear, that she and
Sam were going to drive to Roehampton because
they were *not* engaged? But it would sound too odd,
they were all talking about something else. Sam
was scowling, not enjoying his own ambiguous position. She glanced round desperately, wondering
when their little group would break up.

Just at the moment two footmen came forging
their way through the crowd to make a passage for
an illustrious guest. By what seemed like pure
chance, and certainly without conscious volition on
her part, Edith found herself still beside Melford
but divided from Fanny, Richard and Sam, as the
Royal Duke came on, accompanied by several of his
intimates. She expected him to stop and speak to
Melford, whom he knew well, but he was looking
the other way, caught sight of a distinguished admiral, and stopped in front of him instead. Sam,

next to the admiral, was drawn into the conversation.

Melford whispered to Edith, "Let's get out of this."

He slipped a hand round her arm and when she resisted, his fingers tightened. Making a sudden decision, she allowed him to steer her out of the crowd and through an archway which led into a wide corridor running round the back of the saloon like an ambulatory in a cathedral. It was furnished with tapestries and ancient statues, but although there were lighted sconces on the walls and a few guests walking up and down, it was much cooler and quieter than the scene of the main reception. As soon as they had reached this haven, he broke into speech.

"Edith, what are you doing—have you gone mad? You can't mean to go through with this engagement! You can't marry Sam!"

Edith had let him bring her out here because she wanted to tell him that she was not actually engaged—but this dictatorial attack had to be dealt with first. She was not taking orders from Melford!

"It has nothing to do with you. I shall marry anyone I like."

"Yes, but you don't like him, do you? It's plain that you are perfectly miserable. It nearly broke my heart to see you standing there, pale as a poor little ghost."

Edith was perfectly miserable, and she very much resented being told so by the man who had caused all her wretchedness. He would have done better to keep his mouth shut! Besides which, she thought she had hidden her deeper feelings pretty well. What he had actually seen this evening was her acute discomfort over Fanny's interference.

"I wish you would leave me alone," she said, adding ungrammatically, "It is no business of yours who I marry or what I do."

"It is anyone's business to stop a sleep-walker stepping off the side of a cliff! And that is the kind of state you are in. Wake up, my dear. You are not in love with Sam. If you were, I should be willing to stand back and see you happy. No, not willing, perhaps, but resigned. As it is, I am not going to waste time over the niceties of etiquette when all I want is to marry you myself."

This extraordinary statement took Edith so much by surprise that she wondered if she had heard him properly. She seemed to have lost her mental balance. She came to a halt, and so did he.

Another couple were strolling towards them. On their right was a small, open-fronted chamber beyond two pillars, like a side-chapel in this secular cathedral. He guided her in there, and they sat down on a marble bench covered with velvet cushions. By the time they had made this little détour, a horrid suspicion had entered Edith's mind.

She said in a tight, prim voice, "I don't think I perfectly understood what your Grace was saying."

"Yes, you did. I said I was going to cut Sam out. This is the second time he's stolen a march on me, and I'm not standing for it. And don't look so disapproving, my dearest treasure! You can't deny you are in love with me. You always have been, and now I know you still are."

Edith felt her heart hammering as though it was going to break through her rib-cage.

She said, "I did not think even you were conceited enough to think you would recommend yourself by such a remark."

This startled him, but he said quickly, "Please don't be offended. I didn't mean to sound like a coxcomb. I'm fathoms deep in love with you, so where is the harm in recognising the return of that love when I see it in your eyes?"

Edith instantly averted her gaze. It was true that she found his nearness, his brilliant force and magnetism, almost more than she could bear, but against this there was the shocking contrast with their last encounter, when he had paid her the briefest possible call in order to make his indifference clear.

"Surely you understood? That I wanted to marry you?" he said, misinterpreting her baffled silence. "No, I see you did not. Was this entanglement with Sam meant to bring me up to the mark? I had thought you above such wiles."

Really furious now, she raised her hand to slap the arrogant smile off his face, but he caught her wrist and held it.

"Come, my love. Don't be so cross."

"If you kiss me, I'll scream!"

"You'll ruin yourself if you do!"

He let her go all the same. Even the great Duke of Melford would not care to be caught grappling with an unwilling female if only because part of his reputation rested on the legend that no female in his arms ever would be unwilling.

Edith stood up. "Sam was right about you," she said flatly.

"Oh?" The level brows lifted a fraction. "And what was Sam's verdict?"

"That you never want anything unless there is a good reason why you can't have it. You fell in love with Arethusa while she was engaged to someone else. She remained important to you only while it seemed she could not give you a son. After Bar was born, you neglected her, and your interest did not revive until she was dying. Once you had lost her, you could think of no one else."

She heard him draw a sharp breath, but went on.

"It's been the same with me, hasn't it? You fell in love with me while you had a wife living. At the merest hint that I am going to be married, you are in love all over again. While we were both unattached and you thought I was yours for the asking, your feelings remained remarkably cool."

He, too, had risen. He had gone very white.

"You know I couldn't approach you while I was in mourning. I had to observe the greatest discretion. I always meant to ask you to marry me. Do you think I am trying to deceive you?"

"No," she said sadly. "It is yourself you are deceiving. You are behaving like a spoilt child, Melford. I'm afraid you always do."

There was a moment of incredulous silence while his burning ice look went straight through her. Then he said, "You had better learn to control that poisonous tongue of yours, or nobody will marry you, not even Sam!"

A few minutes later she found herself back among the dazzling assembly of guests and the hot lights; they were no longer in the saloon, but in a lofty music-room, seated on gold chairs while a large lady in purple sang an Italian aria.

Edith crept in as quietly as she could, hoping not to be noticed, but a gentleman in the back row got up and offered her his chair, which she felt obliged to accept, for although there were quite a number of men standing against the wall, all the ladies had seats. She glanced round for Melford. He had vanished. He had come as far as the music-room door with her in a freezing rage, and then stalked away.

She could not see anyone else she knew. The people close to her were all strangers. They eyed her curiously, and no wonder. She felt and probably looked as though she was in a high fever.

She fought to steady her nerves after the recent turmoil, and to re-arrange her ideas. Sam had been

right, and she had been wrong. Melford had behaved exactly as he had foretold. Wanting her again
as soon as he thought she was out of reach, volatile
and unreliable, incapable of sustained affection. She
would not have believed it possible if she had not
heard him just now. In fact, if Sam had not warned
her, she would not have known what to believe.
How extraordinary, she thought, that the great
wish of her life had come true: she had received an
offer of marriage from Melford—and she had refused him. Not because the revelation of weakness
had killed her love stone dead. She still loved him
with her senses and her imagination, if not with
her mind, and she supposed she always would. So
why couldn't she marry him? Love was supposed to
cover a multitude of sins. She had called him a
spoilt child, and they said women could forgive their
children anything. But I don't want a husband who
has to be treated as a child, she thought contemptuously. Of course everyone had faults, and some of
Melford's she would always have been prepared to
forgive: the caustic manner, the habit of getting his
own way, which no one had ever taught him to
curb . . . But she couldn't live with a man so fickle
and changeable that he didn't even recognise the
selfish inconsistency which had made fools of them
both. And, anyway, what was the point of marrying
for love a man who would tire of her in six months.

The concert was over. She had not taken in a single note. She stood up because everyone else did.
Among the sea of unknown faces, she was thankful
to catch sight of Sam. He came towards her.

"What happened to you? I couldn't find you anywhere. Has Melford been upsetting you again?"

"I'll tell you later."

He did not badger her with questions, but concentrated on getting her out of the concert-room and

into the series of apartments where supper was being served.

She heard him saying to one of the waiters, "Can
you find us a table near a window? The young lady
is feeling a little faint."

This procured them a place in the very furthest
room by an open window with a curtain drawn aside
to let in a breath of air. Sam arranged the chairs
so that she was sitting with her back to the room
between himself and the wall. No one else came to
their table. Even the candles in here seemed less
brilliant and numerous than they were in the other
rooms.

"Well," he said bracingly, "a little hot soup and
a glass of champagne, I think. Listening to good
music is always so fatiguing."

She appreciated his kind common sense, and
knew she ought to tell him what had been happening.

So, when she had drunk some of the soup, she
said, "You were right about Mel. Directly he overheard Fanny talking as though you and I were engaged, he decided he wanted to marry me after all.
I have never been so disgusted in my life!"

"I'm sorry," he said slowly. "Sorry that you
should be so distressed. I gather you think worse of
him now than you did ten days ago."

"Naturally. So long as I thought he was grieving
for Arethusa, I could understand very well why he
wanted nothing more to do with me. I was very unhappy, but I did not feel ill-used. I did not blame
him."

"So you were still able to idolise him from afar,"
said Sam acutely. "That made all the difference."

The waiter proffered a dish of lobster. She shook
her head, feeling slightly sick. Sam helped himself,
and began to extricate the coral-pink flesh from a
scarlet claw. The supper guests chattered behind

them, a dowager with a discontented voice complaining on and on about the failings of her daughter-in-law.

Edith knew there was still more she had to say to Sam. It was odd, considering her total loss of faith in Melford, that one thing he had told her this evening was absolutely true.

"You have been very good to me," she said, "but I must go home to Cotebury and stop sheltering behind this pretended engagement. It is harmful to us both. I am not fit to marry anyone, feeling as I do."

"Very well, Swan. If that is what you think best. You have only to let me know if you change your mind."

"I shan't change my mind."

She could not say more without the risk of breaking down in this room full of people. She was sure he understood. She felt too confused to look at him steadily, but was able to read his expression in one brief glance: concern, compassion, and another emotion she could not identify.

CHAPTER FIFTEEN

Fanny was disappointed to hear next morning that Edith felt quite unequal to attending the breakfast at Roehampton. She had not been able to find out what had gone on the night before, but correctly blamed Melford for Edith's feeling too ill to go out. She made a noble offer to stay at home with her afflicted friend, but was visibly relieved when Edith thanked her and said she would be better left alone, she simply wanted to sleep.

As soon as the Weares had gone off to enjoy themselves, Edith got up and dressed. She intended to write to her parents, saying she wanted to come home almost at once, only she could not think of a reasonable excuse. It did seem extraordinary to be running away from London because she had received two such very eligible proposals and could not bring herself to accept either of them. Most people would think she was a fool! That was why she had not confided in Fanny when they got home last night. Fanny would almost certainly advise her to marry Melford now that he had asked her. As long as his capricious passion for her lasted, he would do anything to make her happy, and when it wore off she would still have a very pleasant life ahead of her with all the advantages of his wealth and rank.

It was impossible to explain in words to another person the moral distinctions that were clear in her own mind: she could not marry Melford, whom she loved but did not respect, any more than Sam, whom she respected but did not love. I'm a hopeless case, she thought bitterly, born to be an old maid.

Perhaps she ought to write to Sam. She had not said half the things she wanted to last night. Poor Sam; how much did he love her? How much did he mind her refusing? She saw his face once more in her memory, his expression of concern, compassion and—was it relief? Yes, she thought with a momentary shock, he had been relieved. And no wonder. He had probably realised, sooner than she had, that it would be a mistake for them to marry. He was fond of her, he was sorry for her, and he had got this idea in his head that she would be the right person to bring up Arethusa's daughter, but now that she had released him, she thought he would recover fairly soon and marry one of the many pretty girls who were always delighted to flirt with him. She would be very glad if he did, but it made her feel more melancholy than ever.

She was tidying her dressing-table with the vague knowledge that she would soon be packing to leave, when she came on a bundle of old letters. One of them was carefully written in a round, childish hand. She read a few words, which went like a stab through her heart. ". . . I hope you will come to see us dear Seedif. Papa said you promised . . ." And underneath was Bar's letter, not nearly so well written and much more commanding. ". . . Come and see me soon . . ." Underlined four times.

Poor little brother and sister—she would have to disappoint them, she could never go to Melford House again. It was dreadful to break a promise to a child, particularly to these children whose confidence in the goodness of life had been shattered by

such a heavy blow ... And it struck her that she
could visit them, if she went at once. Today. Melford was going to the party at Roehampton; he had
said so the night before in her presence. There
would be no risk of meeting him, and when he came
home and heard that she had been there in his absence, he could not suspect her of having second
thoughts and lying in wait for him. Ten minutes
later, she set out on foot.

Arriving at Melford House alone, without even a
maid to accompany her, was flying in the face of
propriety, but as she had only come to see the children she could not think she was doing anything
wrong, and the servants, knowing her, treated her
with the utmost civility. She was ushered upstairs
to the old nursery, now the schoolroom, and as soon
as they saw her, the children came rushing to her
with shrieks of delight.

"It's Seedif! Dear Seedif!"

They hugged her with enthusiasm. Harriet had
grown much taller, almost pretty. There was a definite look of Arethusa. Bar had grown, too, but
hardly altered. Dark, beautiful and self-willed, a
painful reminder of his father.

"Not so rough, *mes enfants*. What will Miss Bruton think of you?" said the tall woman who had
been sitting at the table with them.

This, of course, was Madame Villerond, the children's French governess, whom Edith had pri-
vately named the elegant émigrée. Her elegance
was undeniable, but she was well into middle-age
and looked sensible and calm, a cosmopolitan ver-
sion of Mrs. Wells. How silly to have imagined that
Lady Robert would have engaged a dazzling siren
to enter the household of the widower Duke!

She made Edith very welcome, and the children
showed her the new innovations in their world.
Their more babyish toys had been banished, though

the rocking-horse and dolls' house was still there. There was a large schoolroom table, a bookcase, and a map on the wall showing the progress of the war.

"I'm going to be a soldier and fight Boney!" boasted Bar.

"Let us hope that may not be necessary," said Madame Villerond, exchanging a glance with Edith.

Bar was six years old.

Harriet asked if they could dress up in the costumes "Seedif" had made for them. Which they did, Harriet miming an old pedlar woman and Bar prancing about as a bold tom cat.

Edith was glad she had come. Talking to the children had given her a respite from her own gloomy thoughts. She rose to go only when she realised it was nearly time for their dinner, which they had at midday. Bar wanted her to stay and dine with them.

"I shall be having my dinner this evening," she excused herself. "It would be greedy to eat two dinners in one day!"

"My papa is going to have two breakfasts today," said Bar.

"The second one is not a proper breakfast," said Harriet. "It is a sort of picnic that goes on for hours and hours. Anyway, papa did not go to Roehampton after all."

"He did! He did!"

"*Didn't!* Wilson told me. So there."

This announcement had a shattering effect on Edith's nerves. If it was true that Melford had not gone to the outdoor breakfast, did that mean he was in the house at this moment? She was unreasonably shaken. It was an enormous building, and the Duke was most unlikely to visit the schoolroom at a mealtime, if he ever came in here at all. At the same, she was now anxious to escape as quickly as possible.

Her farewells were delayed by Bar, who burst into tears when he understood that she really meant to go away again so soon after she had come back into his life. They reasoned with him, but it was no good. He wanted his Seedif always at his beck and call, as she had been once in the dimly-remembered happy past.

"Come, *chéri*, this is foolish," said Madame Villerond. "Miss Edith cannot stay here. She has other people to please."

"She *can* stay—I want her to. I want her to stay for ever!"

Harriet clutched Edith's hand. "You will come again soon, won't you, Seedif?"

Edith did not answer, knowing she could pay no further visits to Melford House. She kissed the little girl, feeling like a traitor, and looked doubtfully at Bar, who was sobbing loudly and had turned his back on her, sulky but inconsolable.

"Had I better slip off quietly, madame?"

The governess obviously thought so. She had an arm around the little boy and talked to him in a comforting voice, asking Harriet to fetch him a glass of water.

Edith left the schoolroom in a new fit of despondency, feeling that her visit had done more harm than good. If she had thought she might upset Bar so much, she would never have come, but how could she have guessed? Fond as he had always been of her, this outburst of weeping seemed excessive. Unless he associated her with the great tragedy that had overshadowed them all. Walking down one of the wide corridors, Edith reflected that she had been very much involved in Arethusa's last journeys. They had left together for Strenton, reappeared together at Rythorpe, and doubtless the children had been told that when their parents had gone to Bath, she had gone there too. Did that poor little boy still take her for some sort of link with his mother?

She had reached the end of the corridor and was turning towards the staircase, when she heard little feet pounding behind her and a voice calling, "Seedif! Seedif!"

Bar had escaped from the schoolroom and was rushing towards her.

He flung his arms round her, gripping her below the waist and hanging on for dear life, so that she could hardly move. He was surprisingly strong and heavy. Madame Villerond now arrived with two of the servants, and they all began trying to prise Bar away from Edith. It was a ridiculous scene, but it really was very difficult to dislodge the child without hurting him, so desperately were his small hands locked together.

When he was detached from her at last, he threw himself on the ground, his body stiff as though he was in a rigor, his eyes tight shut, his face scarlet, while he bellowed at the top of his lungs.

Various household minions converged from all directions and started giving advice. Edith knelt on the carpet beside Bar, not knowing what to do. Fury and misery had now turned to hysteria, and she was afraid he would work himself into some sort of seizure.

She was actually relieved to hear someone say, "Here's his Grace. He's the only one can quieten his lordship."

And there was Melford, a few feet away from her, attending only to his son and saying in an inflexible voice, "Barlington! Stop that noise this instant—do you hear me?"

Bar paid no attention, Edith sat back on her heels.

Melford, his face hard, repeated, "Barlington! That is quite enough nonsense from you. Now stop."

Edith remembered Arethusa trembling when Melford used that voice to the little boy. Bar's ungoverned rage and anguish subsided into sobs and finally gulps. His eyes opened and the alarming colour in his face receded.

"Well, what a stupid exhibition! I never heard such a din," said his father.

His voice, though firm, was no longer at all harsh or frightening. He lifted the little boy to his feet.

"I want Seedif to stay with us, Papa," said Bar tearfully. "Tell her she mustn't go away."

"I can't tell her any such thing, and if I did, she wouldn't listen," said Melford, with an unfriendly glance at Edith, who had now got to her feet and felt she too would like to indulge in a fit of hysterics if she dared.

"But people have to do everything you say, Papa!"

"Long may you continue to think so. It is not Seedif's view, however."

Poor Madame Villerond was apologising to her employer. "I am so very sorry, monseigneur. We have not had an upset of this kind for so long that I was not prepared."

"How should you be? Bar is getting too old for these performances, and I think he is ashamed of himself. Aren't you, Bar? Say goodbye properly to Miss Edith and then go back with madame to the schoolroom."

A subdued Bar whispered, "Goodbye, Seedif."

She bent and kissed his damp little face and watched him go off holding the hand of the tall Frenchwoman. Various members of the household were vanishing discreetly now the excitement was over. She felt uncomfortable, and looking, she was sure, as though she'd been dragged through a hedge backwards. Her gloves were not to be found, and something very odd had happened to the garland of artificial cherries that had been stitched to the brim of her bonnet. She took it off.

"Your Grace must wonder what I am doing in your house."

"No," he said with a chilling indifference. "You came to see the children."

"Yes, but I shouldn't have come after—after what happened last night. I made sure you would be out. I thought you had gone to Roehampton."

"And I thought you had gone to Roehampton. I imagine we both stayed away for the same reason. But since you are here, there is something I should like to say to you."

He held open a door, and she realised she was being shown into the Grecian drawing-room. She jibbed for a moment. It was a place which had such very vivid memories for her and they increased her confusion, because they were the memories of a girl so different from the person she had since become. However, she could not refuse to go in, with Melford looking so distant and ducal, as though he too had reverted to that former stage of their acquaintance.

She hardly had time to sit down before he began to speak. When he did so, they were immediately back in the present.

"Since thinking over what you said to me last night, I realise that we were at cross-purposes. That you entirely mistook my motives. That is what I want to explain."

Now he's going to try and justify himself, she thought. I wish he wouldn't.

"When I asked you to marry me, you behaved as though I had insulted you. I may have been rash and ill advised, but nothing worse. Did you really suppose that I could do anything so serious on the

impulse of a moment? That having just overheard
the news that you were engaged to Sam, I determined at once to get you for myself, on a mere whim
or in a spirit of pique? You must have a very odd
idea of my common sense, let alone my manners."

This was more or less what she had thought at
the time, though during a wakeful night it had occurred to her that he had probably heard some of
the rumours circulating among Fanny's relations,
many of whom were his close friends.

"I believe there has been some silly gossip," she
said. "I don't see what difference it makes."

"Don't you? Then let me tell you I was not swayed
by gossip. I was given the news in confidence and I
resisted every temptation to interfere. I wasn't going to compete against Sam if you had decided of
your own free will that you would rather marry him
than me. I had no claim on you, after all. You have
said a hundred times that you loved me, but that
was in the days when we had no right to demand
promises and you were entitled to change your
mind."

Edith shifted uneasily, getting ready to protest,
but he went on.

"It was only when I saw you looking so unhappy
that I lost my head and made a fool of myself. With
very little excuse, I must admit, for I'd had plenty
of time to practise indifference. I knew of your engagement before you arrived in London."

"But that's impossible!" she exclaimed. "You
can't have done."

"Oh? Do you think I am lying again, or just deceiving myself?"

"No. At least ... No, of course not. I beg your
pardon. But you must have been misled. Who said
I was engaged?"

"Penelope Dampier. I had asked her for news of
Arethusa's daughter. She told me Caroline's future

was secure because—I can remember her exact words: 'Sam is going be married, and he has chosen the very wife Arethusa would have wished. He has been down to Cotebury to propose to Edith, and she is coming to London almost immediately.' "

"And you believed her?"

"Why shouldn't I believe her? Sam's cousin, who was in all his secrets. Do you mean to say it wasn't true?"

"No."

She remembered Mrs. Dampier trying to congratulate her and suggesting Seddon Park for the honeymoon. She had put this down to Fanny's premature hints, but it seemed there was another explanation. Penelope Dampier must have heard some of Sam's plans in advance, and when she learnt that Edith was coming to London, she jumped to the wrong conclusion.

Melford was walking distractedly about the room. "I took it for granted she knew what was happening. I was in a fever of jealousy and disappointment. Astonished that you should take such a step without warning me. Then I began to realise that Arethusa's death must have brought home to you a much clearer view of me than you ever had before. That you no longer loved me, and would not trust me to make a good husband. You had accepted Sam just before my year of mourning was over, as though you were protecting yourself against me. I was bitterly hurt, but I certainly wasn't going to pester you with unwelcome attentions. I hoped I might avoid meeting you while you were in town. When you came here with presents for the children, I felt obliged to call. I thought a few minutes' conversation in Fanny's company would be all that was required. But you were alone. It was intolerable. You were so cold and correct that I had no key to your true feelings. Until last night, when you kindly presented me with such an accurate portrait of myself."

He was somewhere behind her now, and she could not see him. As she perceived the whole course of their misunderstanding and what it had led to, she was appalled. Each had felt deserted by the other in a peculiarly heartless way. That dreadful day in Fanny's drawing-room when his manner had been so frigid and remote, he was actually thinking that she had engaged herself to another man and was not prepared to tell him so, even out of the kindness due to an old friend. All this might now have been put right, but she was the one who had ruined everything by making such a cruel attack on him. Cruel and, as it turned out, unjustified, for his intentions had never wavered. She could not expect him to forgive her.

After a moment she said, "I am truly sorry. I see now that I made a most terrible mistake. I have only one excuse, and it's not a very good one, because I know that some of the things I said were inexcusable. Only it did seem as though you had changed your mind very quickly. It's less than a fortnight since you told me you would never marry again."

There was such a long silence that she thought he was too angry to reply. Then he said in a strangled voice, "I'd forgotten that. Good God, what a stupid, arrogant piece of play-acting! Can't you guess why I said I should never re-marry? You had made it plain that you wouldn't have me, so my pride insisted on pretending that you wouldn't be given the chance."

She turned round to look at him. He was standing by the window, that marvellous profile cut like a cameo against the light. He went on talking, his words weighed down by a quiet despair.

"Sam was right about the way I treated Arethusa. When the early pleasures of our marriage faded, I became bored and laid the blame on her, instead of recognising that the fault was in myself, in my constant craving for change. Last night I thought you and Sam had been ungenerous. I have spent a year re-living the past and regretting most of it, and I thought you might have credited me with some desire to do better in the future. But now, after the havoc I've created with my own vanity, I can't see why any woman of sense should ever put up with me."

It was himself, not her, he found hard to forgive.

Acting entirely by instinct and without conscious thought, Edith went over to him and touched his arm.

"Mel."

He looked down at her and said, on a questioning note, "Edith?"

When he saw the hope in her eyes, his whole expression altered. Light and life returned as he took her in his arms. As their lips touched and his hands enclosed her, all her painful, unassuaged longings began to be answered, the needs that had been crushed down so often because they could be fulfilled only in furtive haste and guilt-ridden deceit. Now everything was changed, tenderness and pleasure were set free, and eventually every degree of loving was to be enjoyed in its proper sequence. She had never imagined such bliss.

Mel paused only once between rapturous kisses. "Before I get into any deeper trouble, are you or are you not engaged to Palgrave?"

"I'm not engaged to anyone."

"Except me."

"Except you."

They went to sit on one of the couches, enclosed in their private bliss like the gods and goddesses in the medallions. It seemed impossible at first to say

anything except "I love you," "How much I love
you," over and over in all its variations. Presently
they began to talk disjointedly.

How stupid they had been ever to doubt each
other.

"I expect it was a judgement on us," she said
gravely. "Because we had each had good reason to
distrust ourselves."

Now all was explained—and how happy the children were going to be to have their dear Seedif with
them permanently. No second wife could ever have
felt more confident of the welcome she would get
from her stepchildren.

"Bar will be quite insufferable," said Melford, "if
he thinks I have persuaded you to stay with us as
a result of his bad behavior. When, in fact, it's a
result of my own bad behaviour!"

Edith was pondering over the foolish interven-
tion of Penelope Dampier. "I can understand her
expecting me to accept Sam's offer—after all, I
should have been ready to do so once. But surely
she did not imagine my mother would have let me
come to London unaccompanied at such a time? To
choose my trousseau, I suppose, with only Fanny to
help me."

"I ought to have realised myself how unlikely
that was," he admitted. "Though I still don't know
why you did come to London."

"To meet you, of course! I know it sounds forward,
but I didn't see how you were to come to Cotebury,
or how else we were ever to meet again."

It was his turn to be astonished. "But, my dearest love, surely you cannot have thought that I was
expecting *you* to undertake the business of trying
to make us look respectable? I know I've plunged
you into a horribly indelicate situation, but I'm not
quite so lost to all proper feeling that I could sit

back and leave the contrivings to you! That would have been a fine way to treat my bride, I must say!"

"What did you mean to do, then?"

"I have been working on my uncle and aunt for some time. You know what a favourite you are in that family. They are now convinced that it is their own idea to ask you to stay at their house in Surrey some time this summer. I shall come down for a few days while you are there, and during our solitary rides and rambles, we shall get on so well that we shall decide to spend the rest of our lives together."

"I hope Lord and Lady Robert will not disapprove," said Edith doubtfully.

Now that their personal differences had been sorted out, the practical aspects of the gulf between them seemed rather to widen. She felt inept and humble. She had created a lot of unnecessary complications. She was here in his house unchaperoned—a horrible indelicacy indeed! It would shock her mother and nearly everyone else if they knew. Even her bonnet, with the unwinding garland of cherries, looked rather raffish lying over there on the floor. She was afraid she would make an unsatisfactory duchess, and said so.

"You'll learn!" said Melford.

This laconic utterance was rather reassuring. It proved that he was back on form.

Then he said, "You are very young, and it is hard that you should have to be endowed with all my worldly obligations and pomposities. Extremely tedious some of them are. But I'll help you all I can. You have plenty of courage and sense, and you must not let yourself be oppressed by having to live very much in the public eye, or by the idea that people are making comparisons."

For that was the most daunting prospect. She would have to be, not only Melford's Duchess, but Arethusa's successor.

"She was very much admired and loved," he said, following Edith's train of thought without difficulty. "I loved her, more than I realised, until it was too late. You understand that, and you won't be jealous. There is no need, for in spite of everything we were not well suited. She was too sweet-natured and forbearing. She was afraid of my sharp tongue, and because of that I was often unkind to her. Her actual virtues seemed to bring out the worst in me. That sounds churlish: I wouldn't say it to anyone but you. And only to you because I don't want you to feel threatened by the past."

Edith thought it might impose an added strain on a man with such a quick, critical intelligence to live with someone who was too easily hurt. She resolved that if and when he hurt her, she must learn not to show it.

"The truth is . . ." said Melford. "She was too good for me."

It was an odd comment on the unfaithful wife who had betrayed him with his oldest friend. Their eyes met, as they shared the same rueful sense of irony . . .

"That, too, was a good deal my own fault," he said. "At least one thing is certain. I shall take very good care not to drive you into another man's arms."

He drew a finger along one of her eyebrows, down past the cheekbone and under her chin, studying her all the while with those brilliant dark eyes from which the ice had entirely melted. She gazed back unflinchingly.

"You are the girl I ought always to have been looking for," he said, "if I had guessed that such a creature could exist. It was careless of you not to be born a few years sooner! But now we have caught up with each other, we shall make a well-matched pair."

"A pair of prize-fighters?" she enquired, thinking of their sparring bouts and one obvious way in which she differed from Arethusa.

"No, my charmer! A pair of carriage horses. We shall go well in harness together."

And so they would. She knew with a sudden elation that this marriage would succeed. They were made for each other.

FANCIFUL
FREEDOM OF FORM
EMPHASIZED THROUGH
**IMAGINATION AND
EMOTION**

Marian Devon